Knives of the Ring
Volume 3 of the Polaris Chronicles

Bryan Choi & Erica Carson

ISBN: 1-945882-02-6
ISBN-13: 978-1-945882-02-9

Knives of the Ring is a work of fiction. Names, places, and incidents either are a product of the authors' imaginations or are used fictitiously.

Published by Delphinium Press, LLC.
www.carsonchoi.com

The Polaris Chronicles:

Guns of the Temple

Swords of the Imperium

Prince of Maladies

Knives of the Ring

CONTENTS

Acknowledgments

Thanks again to all our beta readers, those who provided critique and feedback, and especially Shay for being a superfan! To everyone who left reviews, told friends about it, bought books for the family, left a copy near the water cooler, or posted about it on the internet, you're the lifeblood of our series!

1

The river's bottom was cool and quiet. Stones smoothed silken by centuries of mutual abrasion formed a mosaic that far surpassed those in the palaces of men. With each passing year, the current pushed the stones ever further from their mother mountains, so no two seasons' patterns were ever alike. Taki Natalis wasn't enjoying the sight, however, because he was busy drowning.

Above where he suffocated facedown in the silt and stones, ball and shot shrieked through the humid summer miasma and tore through metal, bone, and flesh. Hobnails stamped against the riverbed and churned up more silt and blood. Broken spear shafts and shattered muskets plopped into the water, as did their wielders a few moments later. Crimson wafted off the bodies, only to be swept slowly along by the current. Taki's lungs might be filling with water, but most importantly, it was quiet and he ached less. He closed his eyes.

Before he could succumb, a mailed fist grasped the collar of his gambeson and jerked him upright. Taki's eyes shot open, and his pupils constricted when the rays of the beating noonday sun bore down upon them. Pain pierced his chest, and he coughed and sputtered and breathed once again. He flailed vainly, only to feel his captain slap his face.

"On your feet! If you die here, I'll desecrate your corpse!" Lotte Satou snarled. She let Taki stumble aside and raised her rifle to squeeze off a shot.

The blast was close to his ear, and he flinched and suppressed the urge to curse. Rows of Imperial pikemen in glinting cuirasses lowered their spears around him in preparation for a clash. Drumbeats from the rear reached a furious crescendo, and the water at Taki's thighs shook and frothed. The last thing he'd remembered before waking up to his own drowning was the whine of an incoming shell, a flash of light, and the feeling of being crushed on all sides.

Being conscious and aware wasn't much better. Lotte was shouting. Men were screaming and crying for their mothers. A line of Ursalans bearing poleaxes marched steadily toward him with battle lust on their faces. A month after the Teufelsbrucke had fallen, the Osterbrand Imperium had brought war to the Serene Kingdom of Ursala.

"Shoot! Shoot! Kill them now!"

A chaotic staccato of sharp cracks and low thumps followed Lotte's command, and the entire phalanx was wreathed in smoke. Bodies fell. The gold-embroidered battle standard dipped toward the water but was quickly righted.

"Gunners fall back! Pikes, give it to the whoresons!"

Bellows and shouts overwhelmed her words right before men-at-arms rushed the line. Metal crunched and wood snapped as pike points crashed into shields, armor, and flesh. An Ursalan sepoy in a ragged tabard scooted under the tangle of shafts and tried to stick his dagger in Taki's gut.

Taki raised his kriegsmesser and brought it down on the man's helm. Metal split and crimson splattered. That made three kills that he personally knew of, not counting the possible ones he'd inflicted from afar. Though he was a passable swordsman, Taki's true strength was the ability to channel the elements of fire and air. His power gave him a role in the tercio that Lotte had described as a "scampering magic cannon." He hadn't appreciated her description, though it was completely accurate.

"Natalis, aid the left before we crumble!"

"Yes, Captain!"

Taki waded and sloshed around the pikemen, marveling quietly to himself that they stood in stiff formation even in the face of cannon shells. *Must be the famous Imperial discipline.* Joining Aslatiel von Halcon's Alfa Gruppe had not changed his daily life much since they'd set off for Lhasa three seasons ago, but the average Imperial soldier stood to be flogged for near anything.

"No, doofus!" Hadassah Mikkelsen shouted and cuffed him. "Your brains leaking outta your ears? Left is *that* way!" She jerked her thumb toward the flank before marching to the head of the formation with her rifle in tow. A squad of musketeers followed in her wake, and smoke and gunfire followed after them.

Taki wheeled around and frantically pushed his way past armored bodies, both standing and bobbing in the water. The world still spun if he twisted his head certain ways. The farther from the center he got, though, the more the formation seemed on the verge of crumbling. The phalanx had started fifty deep and a hundred wide. Where Taki was now, the flank boasted a mere three rows. Ahead of the wavering front, his longtime comrades Draco Emreis and Karma Gillette fought for their lives.

"Natalis! Blast these guys!" Karma pointed at a packed square of spearmen ahead.

Taki thrust his palms forward. Prana coalesced before him before shooting forward as a blast of concussive energy. The spear column seemed to splint asunder as men were knocked aside like hempen dolls. "What happened here?" he shouted. "Why've we lost so many?"

"Lancers fucked up," Karma said. "Rode off the edge of the ford, got stuck, and got torn to bits by cannon. Then their reserves kicked us right in the jewels."

"But never mind that," Draco said, and pointed. "Backup's here!"

A gilded main battle tank rolled in from the rear. It trundled ponderously along, with much clanking and sloshing, and from its filigreed smokestacks belched a black, vile-smelling cloud that settled on the water and refused to rise. Two orderly lines of wardens in scarlet cowls flanked the ancient weapon, chanting the necessary appeasement mantras and bearing the flowing banners of their order.

Gunfire crackled from the Ursalan side, and three of the wardens collapsed. The others simply stepped over their fallen brethren. The tank's turret rotated with a deeply unpleasant grinding noise. Then, it fired.

A wave of concussive force enveloped Taki's body and squeezed the air from his lungs. Strangely enough, the report itself seemed inoffensive to his ears compared to that of the rifles going off around him. The Ursalan battle line ahead seemed to collectively shiver, then waver, and finally recede. Soon after, the Imperial drums beat an unmistakable rhythm: advance. A throaty cheer went up from the ranks, accompanied by a celebration of gunfire.

"Hah! Knew the bastards would rout when they saw it," Draco said. He dipped his hand in the water and splashed his face in a vain effort to clear away the caked-on silt and gore. "We've won the day."

"Wouldn't be sure about that," Karma said. "Ursalans don't fear the relics like we do. Probably have a plan to trap and kill it later."

"Then that's the wardens' issue, not ours," Draco said. "I'll just be glad to dry out my bollocks and boots, not to mention rest under a roof. God, I just hope there's a town nearby."

"There is," Taki said. "Chalon-sur-Saone. We want the granary."

"Enough oatmeal to shit softly for days," Draco said, and clapped Taki on the back.

Karma tugged the brim of his hat to straighten it and spat. "If we're lucky, the villagers have fled already. If we're unlucky…"

Taki frowned. "Then what?"

"Faith runs deep in these places. To these people, the old man on the throne is a god. They love him more than Emreis loves wenches. And when you combine faith and love, you get some bad shit indeed."

* * * *

By evenfall, Taki smelled something roasting and heard voices singing off key, and thus he knew where the rest of his squad had bivouacked. Slivers of pink on the horizon rapidly gave way to indigo as he stepped delicately over snarling roots and avoided patches of bramble. Eventually, he found them.

Draco crouched and intently turned the hilt of a poniard on which he'd impaled several wild harspuds to roast over a small campfire ringed with mossy stones. Karma, meanwhile, strummed a lute with unexpected skill.

Will the circle be unbroken,
By and by, oh Lord, by and by?
Is a better home awaiting,
In the sky, oh Lord, in the sky.

Hadassah looked up from cleaning her rifle. "Dude, stop. You've sung that exact same verse thirty times already. Isn't there another part to the stupid song?"

"Yes, but I don't remember the lyrics."

She rolled her eyes. "It's annoying when someone knows only one part and then sings it over and over again. Play something else."

"It's important that I practice," Karma said. "I haven't gotten to do this for several fortnights, and I'm getting rusty."

"You *like* practicing incessantly?"

"I enjoy mastery of my pursuits. Besides, maybe the lyrics will come back to me in time."

With that, he started to strum again, only to have Hadassah sing:

Will we eat more tasty pumpkins,
In a pie, in a pie?
Is a better harvest coming
From that asshole in the sky?

"There!" She whacked him with her cleaning rod. "Your second verse. About something useful, too."

Karma smiled at her. "Your voice is as lovely as your flowing crimson tresses."

She slashed him across his crown with her rod. "P-pervert!"

Taki sat down near the fire. "Never knew you were a bard."

Karma shrugged. "Well, I was Duke Gul's manservant for a long while. Guarding the nobility isn't all killing from the shadows. Sometimes you're the cook, sometimes the sommelier, and oftentimes the jester."

"The shittiest jester," Hadassah cackled.

Taki ignored her and cocked his head at the lute. "When'd you get *that*?"

"A chevalier decided he didn't need it anymore, so he gave it to me," Karma said with a wink.

"You know we're not supposed to loot the dead, right?"

"*Imperials* aren't," Hadassah said. "But the Code says *we* can take whatever."

Taki bit the inside of his cheek. "Don't forget, we're in Sir Aslatiel's employ now. We've got to follow their rules."

Her eyes narrowed to slits, and she tapped a knife edge against a bootheel. "So says the new Imperial leutnant."

"Come now, people," Draco said. He plucked the steaming, sizzling harspuds from his poniard and lobbed them gently at the others. "We're all hungry and tired. No arguments until we've eaten, at least."

"I almost didn't find you lot," Taki said. "Why'd you settle in this spot, anyway?"

"Air's cleaner out here," Karma said. He blew steam away from his harspud and tried for a bite but shied away when his lips brushed against it. "Where's the captain?"

"Finishing up with the mayor," Taki said. "He's sold us a hundred bushels, with delivery tomorrow on the morn. That'll last us a good fortnight, so long as we supplement with forage."

"Huh? *Sold* us grain? Didn't we just occupy the town?"

"We did, but we'll pay fairly for our supplies. I got us a good price, too. Only ten rounds of Old Nayto."

"Ten rounds too many, in my opinion," Hadassah said. "I saw inside the stores. There's enough to feed us all for a season, and that includes all the rats. No one could do a damned thing if we wanted to take it. So was shelling out for stuff we already own *your* foolish idea or the captain's?"

"It was hers, actually," Taki said. "We've no idea how long we'll be waiting here, and we're barely dug in. Last thing we want is to anger the locals."

"Doesn't sound like the Lotte I know."

"She's got a lot more to deal with now," Taki said. "There are a *thousand* men under her command. She can't wager their lives."

Hadassah let out a sigh. "And we hadn't seen hide or hair of her for a fortnight until today. Then she just disappears again to haggle with some bumpkin who by all rights should be on all fours licking her hobnails."

"Aw, you miss snuggling with her that much?" Draco said.

"Maybe I do!" Hadassah said. "This...this whole thing just sucks. I thought we were going to bail on the Imps and find Mezeta so we could get our damned pensions back! And instead, what are we doing? We're in the middle of a fucking war with Ursala! You *never* get into a land war with Ursala!"

"I think you mean you never get into a land war with the Imperium," Karma said.

She swatted at him. "That's not the point, smartarse. The point is that we're just being used again, and while I know that may be our lot in life, at least normally we'd have our captain with us. But now she's going along with that one-eyed bastard's whims and can't even spend time with us anymore. I miss her, but I'm...I'm pissed, too! I thought Mezeta was heading *east*. Why are we heading *west*?"

"You realize that none of us actually stand a chance against the woman, right?" Draco said. "I want my rounds as badly as you do, but so long as I can eat my fill, I'd rather not toss my life away."

"The Padishah said he'd help us fight her, so long as we helped him." Taki said. "I say we give him a chance."

"What if he reneges?" Hadassah said. "He has an empire to rule. Why does he give a damn about Mezeta? Or us peons?"

"You've seen how much of a threat she is. No man can ignore that for long."

"I have a theory," Draco said. "Many naturalists say the world is a sphere. So if you go westward, at a certain point it's like you've headed eastward to begin with. Perhaps that's his plan?"

"Don't tell me you actually believe that 'world-is-a-sphere' crap," Hadassah said.

"No, but I do know that if we tried to head east right now, we'd spend years trying to cross the Imperium on foot. Then there's the issue of the storm wall of Goryeo. No one crosses that hellpit alive. Hell, Mezeta's like to be swallowed by some leviathan herself, if she's not torn apart by the storms."

"Which doesn't solve the issue of getting our grad back," Karma said.

"Right. So the best we can do is fight on, take Versailles, and then have the Imperials ferry us east," Draco said. "They'll owe us."

"Oh please, you sound like Natalis," Hadassah said. "Why don't you just accept a commission from fuckboy von Halcon and become a real Imperial already?"

"I won't have you disparage Sir Aslatiel..." Taki stopped. No, it wouldn't do to get into a fight with her. Not over a man who'd disappointed him so.

"Nah, the Imperial discipline is too much for me," Draco said. "We have it good as freikorpsmen. We get paid but don't have to get flogged for tying our laces funny."

"Whatever." Hadassah took a bite off her harspud and glumly chewed on it. "Forget I said anything. Let's kill some chevs. Woo...or something."

Taki sighed to himself, glad that Hadassah seemed to be settling down for the moment. In truth, finding Hecaton Mezeta had become less and less important as each day passed. Lotte had assigned him purser duties for the entire regiment of five tercios, two wings of light horse, and a reliquary. He now saw tables and figures in his sleep, rather than visions of a taunting old woman whose face was increasingly difficult to remember.

Draco broke the silence. "I am disappointed by one thing, though. I never did get to see the Tirefire of Berlin."

"Oh, yuck! Don't even remind me of that," Hadassah said.

"It was our proud namesake!" Draco said. "Or at least the one on Santorini was."

"I bet it doesn't really exist," Hadassah said.

"It certainly does. Elsa swore it true. Smoke column wide as a league and towering high enough to finger God's bung."

"You blasphemer. The Almighty has no asshole."

"So you're saying God doesn't poop?"

"That's right. He neither shits, nor pisses, nor farts, either."

"But since we're crafted in his image, then why must we use the jakes?"

"Because it feels really good in the morning."

Taki opened his mouth in an effort to silence his companions and save his own appetite, but a quavering rumble from afar stifled his words. The others noticed it too and fell silent. Hands dropped and hovered over hilts.

Karma sniffed and grimaced. "Hair and flesh. Coming from the village. Shit." He looked over to Taki. "Well, sir?"

Taki's fingers strayed to his mouth, but he wrenched them away before he could start chewing his nails. He looked back at the others and nodded. "We have to go in."

Draco hurriedly kicked clods of dirt over the campfire while Hadassah screwed her cleaning rod back into place. She opened her rifle's bolt to check for a cartridge, which was present. Karma shoved the rest of his harspud into his mouth and slung the lute over his back.

Taki tugged, ever so slightly, at his blade. It slid smoothly from the scabbard partway, and he pushed it back. Nearby, he spied a waist-high wall of painstakingly fitted stone. It would lead them in the general direction of the town and, more importantly, provide some safety against ambush. "Stick to cover and keep close, you lot. We've got to find the captain and regroup, no matter what."

With measured, loping steps, the four made their way across the scrubby field. The acrid hint of burning human matter in the air gave way to the cloying, rotten-egg smell of gunsmoke. Taki spied out one of the many wooden shacks that dotted the edges of town and drew carefully up to it. Shouts and the clanking of steel rang out on the opposite side. Smoke haze rose in the air and colored the light of the setting sun brown.

If they've set on the townsfolk… Taki's hands grew cold, and his heart raced. It didn't make sense, though. Lotte was firmly in charge of the men and wouldn't allow such a thing. *Or would she?* He peered over the edge of the ridge and gasped.

An Imperial pikeman shuffled unsteadily on his knees, clutching at his gut. His tunic was soaked in crimson, and his face was already deathly white. His gaze met Taki's, and he raised a bloodstained hand.

Before he uttered a sound, a cudgel caved his crown in. Chunks of grayish-pink matter splashed on the packed dirt, and the body flopped over. Standing over the corpse with weapon in hand was an Ursalan. Not an enemy soldier but a milkmaid.

Taki scrambled to his feet, drew his blade, and leveled it at the woman but stopped short of charging her. "Drop your weapon! *Explain yourself!*"

She raised her club and started toward him. "Inferior beings! Die!"

"I'm warning you! Drop your weapon right now!" His arm tensed and shook.

The woman was almost on him when a gunshot rang out. The back of her head exploded into fragments, and she collapsed into a sodden heap.

Hadassah lowered her pistol. "What the hell's wrong with you, Nata? Scared of her raging cunt?"

Taki shivered. "This woman...her name is Jeanne." He clenched his jaw to still the chattering of his teeth. "I talked with her only a bell or two ago! She offered to give me a wheel of cheese. I...it's against regulations."

"And now she just about killed your dumb ass," Hadassah said. "I knew these bastards were up to something!"

"It's why we supped so far away," Karma said.

"Well, we're surrounded," Draco said. He hefted his fighting iron in both hands and sank into a ready stance.

From alleys and around brick corners, more Ursalans started to emerge. None of them were obviously soldiers, most were armed, and all bore an expression of singularly murderous intent.

"We need to get to the church," Taki said. He intoned a sutra under his breath, and prana started to gather in his core. "The captain told me she'd remain there for a while. The mayor was going to introduce her to his burghers."

Draco spat. "You left her alone in the middle of this place?"

"There were other officers, plus at least a hundred enlisted," Taki said. His eyes flitted around and settled on a darkened alley nearby. "I'll blast a path for us. Run with me, and don't fight unless you really have to."

He raised his free arm and mouthed the intonation, and a burst of compressed air issued from his palm. It smacked into a loosely formed group of men and bowled them over like ninepins. Splintery chunks of makeshift shields and flaming torches flew through the air. Taki took off running and forced himself not to examine the townsfolk as he passed them.

Taki burst out onto the main drag and instinctively ducked for cover when he heard the sound of gunfire. He scurried up to an overturned cart and peered around it. No more than a few paces away, Ursalan townsmen crouched behind other makeshift barricades with weapons at the ready.

Some bore what looked like ancient muskets, while most others hefted nail-studded table legs or drying poles with the ends cut into sharp points. Beyond the mob was Taki's intended destination: the high-walled church in the center of town where Lotte was.

We have surprise on our side, Taki thought with a grim smile. He tore at the cuticle of his thumb. *But just barely.* Silently, he signaled to the others. They nodded back and started to gather their energies.

Rapid-fire shots rang out from a second-story window on the church's face, and the townsmen scrambled back in fear, while some of their number collapsed. Taki peered around from his cover at the source, and his eyes widened.

"It's the captain," he barked at the squad. "She's alive! Rush the bastards and make a break for the doors!"

With shouts and ululations, Tirefire the Lesser burst out into the main drag and set on the panicked townsmen with blades and bullets. Taki easily pivoted out of getting impaled with a spear, ran his opponent through to the hilt, and looked up once again at where Lotte was.

"Captain!" He waved his arms at her. "Can you make it down here?"

"Natalis? You need to get out of here! Take the squad and make a break for it."

Taki scrunched his brow. "But we came here to get you!"

"We can't leave the mayor! The loyalists will kill him!" She squeezed off another shot and felled a nearby man trying to sneak up on Taki. "Help me defend the place if you won't leave. One of the Imperials will get the door."

A few seconds later, Taki heard the scraping of wood against metal, and a pair of iron-reinforced doors opened in front of him. A bloody-faced Imperial peered out and frantically gestured for Taki and his group.

"Don't need to tell me twice," Karma said as he rushed in with Hadassah in tow. Draco followed soon after. Taki took a last look around before retreating to sanctuary. The townsmen were amassing behind cover again. He spat. Was there truly no reasoning with them?

The Imperial wheezed and shook as he barred the doors again. The inside was almost blasphemous in its appearance. The pews were shattered, the altar destroyed, and fresh bodies strewn around made the slate floor slick with blood.

Taki swallowed. Among the corpses were Imperials, some of whom he'd made tentative friendships with while the regiments had prepared for war. "You lot, see if the survivors need anything and shore up the defense. I'll go up to aid the captain."

To his surprise, he heard no objections. Gingerly, to avoid stepping on the fallen, he made his way to a set of nearby stairs leading up. The gunfire from Lotte's end had stopped in the meantime. He forced himself to quash visions of her brains evacuated by a lucky potshot. To his relief, he saw her a moment later, surrounded by spent casings and furiously working to unjam her rifle. Huddled in terror nearby were the town's mayor and a handful of burghers.

"Report," Lotte said.

"The town, it's gone crazy," Taki said. "A godrotting *milkmaid* stove in a man's head right in front of me! She's dead now. We had no choice."

"Anyone who murders my people deserves death, Natalis," Lotte said. "Damn my stupidity, though. I should've paid more heed to the warnings."

"Warnings about what?"

"Von Halcon told me to be on edge. To dig in for insurgency, but I didn't think it'd be this widespread or organized. I only hope the main force has rallied well. At the very least these are simply peasants with torches and not chevaliers."

Taki glared at the mayor. "How about him? Did he cause this?"

"Nay, good sir!" The mayor shuffled on his knees and started to kiss Taki's boots. "I had nothing to do with any of this! You lot may be enemies of the crown, but you've treated us right fair!"

Taki backed away with a grimace. "On your feet, man! I believe you, damn it."

"I think him sincere," Lotte said. "But I also find the whole thing suspicious. Most armies don't even mobilize this quickly, much less partisans. I intend to take this man and his burghers with us. Find out if we can expect this behavior in the future."

"And then?" Taki began.

"I'll honor my promises. I'll release him, even if he somehow ordered this business. Do you understand this, sir?"

The mayor nodded.

11

Lotte took another look out of her window. "Too many right now for us to make a break for it. Natalis, do you have your signals? It's a long shot but our only chance right now."

"Aye, Captain," Taki said. His fingers brushed over the small wooden satchel hanging from his bandolier. "I'll fire the green."

He moved to the window and opened the box. Standard issue to Imperial officers, it contained a smooth-bore pipe-gun and a set of red and green flares. He withdrew the chunky-looking gun, opened the breech, and shoved the squat cartridge inside. He took aim at the sky through the bullet-riddled window frame and squeezed the trigger.

Steel crunched against metal and scraped against mail and leather, followed by the sound of yielding flesh. Taki whirled around, and his hand shot to his kriegsmesser. The blade cleared its scabbard even before he saw Lotte fall to one knee with a dagger hilt sticking out from her back. The mayor's eyes shone with malice as he stepped back and reached into his vest.

One of the burghers lunged in from the flank. Much as Taki would have loved to decapitate the mayor where he stood, the immediate threat was too pressing. Taki shifted his hips and slashed the burgher under the armpit. The blade sank into the man's torso and lodged firmly into a vertebra. Taki let go of his hilt just in time to meet a tackle attempt by another townsman. The two rolled on the ground for a short while until Taki punched the burgher's throat and caved the man's windpipe in. An untrained serf was no match for a Polaris of the Temple. Taki kicked the choking man off and scrambled to his feet to help Lotte.

With a subdued, squelching noise, the mayor's head split open between the corner of an oaken table and Lotte's palm. She stepped back and slumped against the wall nearby the window.

"Captain!" Taki rushed over to her, and his hand wrapped around the handle of the knife stuck in her back. It had gone between the plates and punched through mail. "Hold still."

Lotte turned and waved him off. "Leave it in, Natalis. You want me to bleed out?"

"No!" Taki, feeling foolish, loosened his grip.

"Good boy," Lotte said with a wince. "Did the flare go off?"

"Aye." Taki dared a glance out the window. The crackling chaos and gunfire outside had dulled to a low hum, but whatever relief he could take from that was diminished by a new sight: cannons.

"Shit," Lotte muttered. She'd seen the same. "They're loading ship's grape. These walls might as well be parchment against that."

"Can we escape?" Taki said.

Lotte shook her head. "There's no rear door. You shouldn't have come."

"With all due respect, Captain, that's a load of steaming bullshit."

"Watch your tongue, Natalis, lest I flog you for insolence," Lotte said with a chuckle.

"I'd like to see you try!" Taki stopped as he heard rumbling and gunfire outside. The low din of townsfolk massing for an attack was replaced by shouts and screams. His curiosity having gotten the better of any sense of self-preservation, he peered over the sill again and let out a whoop. "It's Sir Aslatiel!"

A wedge of Imperials on horseback thundered down the avenue, firing pistols and throwing lances. At the head of the charge, Aslatiel von Halcon furiously hacked at any opposition that his horse hadn't simply knocked away. He held his reins between clenched teeth, and his free hand held high a spear on which had been tied a ragged Osterbrand war standard.

The mass of Ursalans melted before and crumbled beneath the onslaught, and the Imperial charge swept over the bronze cannons pointed at the church doors. The tarnished guns fell off their mountings and clanked as they rolled unceremoniously across the cobbles.

Aslatiel reared his horse, turned, and shouted at the riders behind him. With perfect coordination, they peeled off into the side streets and vanished from Taki's sight. Only one other remained with Aslatiel. Simultaneously, they dismounted and strode up to the doors.

"Go meet him," Lotte said.

"I'd rather aid you." Taki's gaze flicked over the jutting knife handle. From below, he heard the sound of cheers. "I may not be a surgeon, but—"

Lotte reached over and gently flicked Taki's ear. "I can tell you want to see him."

Taki's lips curled into a smirk. "He's still a godrotting asshole."

"Glad to see you again, Natalis," Aslatiel said.

Shit. Taki turned and gave a stiff-bodied salute to his superior. "Oberleutnant."

Before Aslatiel could return it, someone barreled across the room and nearly tackled Taki to the floor.

"You idiot!" Enilna fixed a glare at him. "I leave you alone for one godrotting battle and find you trying to get yourself killed in the stupidest way possible. Give me your leutnant's chain! You don't deserve it!"

"Sh-shut up!" Taki pouted and swatted Enilna's grasping hands away from his neck. "Why couldn't you have been Lady Lucatiel or Lady Irulan? I'd have been glad to see them and not some annoying brat."

"Shithead!" She crossed her arms. "I can't believe I wanted to sleep with you at one point. Just go die a virgin already!"

"Maybe I will!"

"Then do it right now!"

Lotte cuffed Taki upside the head. "Enough! Von Halcon, do you know how the rest of my men fare?"

"Aye," Aslatiel said. "The Ursalans turned their wrath on the unfortunates in town, but your camp held strong. A small number fell, perhaps less than three squads."

"And the townsfolk?"

"Driven back for now. Riders will round up the rest."

"Why?" Taki said. "Why would they turn on us so suddenly? We treated them fairly."

"For many Ursalans, there is no life without the Sanctissimus Rex. Death is preferable to suffering a foreign presence," Aslatiel said. He glanced at Lotte's wound. "If you had a knife plunged into you, wouldn't you be consumed with the desire to remove it?"

"I admit, my tolerance is running thin," Lotte said.

"Captain, I'll call for a stretcher," Aslatiel said. "You need a surgeon's attention."

"No thanks," Lotte said. "I won't rest on a bed while the rest of my soldiers suffer on their feet. Shpejtspate, lend me an arm."

Enilna chewed at her lower lip but nodded and allowed Lotte to sling an arm over her shoulder. Taki allowed himself to stare at Enilna's back for a second as the two women departed. Since their first meeting, the girl had visibly grown and was now almost a match for Taki's height. The skin on the back of her neck looked like coarse leather after months of marching under the sun, and she seemed more sinewy than ever before. Taki sighed to himself.

"It's easy to forget that she was once a starving orphan," Aslatiel said. He pulled his leather gloves off and stuffed them under his sword belt. "Fated to perish of dysentery or die while giving birth after her own rape. But instead, she's grown into a fine woman and a fine soldier. That's no accident, nor is it because of the will of some absentee god. It happened because of *us*."

Taki paced. "Sir Aslatiel, what are you trying to say?"

"That the Imperial Way—our conquests and all of the bloodshed and suffering they bring—is the only hope left in this world. We are the only people who want to help our fellow men and women for any reason beyond self-interest. No one but we would ever have given young Enilna this opportunity. I hope you haven't forgotten that. I hope you wear your leutnant's chain with some pride. You are, after all, one of our own."

"I still can't forgive you for lying to us," Taki said. "Lying to me."

"About Hecaton Mezeta? Does your ire for one woman really outstrip everything else? Everything we could accomplish for what's good and right?"

"She stole our pensions and our futures."

"How much did she take? Five hundred rounds of Luger milligrad? My sister expends more in one day of battle. If it will soothe your anger, I will take you to the hauptmann quartermaster right now and let you take whatever you wish from the payboxes: five hundred rounds, or a thousand, or ten thousand. You're welcome to it all!"

Taki balled his hands into fists. "I'd rather you apologized!"

Aslatiel shook his head. "I will never abase myself for doing my duty for my Imperium. But I *am* sorry that I've hurt you. I never intended to do that." He placed his hands on Taki's shoulders. "You're a fine soldier, and I consider you a friend."

Taki looked away from Aslatiel's gaze. "I suppose that's the best either of us can do."

"Believe me," Aslatiel said. He dropped his arms to his sides and smiled. "You're much more forgiving than Lucatiel, any given day."

"Where is she now? Your sister?"

"Back with my regiment. We broke through enemy lines a bell after Captain Satou did."

"Did the Ursalans rise against you as well?"

"Not like this. We faced some harassment from scouts, but that was it."

"Have any others crossed yet?"

Aslatiel shook his head. "Only us. Eight regiments still battle as we speak. We're the vanguard."

"So things aren't going as planned," Taki said.

"Battles never go to plan. The Ursalans are skilled fighters, fueled by zealotry, and believe that the highest honor in life is to die in battle for the Rex." Aslatiel peered out the window at the burning town. "I would have liked more time to prepare."

"But the Padishah insisted we move this fast." Taki started to chew on a nail again. "And I'm concerned how slow the supply caravans have been moving. Our last shipment of cannon shells was late by a week."

"*Ba'gshnar*—I mean, His Majesty—has never lost a battle in his life," Aslatiel said. "I'm absolutely certain he has his reasons. Perhaps this is part of his plan to capture Hecaton Mezeta."

But do you really trust him? Taki bit his tongue before the question formed on his lips. It wouldn't do to offend Aslatiel right now, especially after they'd reached a reconciliation of sorts. "So what now? I was only given our strategy up to taking this town."

"After we firmly hold the Rhone valley, we'll make our main camp in the deepwood of Morvan. There's a wealth of timber for stockades and earthworks, plenty of game to feed us, and ample water nearby. We'll be on solid footing to surround Versailles. And the irony is that Morvan is the Rex's personal hunting ground."

Taki bowed his head in thought. "I hear that west of Ursala there's nothing but endless sea. Is that the one the Padishah wants to cross?"

"I imagine it would be."

"What if there's nothing on the other side? What if the world really *is* just a dish suspended in the heavens?"

"Then, Natalis, we'll have gotten to see what no one else has seen, which is of inestimable worth by itself." Aslatiel shrugged. "Let's not tarry overmuch in this place. The town's ruined, and we need to secure the grain stores before the Ursalans try to burn it all."

"Damn it," Taki said. "We paid them for the grain, too. They could've...I suppose it makes no difference now."

"I'm just glad to see you and your fellows unhurt. Let's check on everyone else." Aslatiel clapped Taki on the back, and the two descended to the ground floor.

The shattered pews and desecrated altars had been pushed aside, and the corpses were laid out in rows to restore some semblance of dignity. Taki blinked in surprise, for his comrades seemed earnest about assisting their Imperial counterparts. Lotte sat on a bench with her cuirass off, while Draco tore swatches of linen into strips. A nearby brazier warmed a brace of iron pokers, and Taki looked away, not wishing to think more about what would happen next.

A woman in a full-face helm stepped into the church and saluted to Aslatiel. "We've returned, Oberleutnant."

Aslatiel returned the salute. "Glad to hear it, Kommissar."

The soldier removed the helm, and blond hair spilled out and around Irulan Surenovna's face. She winked at Aslatiel, who gave her rear a subtle caress as they walked together. Taki's cheeks started to redden at the sight, and he looked over to Enilna, who squatted like a frog next to Karma and gobbled down harspuds. She tried to say something to Taki and let out a belch instead. Taki silently griped: *Why can't she be more feminine?*

"Did you capture any?" Aslatiel asked Irulan.

"Aye. They're in the square."

Taki raised an eyebrow. "What happens to them?"

"The guilty will hang. The innocent will walk."

"Even if they're just villagers?" Taki asked.

"We carry out the same justice for all uprisings. Soldiers or civilians, they betrayed and attacked us after we gave them safety."

Taki gritted his teeth and nodded. *He has a point. This is a battlefield, after all.*

The rest of the Imperial riders had dismounted and now leveled their guns at two dozen Ursalan townsfolk huddled together. Most were able-bodied men, with a handful of women; all faced their captors with a look of defiant hate. Taki shuddered involuntarily as he recalled the milkmaid's eyes. *There's really no other way for them, is there?*

"The penalty for murder of Imperial soldiers is death," Aslatiel said to the prisoners. "Any who will swear innocence, speak now, and you will be spared." None of the townsfolk replied. Aslatiel shook his head. "Throw them all in the gaol. We'll hold a real inquest later, when we've got a magistrate present."

"Halt!" Irulan strode toward the group. "Oberleutnant, one of them hides a child under her cloak."

"Surenovna, wait," Aslatiel began, but Irulan had already dragged out one of the women, who was wrapped in a long, mud-splattered shawl. She pulled the cloth aside to reveal a little girl, perhaps only seven, who clung desperately to the woman's waist.

"Goodwife, is this your daughter?" Irulan asked.

The woman spat in Irulan's face. In the periphery of his vision, Taki saw Aslatiel's hand reach for a pistol. Irulan simply wiped the spittle away.

"Your child could not have raised a hand against us. She's innocent. And she needs her mother. Come with me. We'll feed and clothe her and tend to your wounds. We're not evil."

"Inferior being!" The woman swiped at Irulan with her nails and missed.

"Choose for yourself, but I won't let you drag your child into this," Irulan said, and gripped the girl's arm.

The girl resisted a bit but then stepped away. Taki let out a sigh of relief.

"Aslatiel," Irulan said. "Make sure this one's mother comes to no harm."

The girl tugged at Irulan's sleeve.

Irulan knelt down to face her new charge. "Are you hungry?"

The girl smiled and shook her head. Hidden from Irulan's sight, but not Taki's, something glinted in her free hand. Taki reached out on instinct, and a shout formed on his lips. He caught the girl's wrist and twisted to force the knife out of her hand, but it was too late.

Irulan lurched backward and let out a choking gasp. Crimson spurted from between her fingers as she clawed at her throat and lines of blood trailed from the corners of her lips. Her knees buckled, and she fell gracelessly to the cobbles. Shouts erupted, and a gun went off.

The resultant barrage plunged the square into a chaos of noise, flashes, and swirling smoke. Through the choking haze, Taki saw Ursalan bodies slump and hit the ground. The girl squirmed and tried to flee, but he held tight, not knowing what else to do. The sudden onslaught had deafened him, but he could have sworn he'd heard Aslatiel screaming. Behind him, the church doors slammed open with a bang, and yet more cursing buffeted his ears.

As quickly as it had appeared, the gunsmoke lifted. Taki's jaw dropped. The townsfolk lay still in the center of a pool of seeping red. Aslatiel held Irulan in his arms, bellowing at her to move, to talk with him, to do anything. Her skin was porcelain white, and her eyes were open and rolled back in her head. Her arms hung limply at her sides. For what seemed like an entire bell, Aslatiel continued to cajole and beg her to respond. Finally, he laid her down, whispered something inaudible, and kissed her pale lips.

"God, no…" Taki whispered.

The girl in his grasp squirmed; Taki's fingers finally gave way, and he lost his grip on her. He turned and lunged at her ankles, only to hear a gunshot ring out. Crimson spurted from the girl's back, and she flopped face first to the street. To Taki's horror, the girl shook and tried to drag herself away with the little strength she had left.

Aslatiel glided past Taki, leveled his smoking pistol, and fired twice more. The girl ceased to move. The gun stovepiped on a casing. Aslatiel wordlessly cleared the jam and racked the slide again. He pointed it at the body.

"Stop," Taki hissed. He grasped Aslatiel's wrist. "Just stop it! She's already dead!"

Aslatiel drew his weapon hand back, as if to bludgeon Taki across the face. Taki flinched and prepared for the blow, but it never came. Aslatiel holstered his gun and staggered away without a word.

2

A fortnight later, the Liberation Army had plunged claws into the royal Morvan deepwood. What had been an unbroken sea of green was now stripped completely bare and turned to endless rows of tents surrounded by a stockade thick as two men laid end to end and four men high. The air had once been clear and had rung with the songs of ortolans, but a pall of thick smoke now hung over everything while the birds roasted on spits over fires. Hundreds of thousands of Imperial soldiers called the camp home, with more arriving every single day.

Taki coughed and tried to bury his mouth and nose in his scarf in a vain attempt to block out the dust. Thick and choking, it billowed from under the rumbling, armored reliquary passing him, flanked by marching attendants made faceless and monolithic by their robes. He waited impatiently for the armored hulk to pass, remembering a time when he'd almost lost his legs to one of them.

Rumors were that a whole quarter of the Imperium's stock of working relics was now stationed at Morvan. The air was thick enough with musky diesel fumes to make Taki believe it. The path he traveled overlooked a shooting range, and the irregular cracking of muskets and rifles reminded him of popping corn. He passed a troop of Varangians watering their horses, avoided colliding with a column of hussars, and eventually found who he was looking for.

Lucatiel sat on a pile of wooden pallets in a secluded glade, where it was quiet and the air was clear, surrounded by destroyed crates. She was concentrating, honing the edges of her jian with a smooth-worn stone. Taki hesitated to disrupt such laser focus but pressed on regardless. Before he could speak, Lucatiel leapt up from her seat and had her blade leveled at his neck.

"Oh, it's *you*," she said. The jian plunged back into its sheath, and she crossed her arms. "What do you want, Natalis?"

Taki let out a slow breath. The Prince of Maladies was still as unsettling as hell to be around. "My captain sent me to get you. The Padishah's about to address all of the officers. And, well, Sir Aslatiel probably won't—"

"Have the will to attend?" Lucatiel said with a glare. Her sapphire eyes glinted with menace.

"Aye," Taki said. "Do you contest that?"

Lucatiel sighed and shook her head. "We should all be used to losing our friends by now. A day of grief, and then right back to battle! That's *our* way, and that's what makes us different from the sheep living fat and happy in the heartland. Elsa bounced right back after Mikhail died. But my brother…"

"I'd be awash in grief if my lover perished," Taki said.

Lucatiel jabbed his chest with a finger. "I loved Irulan too! In fact, we were *more* than friends. And yes, that's possible between two women, you slack-jawed barbarian."

Taki raised his hands. "I'm an Argead, milady. We invented lesbians."

"Whatever." Lucatiel paced. "That doesn't solve our problem. Aslatiel's useless as he is right now, and I have no interest in commanding a regiment. There's too much inspection, writing reports, and dealing with you bean-counters."

Taki rolled his eyes. "I'm just here to get you to the meeting on time. I don't know why you're ranting to me."

"Because you're not a threat," Lucatiel said. "And you're also a secretive sort, so I know you won't blabber on like the other fools in your group."

"You don't have many friends, do you?" Taki said with a frown.

"No, I don't," Lucatiel said. "Whatever. I don't want to displease *Ba'gshnar*, so I'll come with you. But as soon as that's done, I want you to go to Aslatiel and smack some sense into him. No one else has the guts to call him out on his shit, not even me. But you might. Besides, he's always liked you a little too much."

"Definitely no friends," Taki said.

"Will you promise to help, or do I have to beat your ass first?"

"No need for beatings," Taki said.

After a brief, dusty stroll, Taki finally reached the Padishah's sheepskin longhouse, or yurt, as was the proper term. He was glad to arrive, for it had taken a toll on his neck to periodically look over his shoulder to ensure that Lucatiel still followed close behind. Or, at the very least, wasn't about to shank him. He had figured out quickly that she wasn't one for conversation.

Taki nodded to the two halberd-wielding trebizonds guarding the entrance to the yurt. Because he was an officer, he was allowed to keep his weapons close, even in the presence of the highest authority in the Imperium. Having faced the old man in battle, Taki knew that having a side arm made no difference. The trebizonds pulled their halberds back to allow him access, and he pushed through the tent flaps into the dark and stuffy interior.

A far cry from Taki's expectations, the inside of the yurt was overwhelmingly rustic, almost crude. Even an Argead camp follower's tent had more accoutrements than what he saw before him. The only source of light or heat was a glowing brazier in the center, and everyone from generals to their pages sat uncomfortably on a packed-dirt floor. Before the fire, Chronicler—now Padishah of the Imperium—sat in what looked like deep meditation. Upon Taki's entrance, the old man opened his remaining eye.

"Mind that your flirtation does not interfere with business, young man and woman," Chronicler said.

Laughter sounded from the assembled commanders and Taki felt his stomach turn. With a wave of his hand, Chronicler signaled for silence.

"After much bloodshed, we have gained a solid foothold in the heart of Ursala. No army has managed to camp so close to Versailles since the Fall or strike such fear into the heart of the royal family. Some of you in this room have encountered them up close." He stared pointedly at Taki. "And you will agree with me that they have no respect for honor and decency. Worse still, the Ursalans desire expansion and will stop at nothing short of total domination. Unlike we, who wish to spread the Way to all oppressed people of the world, the Ursalan menace only seeks enslavement. You've seen the effects in their unwitting subjects who throw their lives away in attempts to murder us. But for all the good that we wish to bring to the people of Ursala, I will now reveal to you the most important reason that you fight."

Chonicler paused to toss a lump of dried dung into the brazier. The flames glowed, eager to devour new fuel. Chronicler muttered an incantation and gestured at the fire. A ball of plasma seemed to separate out from the flames and float in midair. Surrounding the hovering, flickering mass was a corona of ash.

"The foolish ancients who brought about the end of our world had many ambitions, and one of the greatest was to climb to the heavens at will. In the skies, well above what we can see with our eyes, there exists a man-made ring that circles our globe. If a man were to traverse the ring, he could reach any point on this planet at will. The same goes for an army. The Ursalans aim to reach that ring in the heavens, and they are very close to doing so. I trust you realize what that would mean for our nation and our way of life." Chronicler gestured again, and the ash ring collapsed into the floating flames and snuffed them out with a violent thump. "But if we can co-opt their ambitions, perhaps ours will be realized sooner than we thought."

"Your Majesty," one of the generals blurted out, "how come your predecessor never shared this knowledge with us?"

"Because he wished to keep it a secret. But I, Shastirch of the Ghazar Khoch Tenger, want my warriors to know exactly why they fight, bleed, and die on my behalf. Honesty is the only acceptable treatment from one fighter to another."

"Then," another general stammered, "you have our redoubled loyalty and respect. Hail Padishah Shastirch! Hail Padishah Shastirch!"

In unison, the commanders in the room chanted their declarations of loyalty. And despite himself, Taki almost felt compelled to join in. The concept of a heavenly construct allowing transport to any part of the globe seemed far-fetched, but then again, the ancients had produced seemingly infinite wonders, even if most of those had degraded into plastic. *And perhaps...* Unbidden hope swelled within. *Perhaps that's how we can finally reach Hecaton Mezeta!*

Chronicler waved for silence once more. "Your cheer gladdens me, my soldiers. However, I did not share these revelations with you for praise. I only wish that you draw strength and purpose from this knowledge, especially since we have lost so many to get here. Together, we will save this earth. Together, we are the last, best hope for humanity. *Uukhai!*"

The resultant cheer deafened Taki more than any line of muskets. Lucatiel wrapped her fingers around his arm and tugged. He stumbled but managed to find his footing as they emerged from the tent.

"Either *Ba'gshnar* has lost his fucking mind, or we're about to actually punch God in the face," Lucatiel said. "This was worth attending! I guess I owe your captain for making me come."

"Wait," Taki blinked. "Why would we want to hurt the Almighty?"

"You don't?"

"No."

She shrugged. "You lack ambition, Natalis. I fail to understand why my brother, or Enilna for that matter, likes you so."

Taki shot Lucatiel a glare. "Can we please not talk about Shpejtspate?"

"What, do you hate her all of a sudden?"

"No, but it's complicated between us."

Lucatiel smirked. "Your equipment doesn't work, does it?"

"It works *fine*, goddamn you."

"You've never used it! Why don't you just tell Enilna the truth and spare her some pain?"

"You're just pissed about me beating you in Pristina," Taki sneered. Now he was heated and wouldn't stand her insults any longer. "Some *nobody* cunt-punted the invincible Prince of Maladies and lived to tell the tale! You'll take that shame to your *grave*, won't you?"

Lucatiel's nostrils flared, and her fingers twitched. For a moment, Taki worried she'd actually try to kill him where he stood. But instead, Lucatiel seemed to relent.

"Enough," she said. "You're right, Natalis. I'm still mad as hell about it. Even now, I can't bear to look at your noodle arms and sunken chest and know that some *manlet* could've ended me. I would've sniped you later on, but it was Aslatiel forbade me. You owe my brother your life. So now it's time for your end of the deal."

"Aye," Taki said. He let out a breath of mixed relief and triumph. "Let's go to your brother. Lead on."

As the commander of Alfa Gruppe, Aslatiel occupied his own tent as he would have occupied his own quarters in Sevastopol. As Taki drew closer to the entrance, he waved to Elsa, who guarded the entry.

Lucatiel pushed ahead. "Has he eaten?"

Elsa shook her head. "He picks at things, is all. And only when I cajole him with all my might. I've tried to be as annoying as possible, but he doesn't seem to respond." She looked at the ground. "He won't even tell me to shut up, Luca. I…"

"It's okay," Lucatiel said. "I know you're trying your best. We'll deal with him."

"Aye," Elsa said. She drew the tent flap open.

Taki's pupils dilated as he stepped in. In contrast to the brightness of the noonday sun outside, the interior was almost pitch black, without even a single candle for illumination. He scrunched up his nose; the tent smelled strongly sour, almost fecal.

"Aslatiel," Lucatiel said. "I've brought Natalis. You told me you had something you wanted to say to him."

Taki's eyes had adjusted to the point where he could faintly make out someone sitting on the floor, leaned up against an unused bedframe. *Sir Aslatiel.* He took a step forward, and his feet collided with a pile of metal trays. Decaying food slopped over his boots, and he grimaced. Aslatiel did not respond.

"We need some light, Sir Aslatiel," Taki said, and snapped his fingers. A small gout of flame burst from his fingertips and cast a pale, flickering glow throughout the room. Taki scanned around, found a candelabrum on a nearby side table, and held his flame to the wicks until they ignited. He looked back at Aslatiel and resisted the urge to gasp.

Aslatiel's cheeks were gaunt, his eyes hollow, and his hair an unkempt mess. He wore only a pair of stained britches and no shirt. Around him were stacked more platters of uneaten food. He did not look up at Taki.

Lucatiel held a hand over her mouth in an obvious attempt not to vomit and stepped over to Aslatiel. She took him by the shoulder and shook roughly. "Honorable Brother, you have a friend visiting. It's impolite not to greet him."

At this, Aslatiel raised his head. "Thank you, Luca. And...I'm sorry, Leutnant Natalis, but I'm not good company right now."

"That's quite all right, Sir Aslatiel," Taki said. He squatted and tried to think of something to say. *Probably shouldn't mention Lady Irulan right now*. He swallowed. "C-can we help you with cleaning your tent up? It needs airing, and the cooks want their trenchers back."

"No," Aslatiel said. "I want to be alone right now."

"Brother, that's what you say—" Lucatiel started.

"Sir Aslatiel," Taki interjected. "You taught me to be frank and not mince words. So please listen to me. The Padishah has just informed us of the true importance of this campaign. I don't understand all the details, but it seems the Ursalans may have stumbled on something dangerous. We must redouble our efforts to capture their capital."

"Is that so?" Aslatiel's voice was distant.

"Yes," Taki said. "And your regiment needs you in command. It is improper to make your sister assume your duties without an increase in pay and rank. My captain also requires your counsel as well as your assurances that the Imperium has not forgotten our needs or our reason for joining."

Aslatiel looked up. Taki held his breath. *Have I reached him? He was always the dutiful type.*

"Sorry to burden everyone," Aslatiel said. "But I just don't care."

Taki bit his lip. "Sir Aslatiel, is this how Lady Irulan would have wanted you to be? Sodden with shit and holed up in your quarters like a moping child?"

"She's dead. The dead desire nothing."

"Then how about me?" Taki stepped forward. In the pit of his stomach, something started to burn. Not nausea or fear or loathing but rather, anger. Unbidden, memories surfaced: the whipping after Vergina,

Aslatiel holding him at gunpoint in Pristina, Hecaton Mezeta ordering him to Athenaeum, the basileus slumping lifeless in a chair. "I'm still living, aren't I? Your sister's still living, isn't she? What about us? Do we not matter to you?"

"Do what you want," Aslatiel said.

"That's not an answer!" Taki brushed past Lucatiel and took Aslatiel by the throat. More memories flooded him: the Black Cross storming the kitchens, the Usurper's pronouncement of death, the tavern brawl. "You screwed up my life, von Halcon! You and your people are responsible for every horrible thing that's happened to me since I became a Polaris. You sank my career and turned me into a kingslayer! So you have to live on, so that all my suffering wasn't for nothing. Otherwise, why the hell am I still here? Why the hell am I still alive?"

Taki clenched his jaw and started to squeeze. He could sense Lucatiel on edge, but she hadn't killed either of them yet.

Just as Aslatiel's features began to darken into a subtle shade of blue, something resembling indignation crossed his features. Aslatiel lashed out with an arm, grasped Taki by the front of his jerkin, and tossed him into a corner of the tent. Platters clanked and upended their contents onto Taki's head.

"Stop blaming me for everything, damn you!" Aslatiel roared, rearing to his full height. He stomped over to Taki and reached down, only to be rewarded by a punch straight to the jaw.

"Bastard," Taki snarled as Aslatiel stumbled back. "Do you know what happened to me after we first met? They fucking flogged me! Because *you people* had to show up!" He charged at Aslatiel's midsection and caught the Alfa commander in a grapple-turned-tumble.

Aslatiel swung a leg around to unbalance Taki and flip him to the ground. "I carried out my orders! What was I supposed to do, consider your godrotting *feelings* and not take the fort?"

Taki swept at Aslatiel's legs with both feet and was rewarded with a boot to his gut. "You plunged me into a world of shit. I killed my liege because of you!"

"Screw off!" Aslatiel reached down again and lifted Taki by the throat. "I didn't tell you to do *anything*! You killed that old fart all on your own! Have some fucking pride in yourself, man!"

Taki kicked out to no avail while trying to pry Aslatiel's iron grip apart. As he started to become lightheaded, he let out a choking laugh. "You too, you son of a bitch!"

At this, Aslatiel let go; Taki crumpled to the ground, gasping for air. He rolled onto his side, hacking and spitting. Aslatiel crouched next to him, but not for another attack. Instead, the spetsnaz offered a hand. "Natalis, I…I apologize. I acted rashly…"

Taki took Aslatiel's hand in his own and dragged himself to his knees. "Don't worry. My captain's dished out much worse. You could take some tips from her, you know."

Aslatiel clenched his jaw. "And I'm also sorry for what happened that day. I was lost in rage. I almost struck you with my weapon."

Taki shook his head. "I understand, Sir Aslatiel. I forgive you. Lady Irulan was a worthy companion. We all mourn her loss."

"She died as she lived," Aslatiel said. He wiped at his eyes. "Trying to aid the oppressed and voiceless. That was her life's dream. And they just turned on her. Down to that godrotting child. But I'll avenge her. I'll avenge her and end this madness no matter what."

Taki let out a guarded breath. "And you'll have my—no, everyone's support doing so."

Aslatiel drew Taki close and wrapped him in an embrace. "My thanks. I'll count on you in the coming days. You are a true follower of the Way. I am grateful to know you."

Taki smiled, even through the stink. "Shall I send Captain Satou by when you've cleaned up?"

"Aye. I have much to discuss with her. And Luca, tell *Ba'gshnar* that I—no, *we*—are back to fighting trim."

Taki got to his feet, saluted, and retreated out of the tent. As he closed the flap, he heard Lucatiel sobbing. Elsa gave him a quick pat on the back and whispered her thanks. Taki shook the cricks out of his neck and started to walk jauntily back to his own tent. He stretched and beamed in satisfaction. Aslatiel was whole again, and perhaps Lucatiel would stop being such a shrew. And then, after Versailles fell to Imperial cannons, Taki would make his case that perhaps he deserved yet another promotion.

"You smell horrible," Enilna said. She scrunched her nose up. "Did you shit yourself in there?"

Taki sighed. "Don't sneak up on me like that. And no, I definitely did not *shit myself.*"

"There's only one way to prove your innocence," Enilna said. She paced around him with a hand tucked under her chin.

"What is this, an inquisition?" Taki started in the opposite direction, but Enilna blocked him off.

"I *said* there's only one way to prove you didn't have an accident. Show me your britches!"

"No! And…and even if I had soiled myself, why in God's name would you want to see such a thing?"

"To prove your guilt, of course," Enilna said with far too much cheer.

"Okay, guilty as charged!" Taki said. "I, Leutnant Taki Natalis of Alfa Spetsnaz Company, Squad Tirefire the Lesser, confess to shitting myself in the presence of the company commander. You happy now? Can I go?"

Enilna shook her head. "You're just saying what you think I want to hear. But as your prosecutor, it's my duty to uncover the truth behind this grave offense. To make sure that the higher-ups *actually responsible* for the crime face justice, and not just some low-ranked fall guy."

Taki crossed his arms. "You're not an army prosecutor. You can barely read."

"I've gotten better," Enilna said. "Irulan made sure of that."

She really knows how to make things awkward, that's for sure. Taki tried to change the subject. "Why all this interest in the law? I thought you were more of a doorkicker."

"Well, I enjoy fighting the padishah's enemies like any proper girl…"

What the hell kind of proper girl enjoys bloodshed?

"But I was talking with Master Emreis, and he told me to start thinking about the future. You know, after my glory days are over. He said I should work on honing my mind as well as my body, so I could do work that involves sitting down in case I lost a foot or whatnot."

Taki cleared his throat. "I would be very careful about Draco's counsel. His mind is a buzzing hive of lies and blasphemy."

"I'm not completely naïve, Taki. He tried to convince me that the world was a sphere that revolved around the sun, but I shut him down real fast. I even used his own sources to prove him wrong, too. He said I had a talent for arguing."

"I concur." Taki allowed a smile to creep across his lips. As obnoxious as Enilna could be, she was entertaining company. On occasion, that was.

"If you must, call me a shrew. But you, good sir, still stink of poo."

"That was horrible," Taki said with a chuckle. "Well, if I still reek, then help me get cleaned off."

Enilna seemed taken aback, and she blushed. "Damn, you're a forward sort…"

"I meant help me wash my clothes, not scrub me down," Taki said, relishing the turnabout.

"You should've said so in the first place!"

Taki cackled and started to walk in the direction of the camp outskirts. "Come on, Prosecutor. Time to get your hands dirty."

The Morvan deepwood was cut through by several small rivers, really creeks and streams, that all served as tributaries to the Rhone far to the east. Access to plentiful, clean water that could not be poisoned upstream was one of the reasons the forest had been picked for the Liberation Army's base. Without water, the army would die of thirst and filth. Soldiers were allowed to bathe downstream of where the water was collected for use in field kitchens and communal troughs. Effluvium from the jakes was painstakingly collected and hauled outside the stockade, as an outbreak of dysentery would fell men and women more surely than any hail of bullets.

Taki was still suspicious and kept his eye on the water's surface for any telltale traces of excrement. He rubbed his shirt against a flat piece of river stone, regretting that he had no lye. He'd found a relatively quiet corner, still within the protection of the stockade but away from the hubbub and press of the camp. Nearby, Enilna was busy beating Taki's leggings clean with a stick. She'd followed him all the way here, surprisingly enough.

"When's the last time you actually washed your clothes?" Enilna huffed.

"Can't remember," Taki said with a shrug. "Maybe after the Teufelsbrucke?"

"That's revolting," she said. "Now *I'll* need to bathe after touching these!"

Taki chuckled. "You're the one who wanted to help me."

She grimaced. "I always thought you were more hygienic. You know, Aslatiel makes us wash our smallclothes once a fortnight. With lye soap, too. It keeps the lice away, and we don't get boils."

"Never had a problem with lice or crotch rot," Taki said. "The Temple was high up in the mountains, anyway. If you wanted to waste water, you'd have to cart it up yourself from the foothills."

"I can't imagine living like that," Enilna said. "Even in Pristina, there was always a stream close by. Of course, you couldn't just drink from it, but that's a given anywhere."

We've not really talked about her past, and definitely not after that festival in Astarte, Taki thought to himself. Especially because the last time he'd brushed up against the subject, she'd ended up crying. He remained silent for a moment, but curiosity quickly got the better of him. "Did you always live there? Well, before you, er…"

"Killed that bastard Khazari duke who wanted to murder every last one of my people?" Enilna said.

"Uh, yes."

"Don't worry," she said with a chuckle. "That memory gives me a smile. But yes, I was born and raised there. My parents were city-bound serfs, really. Not more than slaves to the Khazari, but at least we didn't have to eat dirt in the countryside." She wrung the leggings out and set them aside. "I think I was ten seasons old when they died. Fever of some sort, maybe from breathing miasma. I don't really know. After that, I cast my lot in with the rebels."

"When did your taint manifest?" Taki asked, feeling curious. His control of fire had been an obvious mark of demonic descent, but he'd quickly found that most of his peers were far subtler in their mutations. Most Polaris were like Draco: faster and stronger, but not smarter or luckier, else they'd have avoided the Temple's eye in the first place

Enilna took a seat next to him and drew her knees to her chest. "Around the same time. I didn't know what the hell was going on, but Sunduz—he was the leader—probably did. He trained me to kill, and my rations got bigger. Probably the only reason I didn't get passed around by the older guys."

"Damnation," Taki muttered. His shirt lay forgotten on the rock.

"That was just the way it was." Enilna shrugged. "If you didn't pick up a blade, you served with whatever else you had."

"Doesn't make any of it right," Taki said. "I wouldn't have put it past the duke's men, but the rebels? They were fighting for their own people…"

Enilna chuckled softly. "You're a weird one, Taki. On one hand, you're a kingslayer, and on the other, you're innocent as fuck. I expected you'd be savvier, what with the whipping scars on your back."

"Thanks," Taki said. "Just when I'd forgotten about them, you had to remind me."

"You're welcome! If it's any consolation, I think they make you more trustworthy. Anyone who's gone through life without a flogging is definitely an evil mastermind in my book."

"And *how* many times have you earned the cat-o-nine?"

"Never. I was a model kadet."

Taki rolled his eyes. "You realize that you're an evil mastermind, then?"

Enilna bumped him with her shoulder. "I never said I wasn't."

"So how did you end up in Sevastopol? After you killed the duke, that is."

"I went up to *Ba'gshnar*'s and told him I'd kick his ass if he didn't let me join," Enilna said.

"*Right.*"

"Actually, it was annoying afterward. I barely escaped from the rest of you and nearly got killed a few times trying to make it back to Sunduz. I was sure I'd earn his praise for offing Duke Gul. I even showed him Lotte's gun as proof." She sighed. "Then, Sunduz took it away and told his brothers to kill me. He said the movement wouldn't ever accept a girl like me as their savior, and that the honor would go to him. But Aslatiel had tracked me down. You should've seen the look on Sunduz's face when Irulan stepped in and made the old bastard piss himself!" She grew quiet and wiped at her eyes. "Ah, Taki, I can't believe she's gone. Why her, out of all the *assholes* in the world?"

Taki edged closer and tentatively put an arm across her shoulders. He pulled her close, and she shivered and let herself cry for a while. When she was done, she turned her head and planted a kiss on his lips.

"I don't want you to get the wrong impression," she said. "I'm not some weepy little wench who cries for anything and everything."

Taki pressed his forehead to hers. "Your mentor just *died*. I'll let this one go."

"Thanks," Enilna said. She glanced over at Taki's waist. "In return, I'll forgive you for that."

Taki's hand reflexively shot down to cover himself. "Sorry, I can't help it. I'm a man, and my clothes are wet and…"

"And we've never done it normally like every other godrotting couple gets to," Enilna said. She twisted her body and swung a leg over to straddle him. "It's annoying and stupid that we're always getting interrupted in some way. So while I have you naked…"

"Near naked," Taki said.

Enilna rolled her eyes. "Stop killing the mood. As I was saying, while I have you here, I'm going to do what I promised."

"During the siege?"

"Yes, now don't speak another word." She started wrestling her sodden shirt off. "I swear. It'd take the padishah himself to fuck things up this time…"

The sound of a horn slashed the air. Enilna whipped her head about to glare at the source and immediately leapt off Taki, who scrabbled for his clothing and held it as a dripping wad over his nethers. Atop the bank, Aslatiel, Lotte, and the rest of their squads were on horseback. Hadassah pressed the Imperial signaling horn to her lips and tooted it again.

"D-dammit!" Enilna shouted at the group. "What's the matter with all of you? How long were you staring?"

"Rest assured, we didn't see anything impressive," Hadassah cackled. "Get dressed, you two, and come with us."

Taki struggled to force his limbs into his dripping clothes. "What's going on? Why are you all here?"

"The padishah has summoned us. There's no time to waste."

* * * *

When Chronicler's yurt wasn't full of Imperial officers, it seemed much larger inside than its humble outward appearance would suggest. The only problem was that it smelled just as musty as it had when packed with bodies, and it was just as dim.

He's the most powerful man in the Imperium, maybe the world, and yet he carries on like a poor shepherd. Taki stole a quick glance at the faces around him. Their expressions confirmed for him that they probably thought the same. Aslatiel and Lucatiel, however, seemed completely at home.

"Drink your fill, young hero," Chronicler said.

Taki tensed, uncomfortable with the man's attention. He glanced down at the cup of pocha sitting on a wooden minitable by his knees. The stuff had revolted him in Xizhang and looked and smelled equally unpalatable now.

"Your Majesty," he said, and brought the bowl to his lips. He tipped it slightly to allow the stuff to wash over his lips but didn't open them. Disgustingly, everyone else seemed to relish theirs, even Hadassah, who Taki was sure hated the stuff.

"I understand that it was you, Taki Natalis, who brought Aslatiel out of his abyss of mourning," Chronicler said.

Taki set his bowl down and tried not to make eye contact. "I, uh...I just did what any friend—I mean, soldier—would do for his commander."

"Even Lord Buddha frowns on excessive modesty," Chronicler said. "If you render a great service, it is virtuous to be given and to accept a great reward. Please accept this as a token of my gratitude."

One of the Imperial Cult attendants who stood silently in the shadows padded up to Chronicler, bearing a box. He or she—it was impossible to tell behind the featureless armored niqab—opened it to reveal a palm-sized medallion. It shone more intensely golden than brass, and its surface was etched with painstakingly detailed dragons and fu-dogs that chased each other around pictograms impossible to comprehend. A tiny line of holes marched across the diameter, the only detraction from a piece both stunning and impossible to duplicate.

"That's beautiful," Taki whispered despite himself.

"It is," Chronicler said, and then snapped the medallion in two. "Aslatiel and Lucatiel are my children, though I am not their sire. For assisting them, I will grant you any wish within reason. All you must do is present your half to me when you are ready. I will honor your request, even if we should be mortal enemies at the time. Think well on your choice and its wording, for once this coin is made whole again, I will no longer owe you a debt." He handed the coin-half to Taki.

"I don't know what to say, Your Majesty," Taki said, taken aback.

"Then don't say anything right now," Chronicler said.

"Whoa," Hadassah said. "So Natalis could make you run around naked in front of your troops while thrusting your member in a pie and shouting, 'Gimme all your buttholes!' and you'd do it?"

"Jesus, Dassa!" Draco hissed.

Chronicler let out a belly laugh. "He certainly could, young madam. But then I'd be forced to execute him for wasting food whilst others starved."

"I suppose he'll just have to settle for getting laid, then," Hadassah sighed.

Taki reddened. "I'm not going to use it *go wenching!*"

"Indeed you should not!" Aslatiel said. "The padishahs have only given these coins out a handful of times in the entire history of the Imperium. Until now, even I thought they were more legend than fact. I never thought I'd actually see one in person." He clenched a fist and held it to his chest. "And to think that my selfish grief could have burdened you so, *Ba'gshnar...*"

"Do not scourge yourself on my behalf, Aslatiel," Chronicler said. "I gave the gift freely. Yes, out of gratitude, but mainly because I wish to see exactly what young Natalis will use it for. He fascinates me, especially after our little talk at the Hot Gates."

A chill went up Taki's spine as Chronicler glanced at him again. For a moment, it almost felt the same as when Chronicler had piled the full force of his will on Taki's soul and almost crushed it out of existence. He squeezed the coin-half in his hand. The metal was cool to the touch and seemed to soothe his jitters. *Anything within reason?*

For a moment, Taki considered asking for a promotion to oberleutnant. But if Chronicler could give him anything, then why not a promotion to general? Or even feldmarschall? Taki shook away those thoughts. It would not do for him to suddenly assume a position he had no training for and could be removed from at will. Perhaps it was wiser to simply ask for his freedom and a hundred thousand rounds of Old Nayto. Or, as Hecaton had once demanded, a million. With that many rounds, eight generations of descendants could spend frivolously every single day of their lives, even if they all lived to a hundred and sired a dozen children each.

Stop, you idiot, he thought as he took a deep breath. He was dealing with Chronicler. There was always a catch when dealing with these vipers masquerading as men. The coin-half might prove useful some day, but for now it was just another source of peril. *After all, would you trust Hecaton Mezeta with the same?*

"Your Majesty," Lotte said, "forgive my bluntness, but I feel that you've really passed on a great burden to young Natalis, in guise of a gift. I also sense that he was not the true reason you assembled us all today."

Chronicler grunted. "Your candor is refreshing, Captain Satou. I am pleased that you decided to stay with us. Indeed, I called you here for another reason as well. Do you remember my address to the officers?"

"Aye," Lotte said. "The revelation was disturbing indeed, though I still find it far-fetched to imagine an enormous ring encircling our world from the heavens. Particularly one fashioned by men."

"Captain Satou, do you know that humanity once traveled to the stars and back? That the crumbling stone hovels that we claim as our grand palaces actually used to stretch to hundreds of meters in the sky? That we once had a means of sending letters and pictures to each other over seconds instead of months or years?"

"Those claims sound equally ludicrous."

Chronicler fixed her with a stare. "But they are not. Consider the Argead *Ooss* and the God Hand you once tried to kill me with. Consider the relics you've seen that come to life when imbued with your prana. You all worship the Ancients' rusty butcher tools but cannot comprehend the magnitude of horror that those foolish people unleashed on each other with the blink of an eye."

"Humbly begging your illustrious pardons," Draco said. "But I believe His Majesty. I've read some works that tell of these things, and even of the ring suspended in the heavens. *Kether Elysion,* the hidden refuge of Prester John!"

"Draco, those works were written by madmen and heretics for the sole purpose of selling books," Hadassah said. "There's no silly castle in the sky. The garden of Eden is a metaplastical construct."

"'Metaphysical,' my dear," Lucatiel interjected.

34

"Aye, thanks Luca," Hadassah said.

"This has nothing to do with philosophy," Draco insisted. "You see, after being forced from out of the Orient by the White Huns, Prester John reformed his kingdom in Ethiopia where he reigned in peace for over a thousand years. But shortly before the Fall, his lands were overrun by an invasion of the heretical Gammadion Cross. The good prester realized that the terrestrial world was too awash in sin to merit his continued ministry. So he set his sights to the sky. He was resolved not to repeat the same mistake as when he'd constructed Babel, so he built his new stronghold—his new *Sephira*—at a respectful distance from heaven but still elevated above the blasphemous clusterfuck of Terra Mundus. In Kether Elysion, Prester John now waits for enlightened men of the faith to travel to *him*. Once this happens, his kingdom shall return and bless us with another millennium of virtue."

Hadassah's eyelids twitched. "Draco, what in the Almighty's name have you been smoking?"

"Young madam," Chronicler said, "your friend speaks the truth, though a convoluted and somewhat incoherent version thereof. Kether Elysion is real, though whether it was constructed on the orders of some immortal prophet or through a rare moment of global unity is up for debate. The Ancients certainly had the capacity for such an undertaking, even if it seems impossible to us in the present day. Remember that we are but insects staring up at the cathedrals of men. What is incontestable is that Kether Elysion has long remained in the sky, for centuries out of all practical reach, until now."

Lotte frowned. "And you say that the Ursalans have somehow devised a means to reach this…ring called Kether?"

"Two, in fact. Their first effort ended in failure and the destruction of their old capital."

Draco clapped his hands together. "The Tirefire of Berlin!"

"A *tirefire?*" Chronicler frowned. "Is that what you believed had happened? That's utterly ridiculous."

"But…" Draco slumped in disbelief.

"Berlin burns because they attempted to construct a spire to Kether Elysion. It stretched many leagues in the sky and threatened to give them purchase on the ring. But my spetsnaz sabotaged it and brought the tower down on their heads."

"Ugh." Hadassah rolled her eyes. "So all our punishment in the kitchens was because of bullshit that never happened. Figures."

"The second attempt is the one I am concerned with," Chronicler said. "The Ursalans learned from their mistake in Berlin and have centered the new spire over Versailles. Only the royal family and their guards may cross through the Aegis, so I cannot slip infiltrators in like last time. It will take a long, bloody, and costly siege to break through and take the spire."

Lotte rubbed her hands together. "What will happen if the Ursalans reach their goal?"

Chronicler let out a slow breath. "The total destruction of everything you cherish. The Ring is not only a scientific marvel but also a weapon. First, it could allow an army to deploy at any point on the earth. And second, its sheer mass means that if it ever crashed to the ground, humanity would perish for certain. That is something I cannot permit, Captain. I hope you share my sentiments."

"A disturbing revelation indeed," Lotte said. "So what is our role in preventing this calamity?"

"I'll be frank. There is no way for my army to break through Versailles on its own. A true siege would take years to accomplish its goal and cost millions of Imperial lives. Meanwhile, rebellions would spring up all across the rest of the Imperium and fracture my nation for good. You've already witnessed this once, for the Mandate of Heaven were a direct consequence of the war we waged on the Dominion. But most importantly, the Ursalans will definitely complete their work on the spire in that time. All else will be moot."

"Then why invade at all, knowing you cannot win?"

Chronicler huffed. "I will not simply stand by and do nothing in the face of another Gotterdammerung. And now, things have changed. Now I have *you* all gathered in my tent: the greatest warriors in the Imperium. I need your help."

"Uh," Hadassah said, "if we're the best you've got, then you're in deep shit, old dude."

"Hush," Lotte said. "So what is it you'd have us do, Your Majesty?"

"At the southern end of the barrier that surrounds Versailles, there is a castle with a gate," Chronicler said. "It is guarded by an Ordo of Templars, whose grandmaster has been charged with possession of a key-sword. This key, if plunged into the proper lockstone, will open the Aegis in a way that cannot be undone. My army will be able to take Versailles afterward. Do you understand what I ask?"

"Indeed. I also could not help but notice that you never once called for the spire's destruction," Lotte said. "So what will happen when you manage to take it?"

Chronicler chuckled. "Astutely observed, Captain. The simple answer is that I will use Kether Elysion to bring the Imperial Way to every corner of the globe. World conquest, in no uncertain terms."

"Then what makes you better than the Ursalans?"

Aslatiel started and almost rose from his knees. "Satou, I urge you to watch your words!"

"Temperance, Aslatiel," Chronicler said. "She asks a valid question, and I will give her a valid response. *Someone* must unify the world if we are ever to restore our old glory, Satou. Would you rather we all prosper on the Imperial Way, or would you rather we were all slaves withering away on a dying husk of a world?"

Lotte shifted her knees. "And how do you know that the Ursalans intend the latter?"

"Because the Ursalan royal family is definitely not of this world. They don't care about human beings because *they are not human themselves.*"

"Then what are they?"

Chronicler shook his head. "Unfortunately, I have no idea. All I know is that they must be stopped, and that we are running out of time. Aslatiel, do I have your support?"

Aslatiel bowed in place and pressed his forehead to the ground. "In all things, Your Majesty."

"And, Satou, do I have yours?"

Lotte was silent for a moment. Then, she pressed her palm to her chest. "Yes, but on one condition."

"That being?"

"If Kether Elysion can truly take us to any point on the Earth, then your first act will be to take us to Hecaton Mezeta. You've already promised us this!"

"I will do better than just that," Chronicler said, "for the first place to fall under Imperial reign will be my homeland, where Mezeta travels even now. I intend to face her once and for all, and bring the light of the Way to all of my cursed brethren."

3

For the umpteenth time, Taki found himself again staring at and fondling the coin-half Chronicler had given him. As far as he could tell, the thing was simple solid gold but at the same time seemed otherworldly. The metal was always cool to the touch, even when it had rested flush on his bare chest for an entire afternoon. Using some hide scraps and a suturing needle, he'd managed to attach it securely to a leather neck strap that he wore under his shirt, padding, and brigandine. He had initially expected his squadmates to badger him about it, but to his surprise, no one had asked to see the thing, much less attempt to pilfer it.

"Careful about molesting it overmuch," Lotte said. She reclined next to him with her back against a mossy fallen log. "Gold is very soft, and even your fingers can deform it with the right amount of effort."

Embarrassed, Taki shoved the coin back under his shirt. "Sorry, Captain. I'm not obsessed with it or anything, I promise."

Lotte chuckled. "Don't worry. It's far better that you're constantly rubbing that, rather than your nethers. Many men tend to do that when their hands are idle."

"I'd like to think I'm more polite than many men," Taki said with a shrug. He sat up and stretched, blinking as a ray of sunlight caught his eyes.

It had been a day since setting out from the Imperial camp. Alfa and Tirefire had left, along with the two thousand troops they each commanded, to scout and raid along the southern frontier outside the Ursalan Aegis. Their real mission, however, was to get closer to the southern gate, where the key-sword was. For now, the regiments took a final rest in the northern end of the deepwood, where cover was thick and the air still.

Lotte toyed with the hilt end of the knife at her belt. "So have you thought about your wish?"

Taki shook his head. Then, he nodded. "Maybe too much. But everything I think of always has some downside or goes horribly wrong in my head. I've considered the obvious, of course. A palace in the Dominion for all of us to live in, with a feast of eggs and meat every single day. Exarch of the Temple. A million rounds and a pony…"

"Why a pony?"

"No good reason," Taki muttered. "But the problem is that the more I dwell on it, not only do I desire more, but also I start thinking about how everything could be taken away at any minute. Hecaton Mezeta could just waltz in at any second and screw my life up again, for one thing. What's so funny, Captain?"

Lotte covered her mouth to stifle a giggle. "I'm sorry, Natalis. I didn't mean to laugh. It's just that you're very sweet, thinking of giving us a palace to live in."

"Who else would I want that for?"

"Let's be real, Natalis. We're all criminals here, including myself. We've done nothing but treat you badly since we've met you."

Taki frowned. "That's true, but we've been through a lot and survived. That has merit on its own. Plus, you're the first woman I ever kissed."

He was rewarded by seeing Lotte's face go pink for a split second. Buoyed by confidence, he reached out and caressed the scarred side of her face. With gentle pressure, he pulled her closer. Lotte's eyes closed partway, and her lips brushed against his, but she abruptly turned away.

"We shouldn't."

Taki tensed. "Why not?"

"I'm still your superior. What I did wasn't right. I…I took advantage of you."

"But I enjoyed it. I may have found the will to survive the Hot Gates because of you."

"And I'm glad. But there are differences between us. There have always been differences. I'm supposed to protect and teach you, not *coerce* you."

"I've changed," Taki insisted. "I'm no longer some naïve recruit who didn't know how the world worked. I've gotten stronger and wiser."

Lotte clenched a fist. "I know. I…I must go and inspect the men."

To Taki's consternation, she climbed to her feet and plodded away. He knew better than to pursue her. *Damn it,* he thought, and again pulled out his coin-half and stared at it. Perhaps the padishah could make her more agreeable…reason, however, prevailed, and he put the coin-half away. It was easy to fall under the sway of darker temptations with that damned thing hanging from his neck. For a brief second, he considered just burying the thing and being done with it. *Also a bad option.*

For now, Taki reasoned, he would make a promise to himself. He would only consider using the coin-half to better another's lot. The padishah was banking on him to make a stupid, selfish, shortsighted wish, so outsmarting the terrible old man would be the greatest pleasure of them all. *Yes, only to help someone else. That's a choice I can live with, and more importantly, won't screw me over.*

* * * *

"I still prefer my version over the truth," Draco said. "My story is more romantic. It's a tale of futile struggle against inexorable fate, except the good guys win!"

"Emreis," Taki said, "the Ursalans aren't the 'good guys,' and there's nothing romantic about making a city burn for years under molten tires. I'm glad the truth was less *absurd.*"

"One man's absurdity is another man's philosophy," Draco said. He pulled on his reins to dissuade his horse from gobbling a low-hanging shoot.

The regiment marched along a winding forest path that at some points was only narrow enough for three men abreast, or two on horseback. The northern border of the deepwood was less than a bell away. The hairs on the back of Taki's neck had been up for hours as the column trudged along. There was no doubt that they were all being watched.

Elite Ursalan rangers lurked in the trees, ready at any moment to strike with their bows and poisoned arrows. Taki had been told to ignore the threat—the rangers' job was to report on Imperial movements so that an Ursalan force could be poised to intercept. As soon as the Imperials entered a suitable ambush zone, the Ursalans would wipe the Imperials out. But Aslatiel had a plan to deal with this, or so he had claimed. In the meantime, all Taki could do was talk away his anxiety.

"I don't know, Emreis," Taki said. "I'm a bit excited, actually. I want to see what their spire looks like and if it actually connects to something floating in the sky."

"Don't you think we'd have seen a gigantic ring floating overhead? Look at the sky. Well, when the trees aren't blocking everything. *Then* look at the sky. Nothing but blue and clouds."

"What if the ring's painted to look like the sky?"

Draco frowned. "I'll concede that point. Those ancients were a wily sort. Ah! But then how would you avoid blocking the sunlight at certain times of the day?"

"If I were an ancient and wanted to avoid complaints," Taki said, "I'd have it so that my ring spun around freely, so that its shadow coincided with dawn or twilight."

"But then you'd have to accept that the world spins around the sun."

"My way works fine no matter if you're faithful or a heretic. The important thing is that the light is constantly changing location, as is the darkness."

"Oy, Natalis, be careful," Draco said. "That sounds like moral relativism, you know."

Taki sucked his teeth. "Aye, my bad, Emreis. Forget I said anything."

"No problem," Draco said with a pat on Taki's shoulder. "I'm here to watch out for you, eh? Hell, not that long ago, I was your senior corporal. But I knew you'd outrank me one day."

"First time we met, I seriously thought you were going to kill me," Taki said.

"Did I really seem that fierce?" Draco grinned. "That's a relief. Well, it all worked out in the end. Except for Mezeta stealing all our pensions. Ah well, she was always in love with the smell of her own poo. Was only a matter of time until she screwed us."

Taki laughed. "Aye, a pox on that hag. I wonder if she'll even be able to give us our grad back when we find her."

"Course not," Draco said. "She'll have spent it on trifles. But don't worry about funds. From what I hear, the Ursalan exchequer is a literal sea of milligrad. Bring a goodly sack, and we'll be set for life."

"If we get to that point."

"Have faith, Natalis. There's no way we should've survived all we have, and yet here we are. At this rate, you might even get to rut with a woman before the year's end."

Taki's expression darkened. "I'd have tumbled many a time if not for idiocy from you all. I don't go and make a ruckus at your tent when you're fucking Lady Elsa."

"Oy!" Draco tried to shush him. "Quiet about that, hear?"

"We all know about you two," Taki said and shrugged. "Frankly, the captain's glad of it."

"That's a relief, then," Draco sighed. "I've no desire to cause friction. And now I can help you, eh?"

"I don't need help," Taki said. "Just for everyone to keep a distance."

"Come now, that's no way to treat your best friend."

"We're best friends?"

"Aye. You contest that?"

"Perhaps."

"With an attitude like that, we'll never slip past the guard," Draco tut-tutted.

Ahead sounded a horn signal to stop the advance. Taki scanned his surroundings. They were practically at the edge of the forest. At this point, his real task would begin. He motioned to Draco, and they both cantered up the side of the column until they met up with Aslatiel at the fore.

"Natalis, Emreis, are you both ready?" Aslatiel said.

"Yes, Oberleutnant," Taki said. "We're ready."

"Good. I don't need to tell you how important this is to our success. The Padishah's relying on you."

"No worries, Master Aslatiel," Draco said. "I've played an Ursalan lord before. I can do it again. Just make sure you lot cause a big enough ruckus out there."

Aslatiel's lips thinned in a predatory grin. "You don't need to worry about that, Master Emreis. I don't intend to be a mere distraction. I aim to win the field, and if the opportunity presents itself, I'll just take the damned Aegis and be done with it."

"Godspeed," Taki said. *It's good to see him in fighting trim again.* Taki looked over to Draco. "Come along, then. We've no invitations, so we'd better at least show up on time."

Hadassah, who had snuck up next to Draco, slipped a foot out of her stirrup and kicked Draco's shin.

"Ow! What was that for?" Draco bent over and rubbed at his leg.

"This is all a bad idea, and someone's gonna get killed," Hadassah said. "Of all people, they picked you and Natalis to sneak into a freaking Templar fortress? Who do you think you are? Imperial Special Forces?"

"Well, *yeah*. That's kind of what we are."

"*Definitely* special. Ugh! Why can't they send someone more competent?"

Draco huffed. "I'm plenty competent! You're just jealous that you weren't chosen. When I come back with that key-thingy, I'll be a damned hero. And you'll be stewing in your own juices."

"Switch with me. I'll go," Hadassah said. "Natalis won't mind. He loves female attention."

"Doesn't work like that. I'm the only one who looks enough like an 'inbred sack of shit.' That Chung-Kuo woman said so back in Astarte, remember? You just want to steal my glory."

"It's not about your stupid glory!"

"Then why are you being such a shrew?"

Hadassah kicked him again.

"Stop that," Draco hissed, and pulled his reins to move away.

"I bet you'll screw up and look *real* stupid," she snapped, and cantered away.

"Everyone else is ready," Aslatiel said. "Are you two finally prepared to set out?"

"Aye, sorry," Draco said. He stared off at Hadassah, grinding his teeth.

Aslatiel raised his sword aloft and reared his horse to face the rest of the troop column. "Signal the rear and light fuses! Victory for the padishah! *Uukhai!*" he shouted, and chopped his sword down.

From the back of the column, thumping noises reverberated through the stillness of the forest and sent roosting birds screaming and flapping in the air. The explosions drew nearer and branched out, and a thick cloud of choking, purplish smoke descended rapidly over the column.

Taki tapped his horse's flanks and rode out, with Draco behind him. The ground trembled in his wake as the regiments started a march. Aslatiel's plan had been simple: Under cover of smoke, the regiments would split and emerge from the forest to pincer the waiting force of chevaliers. In the confusion, Taki and Draco would slip away.

A bell later, the pair emerged from the tree line onto a path leading down a ridge. Far to the east rose the characteristic smoke column of a raging battlefield, where Taki knew the rest of his friends fought for their lives. He shook his growing trepidation away. It was time to concentrate on the task at hand and the reason for Aslatiel's gambit. Ahead, the Aegis awaited.

The last solid bastion of Ursalan defense, it was a massive curtain wall at least forty meters high and several meters thick. A deep ravine encircled the outside, having directly lent matter to the wall's construction. Four solid gates, one at each compass point, allowed entrance and egress and were wide enough to accommodate an entire company standing shoulder-to-shoulder. Each gate sat under a castle built directly into the wall and was manned by a Templar Ordo appointed by the Sanctissimus Rex. Beyond the gates, no one quite knew what Inner Ursala looked like.

Taki looked up beyond the top of the Aegis. A thin, white column rose from the ground. It grew thinner, almost disappearing as it reached skyward, but it obviously pierced the clouds. The spire was barely visible, for Versailles itself was many leagues away, yet there was no question as to what it was.

"Emreis, your letters patent—" Taki began.

"In my satchel," Draco said. "Fifth time you've asked. Relax. I've been the Viscount of Brittany before, remember?"

"I do," Taki said. "It's just that we can't screw this up."

"We got through Astarte fine."

"We didn't. We had to fight a princess, and Sir Mikhail died."

"But that wasn't because we played our roles poorly," Draco said. "All we have to do is slip in, steal this key-sword thing from the grandmaster, and leave."

"You make it sound so simple," Taki said.

"Because it *is*," Draco said. "The captain's fighting for her life out there to draw the Templars out and make things easier for us. In my opinion, she's got the harder job. So loosen up."

Taki clenched his teeth. Draco was right, of course. The regiments they had split from had already forced the Ursalans to sally out of their watchtowers and battle Imperial forces on the ground. If plans worked out, the Templar castle would only possess a skeleton crew. The Ordo grandmaster might even have left to join the battle. For now, all Taki could do was ride on and keep a cool head.

Shortly after making the descent from the ridge, the pair rode by the first peasant huts and fields. Purple amaranth grew in orderly rows, while large wooden tripods accommodated climbing long beans. The commoners working the fields seemed to pay them no mind, to Taki's relief. In contrast to what he'd seen in the desolate, ash-strewn Silesian fields, the outskirts of the Aegis seemed positively bucolic. There were no trees full of hanged corpses and piles of bones lining killing fields, no rogue chevaliers to raid farmsteads for plunder and rape.

Taki bit his lip. If Draco and he were successful, the place would turn to yet another war zone: a hell of ash and corpses. The Ursalans would probably all turn insurgent, and the Imperium would be forced to deal with them. He closed his eyes. *That isn't what I want.* But if those princesses, like the one who'd killed Mikhail or the one who'd drained Taki's blood, were allowed free reign…

"We're drawing closer," Draco muttered. "Time to get our theater faces on."

The packed earth of the peasant homesteads abruptly gave way to what Taki recognized as concrete: that creepily uniform product of the ancient world that was neither true stone nor clay. Ahead was a roadway marked by statues of chevaliers on horseback. A large, raised plinth boasted a trapezoidal structure of granite, which was guarded by heavily armored riflemen. The Queen's Right, Taki remembered. A physical manifestation of the royal family's power over all their subordinates. With the key-sword plunged into the appropriate slot, the gates would open and stay open, regardless of what the Templars wished.

A pair of burly halvidars crossed their poleaxes when Draco approached the gate. "State your business," one of them said.

Draco reached into his satchel and pulled out a bulky scroll, which he let unfurl under its own weight. The yellow lambskin was festooned with wax seals and sewn-on annotations made of parchment. Notoriously difficult to forge, the letters patent were unassailable proof of the viscount of Brittany's lineage and station. "The Vicomte de Bretagne wishes to pass. Let me pass, posthaste!"

He's gotten better at this, Taki thought when he heard Draco's nasal delivery. It dripped with just the right amount of condescension mixed with undertones of boredom that betrayed a life of idle hedonism.

"Who's the other one?" a halvidar asked.

"De Boron, my poet and lutenist," Draco said. "He chronicles my travels and such, and mostly eats and lies about. Now, how long will we be forced to wait here? My ass chafes."

The soldiers peered at the letters patent. It was painfully obvious that neither could make sense of the chaotic scribbling, much less verify its authenticity. Draco huffed and shifted in his saddle. Eventually, the soldiers shrugged and waved the pair through. Taki let out a silent sigh. So far, things had gone to plan. A viscount was the lowest rank allowed free passage in and out of the Aegis and also one that would not merit attention or ceremony.

The gate was composed of two monolithic slabs that opened out and away from each other on well-worn metal tracks. They were open partway, just enough to allow Draco and Taki to pass single file through the gap. As he rode through, Taki noted that the doors were as thick as two men laid down end to end. There was no way for cannonry to blast through this and no way to brace the doors against closure. Any army that attempted to lay siege to the Templar Ordo would simply be picked apart by cannonry and ballistae. The hairs on Taki's neck stood on end as he finally crossed the threshold. He stared at his surroundings in wonderment. This was the beating heart of the enemy.

Murder holes perforated the arched ceiling overhead, each one a way to dump boiling oil—or, in a pinch, just rocks—on assailants who managed to somehow get past the gates. The place could be made a deathtrap without its defenders risking a man. But what struck Taki most was the sheer amount of armored reliquaries berthed within. A column of a dozen black hulks rested in the middle of the passage, each of them in more pristine condition than the one Taki had ridden long ago in the service of Gul Hekmatyar.

"Glad Dassa isn't here," Draco whispered. "She wouldn't be able to control her damned self. We'd end up trying to steal these and forget the mission."

Taki scrunched his brow. "The Templars probably lack fuel. That's why they're just sitting here instead of going to battle."

"So even the infamous Ordos have the same problem we all do." Draco smiled. "Good to know the bastards aren't totally invincible. Oy, how're we getting into the castle, anyway?"

"Once we're on the other side, we'll find a stable for the horses. Then, go in through the rear. You're a noble, so the rank-and-file won't bother us. Then...we'll have to see about getting up to the grandmaster's chambers."

Draco nodded, and they trotted toward the end of the passage. When the sun shone again on Taki's face, he blew a small sigh of relief. The regiments had done their jobs, for the entire place seemed almost empty save for the gaunt, gray-robed servants who padded along silently like mice. Draco leaned over, looking preoccupied. "Say, Natalis, doesn't it feel sort of strange on this side of the wall? I mean, compared to the outside."

Taki nodded. "I think I know what you mean. The peasants outside were just...people, but all of the servants here seem totally different. Placid, I guess."

"Aye, like drones," Draco said.

"Don't think on it too much," Taki said. He pointed at a nearby row of stable berths that looked to be for common use. "Here, let's drop off the horses and get inside."

He signaled to a servant who looked to be a groom, and swung out of his stirrups and to the ground. "We'll be back soon."

The groom nodded silently and obsequiously. Taki resisted the urge to raise an eyebrow when he saw what appeared to be a tattoo on the man's forehead: a crimson, solid hexagon without any other ornamentation. *A mark of ownership? Or perhaps some sort of elevated status? Either way, he's unlikely to raise an alarm.*

"You saw it too?" Draco whispered.

"Don't gawp at every little thing," Taki whispered back. "Let's get inside."

After a quick climb up a set of sweeping stone stairs, Taki stepped onto the massive landing set over the archway. He stole a quick glance north, at inner Ursala. Most of what he could see appeared to be undeveloped land, but the spire was more visible now, a glinting, silvery needle pricking the sky. He tore himself away from the sight and strode into the castle.

In contrast to the rococo excess he'd seen in Astarte, the inside of the Templar stronghold was oppressively Spartan. Its main hall was a high-ceilinged space broken up by load-bearing columns and ornamented with the rearing-lion standard of the Ordo Arsalan. Draco tapped Taki's shoulder. "Company."

Taki nodded and steadied his posture. *The most important thing is to be calm. Draco's a noble. We have the right to be here.*

A double line of Ursalan chevaliers marched into the hall, all bearing spears and rifles. Wordlessly, they lined the periphery of the grand hall. Taki bit the inside of his mouth. *Stop panicking!* A giant of a man stepped in, flanked by two hulking, fully helmed Templars. He towered almost half a meter over Taki's and Draco's heads, and unlike his counterparts, wore no helmet.

Taki flinched. This was the first time he'd seen a live Templar's face. The man's features were nominally human, but utterly devoid of all smoothness normally gained by fat. Furthermore, every strand of facial muscle bulged with hypertrophied power, lending the man a grotesquely leonine look. Save for a closely-cropped tonsure, there was no other hair that Taki could see. Heavy Templar plate covered the rest, with an Ordo tabard the only thing that differentiated his armor from that of the pair behind him. A slab-like greatsword hung from his belt, but it was what he held that made Taki start to sweat. Gripped in one of the man's massive fists were chains connected to a pair of leashed, mangy-looking lions. The beasts growled and flopped at the man's feet. He peered at Taki first, then Draco.

"I am Cassius of the Ordo Arsalan. A Templar in service of His Supreme Majesty. Who are you?"

Draco blinked. "Uh, wow! So *that's* what you lot look like under your helmets? Can't say I expected this. Kind of thought you'd be more, uh, sewn together."

Taki's stomach turned, and his knees buckled.

Cassius seemed unaffected. "I am Siridar of the Ordo. My kind are *born* Templar, not constructed like our lesser brethren. Now identify yourselves."

"I am the Vicomte de Bretagne," Draco said. "And that's de Boron, my poet and lutenist. He chronicles my—"

"He has no lute," Cassius said.

"We lost it fleeing from Chalon-sur-Saone," Draco said. "One of those Imperial jackanapes robbed us at gunpoint! I've come to petition the Ordo for aid. We simply *must* take the south back from those mongrel hordes."

Taki began to breathe easier. After Draco's outburst, Taki had expected gunshots.

Cassius glowered. "The Imperium will fall soon, Viscount. The Ordo Arsalan guards the Aegis under royal mandate. We are not at your *beck and call*. Find somewhere else to levy troops."

"Take me to your grandmaster," Draco said. "Surely a man of such wisdom and power will see the virtue of my request."

"The grandmaster currently battles the mud-skinned hordes in His Supreme Majesty's name. When the Imperial dogs are crushed, he will return."

"I'll be sure to thank him for his service," Draco said with a wink. "Oy, I bet you're pretty steamed to not be out there stomping heads. I hear the Prince of Maladies is among them. I've seen her from afar. Beg pardon for the blasphemy, but God's blood, she's a cutie pie! Bet you'd enjoy snapping her in two, my burly friend."

Taki's palms grew clammy. *Jesus, Draco, rein it in!*

"Little man, you try my patience," Cassius said. "Were it not for your station, I'd gladly pick your tongue out, shave your head, and cast you among the thralls. Now depart from here before I lose my grip on Scelestus and Circuitus. It is past their feeding time."

Draco stumbled back as the two lions abruptly tried to pounce on him. Fanged jaws nearly closed on his neck, barely held back by spike-lined chokers that bit deep into the beasts' flesh. Taki's eyes widened, and he skittered out of their range. Draco grimaced and huffed.

"Well, if *that's* how you're going to treat the peerage, I see we have nothing further to discuss. We'll be off. Expect a formal complaint in the post!"

"M-milord," Taki croaked on a dry throat. "To the stables…"

The pair stepped back to the threshold and haltingly made their way down the stairs. When they reached the stables, Draco promptly threw up.

Taki rubbed his temples in consternation. "Well, shit! What now?"

"It was a *success*, that's what," Draco said. He spat and wiped at his mouth. "We know the grandmaster's away. That means we can sneak into his chamber without having to face the bastard."

"Christ, Emreis! You were doing well, too, until that last bit about Lady Lucatiel. Were you *trying* to get eaten?"

"I might've gone a bit overboard. But what was the alternative? Hang out there under guard till the grandmaster came back? Better that he threw us out."

Taki groaned softly and scanned the surroundings. Fortunately, they were still alone. The strangely marked groom from earlier was nowhere to be seen. "So how can we get in?"

"I'll take care of that," Draco said. "Pass me the rope from the saddlebags, will you? The longer one."

Taki raised an eyebrow but tossed Draco the coil anyway. Draco spat on his hands and rubbed them together, and then took a final glance around. Then, he took off with a sprint toward the castle and leapt in the direction of an arrow slit about a story's height from the ground. To Taki's surprise, Draco's fingers slipped perfectly into the forbiddingly narrow space, and Draco now hung precariously from the impromptu handhold. *Just like when we first met,* Taki remembered.

Draco looked around, let his arms stretch, and braced the balls of his feet against the smooth stone of the wall. In one explosive motion, he then launched himself upward and latched on to another arrow slit above the first one. This process continued several more times, to Taki's amazement, until Draco finally pulled himself onto the battlements at the top of the castle walls. A few minutes later, the end of the rope made its way down to the ground.

When Taki finally pulled himself over the top and onto the ramparts, he was almost out of breath from the effort of climbing. He collapsed on the roof, only to see a sentry slumped lifelessly nearby. Not only had Draco managed to make an impossible climb, but he'd also managed to take an enemy by surprise just after doing so.

"Emreis, you're...you're pretty amazing," Taki said.

"Thanks. Though I'm really losing my touch," Draco said. His face was flushed red, and his hands shook noticeably. "Used to be able to do this crap on the regular, and much more cleanly. The naik nearly wrestled me off. Ah, maybe after this is over, I'll do more sit-down work. Okay, on we go."

"Wait," Taki said. "Rest a bit. You're not nearly replenished enough."

"Can't hang out here forever. More will show up, and they'll find the body soon enough. We're on the clock here."

Taki grimaced, knowing Draco was right. "We're near the grandmaster's chamber, anyway. Might be able to drop in through his balcony. Then, we'll use the rope to climb back down and leave on our horses."

"Good plan," Draco said, and painfully got to his feet. "We owe the captain, that's for sure. Place would be swarming with men if there weren't a battle on right now."

Taki nodded and jogged over to the precipice over the outer wall. A few meters below it was a small stone observation deck that led into the grandmaster's chamber. From there, the Templar leader could survey the lands south of the Aegis as far as the eye could see.

He took another coil of rope and tied one end to a crenellation and let the end fall onto the deck. Then, he shimmied down the rope partway and dropped to the deck with his knife out. Draco landed next to him a moment later.

"Don't hear anything, thank God," Taki said. He padded to the door to the inside, glad to find it without a lock. Cautiously, he opened it and slipped inside.

"The hell is that?" Draco pointed to what looked like a man-shaped cage partially submerged in a stone-lined vat of glowing, steaming liquid.

"I'd say that's probably the grandmaster's bed," Taki said. "I don't see a normal one around here."

Other than the strange contraption in the middle of the room, the rest of the chamber seemed downright normal. It was as Spartan as the rest of the castle seemed to be; the only other pieces of furniture present were a large metal desk and a number of bookshelves and display stands. Tapestries of the Ordo standard draped the walls.

"Any idea where the key-sword might be? Hell, now that I think about it, I'm not sure what it's supposed to look like. Is it just a sword that looks vaguely key-like, or the other way around?"

"I think that's it," Taki said. He walked up to one of the display cases, raised his palm, and concentrated his energy. He quietly intoned a sutra, and a thin stream of luminescent plasma shot out. The thin metal hasp steamed, turned yellow, and then started to visibly stretch. Then, Taki wrenched the lid right off.

"Smooth move, Natalis," Draco said.

"Thanks. The container's usually weaker than the lock. And now, we have what we came for."

He reached in and pulled a peculiar-looking object from out of the case. It seemed like any other short sword, except that its blade was irregularly and unevenly serrated. Intricate patterns of engraved dashes, dots, and lines decorated the flat of the blade. *Almost like a language.*

Draco let out an appreciative whistle. "Looks valuable. All right, let's wrap this up and get out of here."

"You don't need to tell me—"

Taki heard the growl and moved to dive out of the way, but it was already too late. Claws dug deeply into the meat of his shoulder, and a crushing force bowled him face first to the floor. He'd had the wind knocked out of him before, but this was by far the worst. Not only was he choking, but he was also completely unable to move. Whatever had fallen on him was at least several hundred kilos, not to mention angry and covered in fur. Dripping jaws started to clamp down on the back of his neck. Taki squeezed his eyes shut and prepared for the end.

"Bad kitty!" Draco growled.

Taki heard a thump above him, and the massive weight was abruptly lifted off his back. Instinctively, he scrambled to his feet. The gouges on his back burned like hot irons plunged into his flesh, and his hands tingled painfully. Draco, on the other hand, had his arms wrapped around a lion's throat.

"Little help 'ere!" Draco grunted. Deep gashes marred the junction of Draco's neck and shoulder, and crimson smeared on the floor. The lion was on its side, thrashing madly and trying to flip Draco off its back. For some reason, Babu, who had once been Tirefire's mascot, came to Taki's mind. He'd only seen the fat tom in one scuffle, against an equal-sized rat that had tried to steal Hadassah's cheese wheel. Babu had raked his back claws against the rat's belly, disemboweling it and leaving the innards strewn around the barracks. Disgustingly enough, the rat had continued its melee long enough to chomp off one of Babu's ears before succumbing to its wounds. If a lion fought anything like a cat…

Taki aimed his palms at the lion but decided quickly against using a sutra. There was too much of a chance he'd hit Draco. Desperate, he picked up the key-sword he'd dropped and beat the lion about its head with the flat of the blade. The creature yowled and squirmed out of Draco's grasp and hurtled through the door leading to the castle interior. Shouts sounded from the hallway.

His entire body shaking madly, Taki started to drag Draco by the collar toward the balcony. A blood trail streaked and smeared over the cobbles. Draco groaned and cursed.

A helmeted Templar burst into the chamber, wielding a wickedly curved glaive. Taki dropped the key-sword, intoned a sutra, and then sent a *khala* burst right into the Templar's midsection. The impact blew the Templar off its feet and sent it crashing into one of the bookstands. When a second Templar entered, Taki immediately repeated himself.

The edges of Taki's vision blurred, and his consciousness faded to light gray for a moment. He scrabbled to pick the key-sword back up again but found his fingers too clumsy to wrap around its hilt.

"Leave me here, Natalis," Draco said. "Get out with the damned key-thing. I'll be fine."

"Don't be ridiculous," Taki snapped. He marshaled his strength and wrapped an arm around Draco's midsection to pull the man up. Draco's eyes widened, and his hand shot to his waist. The LeMat was out in a split second and fired.

A halvidar fell midcharge, clutching at his gut. Draco drew the hammer back and fired again to fell another man. The chamber was practically filled with enemies now, both Templars and their subordinates. Draco continued to fire, and when he ran out of rounds, flipped his hammer down to activate the strange pistol's shotgun barrel. A large, imposing shape loomed in front of the pair, and Draco fired again. Taki's vision faded in and out, but in a moment of clarity, he saw Siridar Cassius on the downswing with a cudgel. Then, he saw no more.

* * * *

When Taki woke again, he was naked, freezing, and tied to a post. He squeezed his eyes shut in an attempt to break away a red crust that obscured his vision. His own dried blood, he figured from the way his scalp ached. That was right: the Templar had smacked him unconscious, and now he was at their mercy. Draco and Taki had failed their mission, for there was no way the Templars would have overlooked the theft of the one object their Ordo was charged with defending. *Fuck my luck,* Taki thought. He looked around. They were probably still inside the Templar castle, though where within he knew not. Across from Taki, Draco was similarly restrained.

Siridar Cassius stood before him, holding the key-sword. One of the lions loafed nearby, licking at a spot of congealing blood on the floor. It was hard to say whose blood. "I knew you two were Imperial scum when I saw you," Cassius said.

"I dare say, good Templar," Draco said, "you've proven to be the worst host in Ursala! The Vicomte de Bretagne demands that you—"

Cassius spun around and punched Draco in the gut. Draco's eyes rolled back in his head, and he vomited blood. Cassius turned back to Taki.

"You're the officer," he said. "What is your retrieval signal? A flare? What color?"

Taki remained silent. *Would biting my tongue really make me bleed to death?* He moved it between his teeth and started to clench. When the pain grew too great, he started to retch. Cassius watched this impassively.

"What is your signal?" Cassius rested the point of the key-sword against Taki's throat. "Tell me, and I will give you a soldier's death."

Taki shook his head.

Cassius shrugged and walked over to Draco. To Taki's surprise, he pulled out a key and freed Draco from his shackles. Draco collapsed, only for Cassius to lift him by his hair.

"The signal, or he dies in agony."

Draco spat a wad of bloody mucus to the floor. "Do you seriously think we plan that far ahead? We were just going to ad-lib it. Come up with something on the fly. We're *Tirefire the Lesser*, you piece of shit!"

Cassius snarled and plunged the key-sword right into Draco's gut. Taki shouted and bucked against his manacles while the Templar started to saw upward. Draco convulsed, vomited once more, and then his eyes rolled back in his head. Cassius let the body drop with the sword still embedded. The lion loped over to Draco and started to lap blood straight from the wound.

"Y-you *fuck*," Taki snarled, unable to form even a coherent curse. "I'll kill you! I'll kill all of you! I'll kill your fucking cat!"

Cassius gripped Taki's face in one of his massive hands and squeezed to force Taki's mouth open. "In the end, it matters not what you say. We will defeat that puny expedition regardless and then lead the charge all the way back to the Imperial camp. *You* will remain alive as long as needed to extract your useful components. You too will serve His Supreme Majesty in your own way. Now accept His blessing."

The Templar reached into a pouch to withdraw something that made Taki almost faint to behold. About the size and length of one of the Siridar's fingers, the object looked like a writhing, angry grub. Cassius brought it closer to Taki's mouth, and Taki screamed and writhed.

"Choke on this, pervert."

Cassius spun around, only to have his head bisected by a blade. The Siridar collapsed to his knees. His hands shot up and pressed against his temples, as if trying to mash his split parts together. Draco panted next

53

to him, holding the key-sword. Rivulets of blood gushed from Draco's massive wound and pooled at his feet. Near where Draco stood, the lion sprawled lifelessly on the floor, its head turned at an unnatural angle. Cassius reached for Draco but in doing so let go of one side of his head. The half cranium flopped to one side, and the massive Templar finally collapsed and then moved no more.

"Draco?" Taki whispered.

Draco reached down and swiped the keyring off Cassius's belt and undid Taki's manacles. Taki stumbled and nearly fell as his legs now took on all of his weight. He looked over at Draco, who'd taken a seat next to the Siridar's corpse.

"God's blood, man! I'll never doubt you again," Taki said as he lurched over. "That's a bad wound. Let me heal you, and then let's get out of here."

Draco pushed Taki's hand away. "Save the prana, Natalis. Won't do any good. I'm done."

Taki blinked. "What do you mean, done?"

"My writing career is over. I won't get to see that ring or the spire." Draco chuckled, and a rivulet of black streaked from the corner of his mouth. "But...I prefer my version, anyway."

Taki fell to his knees. Draco was almost completely white.

"Do me...a favor. Tell Dassa...to take care...of herself."

Taki wiped at his eyes. "I will, my friend. My best friend."

Weak in the knees and under a cloak of misery, Taki forced himself to his feet. He took the key-sword in one hand and Cassius's keyring in the other. The clothing, ammunition, and supplies he'd taken into the fort were nowhere to be seen, and he decided not to waste time getting them back. He padded his way to the doorway leading out from the torture chamber. He took in a breath and pressed his palm to the ground. Aslatiel had taught him the sutra during Taki's recuperation from imprisonment within the Teufelsbrucke.

He envisioned his prana diffusing into the earth in waves emanating from where he crouched. Now, he could sense every footstep and breath within the castle, even if the impulses were weak and moved frequently. As Taki had suspected, he was underground. Just outside, a chevalier stood guard. Beyond the lone sentry, however, there were few others on this level.

Taki bit his lip in thought. *Take out the sentry, get to the surface, and run to the Queen's Right. I'll die for sure when they catch me, but I'll make sure none of us perished in vain...* He gazed at the bloodstained key-sword. *So much trouble over this blasted thing. Guess we weren't some sort of elite special forces after all.*

After spending as much time as he could to regenerate his depleted stores, Taki struck the sword's hilt against the door, twice. With any luck, the sentry would think it was Cassius beckoning for assistance. Taki held his breath and waited. A few seconds later, he heard a latch raising, and the door swung open.

Taki charged the chevalier and sank the key-sword into the man's midsection while simultaneously pressing a hand over his victim's mouth. They both slammed into the opposite wall with a dull thud. Taki withdrew the sword and then punched it through the tabard over the chevalier's chest. The wall stopped the sword from going entirely through, but it had penetrated enough. The chevalier's eyes rolled back in his head, and he slumped silently to the floor. Taki wrenched the blade out and was rewarded with a disgusting squish.

He glanced at the dead chevalier. The man had actually been around Taki's height and weight. Up close, the damage and bloodstains would be obvious, but from afar, other soldiers might not notice an interloper. Taki hooked his arms under the corpse's shoulders and dragged it back into the torture-chamber-turned-charnel-house. When he emerged into the hall again, Taki felt more human, if still just as desperate.

A half bell later, Taki surfaced nearby where Draco and he had stabled their horses. To his regret, the mounts were nowhere to be seen. He did not want to think of the fate that might have befallen the animals, and he pushed the consideration from his thoughts. The important thing was to keep calm and make his way to the outside, to the Queen's Right. Thankfully, the gates were still open a crack, as they'd been when he'd crossed. Unfortunately, the archway was teeming with Ursalans.

Most of them appeared to be infantry, and many seemed to be injured. *At least I'll fit in,* Taki thought. *But where are they coming from?* He barely evaded being trampled to death by a squad of riders who barreled down the midway but avoided the temptation to curse at them. All around him, he felt the unmistakable sensation that the entire place was preparing for a siege. That meant the gates would likely close soon, as soon as the last stragglers made their way in. The time to reach the Queen's Right was dwindling.

Taki upped his pace. He initially affected a limp, in order to better mimic a wounded knight, but midway through, he abandoned the pretense. He cut around huddled groups of infantry and lines of scurrying, gray-cloaked servants, all the while studiously avoiding eye contact. The gate entrance was only a few steps away. Someone stepped in his way. Taki looked up to see an armored halberdier.

55

"No one may leave, Sir Knight. Siridar's orders. Gates are closing soon."

Taki clenched his jaw. *Think, damn you! Come up with some excuse!* He cleared his throat. "Make an exception for me, good man. My horse is still out there. I had to dismount to help another fellow in."

"What's your name?"

"G-giles, of Rouen."

"Beg pardon, Sir Giles, but the Siridar forbade—"

A gray servant shuffled up to Taki and signed to the halberdier while bowing obsequiously and trying to kiss the man's hand. The halberdier stepped back and shook his hand, as if trying to cleanse himself of imaginary filth.

"Ugh, fine, go. Just get your thrall off me," the halberdier said.

Taki blinked in surprise but pressed on. In a few strides, he was outside the gates. What greeted him was far more grim than the idyll he'd seen earlier. A ragged mob of Ursalan infantry trudged toward the gate without any semblance of order or rank. Taki's suspicions from earlier had proven correct: this was an army on the retreat. Taki smiled despite himself. Now, he'd do his part. He started to walk to the Queen's Right.

Someone grasped his wrist. Taki turned his head to see who and grunted in surprise when he saw the same groom who'd taken his horse and, he now realized, had also accosted the halberdier. The groom pointed at the Queen's Right and made a cautionary gesture: it was still guarded by a pair of soldiers with relic rifles. Taki squinted.

"Why did you help me?"

The man shook his head.

"Ah, sorry. I should've known. You're mute, aren't you?"

The groom opened his mouth so Taki could peer in. Taki frowned as he realized that the man had no tongue.

"Is this…is this what they do to you here?"

The groom nodded.

"How many are there of your…kind?"

The groom shrugged and gestured widely with his arms.

"You know I'm with the Imperium, right? And you won't try to attack me?"

The man bowed.

"Thank you, that's a relief," Taki said. "I have something that might help you. Help all of you, in fact. But I need to get to that stone."

He started to chew at his cuticles but stopped when his teeth hit the leather of his gloves. Reaching the plinth would be difficult. It would take too long and drain too much of his energy to hit both guards with sutras, and he was in no condition to engage them with one blade to his name.

The groom tapped Taki's arm again. He pointed to Taki, himself, and then to the guards. Then, he closed his fists and made a punching motion in the air.

Taki shook his head. "You're saying attack together? But you're unarmed, and they've got rifles. It's not your burden to take on. You've already helped me when you didn't have to, so if you wish, you can go back."

To this, the groom crouched in front of a patch of loose dirt. Using a finger, he traced a lopsided circle and then added sixteen triangular rays to complete an Argead star. Taki's eyes widened: the sixteen points were only depicted on the battle standard of the Dominion Army.

"Hoplite?" Taki whispered.

The groom nodded and crossed his arms.

Taki clenched his jaw. *If he goes further with this, he'll die. So I need to tell him now.*

"I'm Natalis, once a Polaris," Taki said. "But I need to tell you, I'm with the…Imperium now. All Argeads are. We lost to them, and now the basileus is a vassal of the padishah. If you help me, you're aiding the Imperium."

The man gave off a grim smile and let out a hoarse barking sound that might have passed for a laugh. Then, he again pointed at Taki, himself, the guards, and finally made a jab in the air.

Taki smiled and wrapped his fingers around the hilt of the key-sword. "Okay. Thank you. I'll get the one on the left. You take the one on the right."

By now, the number of retreating Ursalans streaming toward the fortress had dwindled to a mere handful. Taki and the groom had wended and wove their way to within a few meters of the plinth and now stood a few meters away from the guards.

"You," one of the guards barked at Taki. "Stop tarrying here. And get your thrall out of my sight."

Taki chuckled. "Can you tell me where the jakes are? We're from the Dominion."

Before the guards could shoulder their rifles, Taki rushed up, grabbed the fore-end of one of the rifles, and smashed his palm right under his man's chin. A fireball erupted from the top of the guard's head, and the body flew back into the Queen's Right with a clanking thump. Taki spun the rifle into a ready position and disengaged its safety toggle. The groom had managed to get his man to the ground, and they rolled in the dirt, kicking and struggling. Quickly, however, the guard regained his footing, brought his rifle to the ready, and brought it to bear on the groom. Taki pulled his trigger. The guard fell to his knees and then the ground and then moved no more.

"Get his rifle and cover me," Taki said, fumbling to bring the key-sword out. By now, the commotion had attracted attention from the castle. Halberdiers streamed out of the gate, bowling their counterparts over in the rush, and ran toward the Queen's Right. Gunshots rang out, and one of them tumbled to the ground. Taki looked over and saw the groom crouched nearby, firing the rifle. *I'll make sure he gets home to the Dominion. We'll find out who he is and make sure he's rewarded richly for his service, and all the more so for what he's had to endure in this hell. I'll make sure of this, even if I have to use my coin-half for it.*

He turned his attention back to the Queen's Right. From the limited information Aslatiel had possessed on the object, it seemed as if the key-sword had to be inserted somehow. *But where?* Taki realized in a panic that no matter where he looked, there didn't seem to be anything resembling a receptacle. His breathing quickened. He'd come all this way, only to be stymied by his inability to find a hole. Frustrated tears flooded his vision; the irony wasn't lost on him.

The halberdiers were almost to the Queen's Right. The gunshots abruptly stopped, and to his horror, Taki realized that the groom had run out of bullets. Seemingly undaunted, the man simply gripped the barrel of his rifle in his callused hands and prepared to use it like a club. Taki glanced behind him. Now presented the only other alternative: to escape with the sword and regroup with the army. But that would mean leaving his new companion behind as a sacrifice. Taki's stomach turned, but he willed away the nausea. *It can't be helped. This will all be for nothing if I fall here and lose the key-sword. Draco's death will have been in vain.* He started to step away.

The sound of a horn blasted through the air and made Taki's hairs stand on end. He recognized it from earlier, although this one was louder by far and made by a multitude of people. He turned again, looked at the ridge, and saw the full strength of the Imperial Liberation Army descending the incline. A chant carried through the air, initially subtle but noticeably stronger by the second: *"Uukhai! Uukhai! Uukhai!"*

The halberdiers stopped in their tracks, hesitated, and down to the man started to sprint back to the gate. The groom backed away to the cover of the Queen's Right and fell, panting, to his hands and knees. Taki knelt by him. "We did it, Hoplite. We all did it."

A detachment of horse broke off from the front of the column and started to speed toward Taki. He recognized the standard of Alfa Gruppe. Tears, this time of relief, flooded his eyes again. So elated was he that he failed to hear the thumping behind him.

A gigantic, mailed hand descended from above to grasp Taki by the throat. Just before he'd have been caught in the crushing embrace, someone crashed into Taki's side and bowled him out of the way. He scrambled to his feet and grasped for a rifle that wasn't there anymore. Taki looked up at what had just tried to kill him and gasped.

Siridar Cassius stared back at him with blood-blackened eyes. The man's head was now bound tightly together with what looked to be steel wire that cut gruesomely into the overdeveloped meat of his face. Whoever had performed this act, however, had failed to perfectly mate his severed features. His lips, his nose, and even his eyes were noticeably askew, and the junction still leaked blood and gore. But most pressing, Cassius had taken hold of the groom and lifted the man in the air by the throat. The groom kicked and struggled, only to be flung back toward the gates. He rolled and skidded on the ground and then tried to crawl to his knees, only to be set on by a group of halvidars. The burly sergeants took the groom by his arms and started to drag him back to the gate.

I have to save him! I have to save him! Taki's eyes widened in panic as he saw his newfound ally disappear into the press of men. So distracted was Taki that he almost failed to block when Cassius stomped a boot right into his chest. The impact knocked the wind out of him and sent him rolling in a heap. Adrenaline gave Taki the strength to get to his knees despite the pain that drenched him. "Out of my way!"

Plasma coalesced in a vengeful corona around his body, and he hurled a stream of raging light in Cassius's direction. The blast hit the Templar head on and spun him aside. The remainder of the beam went wide and gouged a deep, glowing crater in the Aegis.

Cassius skidded to a stop, still on his feet. He lowered his arms from a guard stance and fell to one knee. Black smoke spewed out from him and stained the ground. His chest plate and vambraces glowed red and cratered, dangling loosely from shattered bindings. A moment later, they crashed to the ground. Impossibly, Cassius stood back up, raised his greatsword, and tromped forward.

Taki, on the other hand, couldn't move. His stolen armor had been reduced to singed rags. His hair smoldered, burnt nearly back to his scalp. But most of all, he simply hadn't the energy to do anything, even pick up the key-sword that rested beside him. Cassius advanced like inexorable fate. *I did my best*, Taki thought, and closed his eyes.

"Natalis, I don't recall giving you permission to die," Lotte said, and cuffed him lightly on the cheek. "Complete your mission."

Taki's eyes fluttered open, and he gasped. Lotte strode past him toward Cassius, her armor battered and bloody and missing segments. She held her blade out with grim purpose.

"Captain!" Taki croaked. "Draco..."

Lotte didn't turn her head. "I know."

Arms linked under Taki's and dragged him to the Queen's Right. He turned his head and saw Enilna on one side, Lucatiel on the other. When they reached the monolith, Lucatiel drew back a fist and punched it into the granite right over an engraving of the Royal Seal. Contrary to Taki's expectations, she didn't break her own hand but rather broke through a thin layer of stone. As the shards fell away, Taki saw it: a slot the width of the key-sword. Enilna pushed the blade into Taki's grip and closed his fingers around it. Together, they jammed the mysterious key into the slot and turned it with all their might.

A deep rumble emanated from below, while the ground shook as if undergoing a temblor. Blasts rung out from the Templar castle, and the gates seemed to jump away from their hinges. The massive slabs crashed into the moat and sent up white plumes as high as the Aegis itself.

Taki opened his eyes and lowered the hand he'd put up to shield his face from the onslaught of dust and spray. He was thoroughly drenched, and his entire body stung like mad. He raised his head to look to the last place he'd seen his captain.

Lotte stood over what remained of Cassius's body. It had been thoroughly dismembered, his bound head smashed to unrecognizable chunks. Pieces of metal ensnarled with flesh were strewn about around the threshold of the castle. Her victory was framed by the archway, devoid of obstacle and aimed straight at Versailles.

4

I have to stop waking up like this. Taki turned his head and surveyed his surroundings. From what he could tell, he was back in the musty-smelling bell tent the squad had inhabited before setting out from the Imperial camp. Everyone's spare possessions were strewn around in the same ramshackle way they'd been right before the Aegis expedition, and Taki's shirt, leggings, and even smallclothes hung from a line overhead. *How did I end up back here?*

Curiosity overpowered his desire for more sleep, and Taki sat up on his pallet. His skin burned in large swatches across his chest and back, and his muscles all felt as if they'd been torn and then sewn back together and then torn again. He glanced down at his torso and realized it was mostly covered in bandages. Taking a deep breath made him slightly nauseated, for he still reeked of burnt hair. He pulled his blanket aside right as Hadassah raised the entrance flap and stepped inside.

"Aim your gun somewhere else," she said, and planted her hands on her hips.

Taki blinked and realized that other than the bandages, he was still in the nude. Reflexively, he pulled the blanket back over his body. "Sorry! I didn't know you were coming in."

Hadassah smirked. "Oh, whatever, it's fine. Not like I haven't been changing your dressings and cleaning your bung for the last fortnight."

Taki reddened and pressed the blanket down further. "*A fortnight?* Was I out for that long?"

"Helpless as a baby. You collapsed right after the gates went down. What a sight that was! The captain freaked out, thinking you might be dead or your brains had turned to potato. But if you're awake now, then you just overdid things and needed a rest. It happens to your type."

Taki looked at his hands, which boasted raw patches where the blisters had sloughed off. "How'd I end up back here?"

"You started out in the hospital, but I moved you here quick-like. The surgeons don't wash their hands, and have you seen the fronts of their aprons? Gross as hell! I think I saw an ear plastered to one of them, all dangling and drying out."

"But the gore is a sign that they're busy…"

"No, it's a sign that they're coated in millions of tiny monsters that want nothing more than to eat you from within."

"Huh? What sort of blasphemy is that?"

"It's called 'germ theory,' you damned plebian. And you fight the monsters with 'antisepsis.' Luca taught me all about it and now everything feels dirty all the time and it's kind of driving me batshit, to be honest."

"How the hell does the Prince of Maladies know any of this?"

"Because she's probably read more books than Dra—" Hadassah stopped and bit her lip. "Anyway, the point is that Luca isn't just a violent, overpowered psychopath. She's a *well-read*, violent, overpowered psychopath. Damn you, Nata, stop interrupting me when I'm talking."

Despite himself, Taki let out a chuckle. It hurt where his belly met his groin, but he didn't mind. "I'm sorry. By the by, where's everyone else?"

"Inside the Aegis. The fighting's gotten crazy. You got our foot in the door, but the Ursalans are trying everything to slam it shut."

Inside…a hollow feeling twisted in Taki's gut as the memories flooded back. "Mikkelsen, there was a servant, a groom who helped me escape. Right before the gates went, he was recaptured by the Ursalans. Has anyone seen him?"

Hadassah shrugged. "No idea. It was a total clusterfuck. You know anything more about this guy?"

"He has a tattoo of a hex on his forehead."

"Can't say I've seen anyone who looked like that, though it would stand out in a crowd. In any case, I've been taking care of you and doing not much else, so someone else might know more. We should get back soon, if you're feeling better. Everyone who can walk is battling assholes."

Taki sighed. "I'm sorry I've been such a burden. I know you'd rather be helping the captain."

Hadassah drew up and flicked Taki's forehead. "Less than a few minutes awake and you're already pissing me off. Look, Natalis. Without you…and without Draco, we wouldn't be this far along."

"Sorry, you're right," Taki said, unable to meet her gaze. "Look, Mikkelsen, before he died, he—"

"No," Hadassah said. "I don't want to hear it. Not right now, anyway."

"Aye, sorry again."

She sighed. "It's fine. Hey, do you think you can walk?"

"Don't know until I try," Taki said. "Might need a little help."

"Here, I'll help you up. Just, uh, keep your manhood under wraps."

After Taki had gotten to his feet and painfully dressed himself, he stepped out from the tent with Hadassah.

"Good," she said. "Come along now. It's not far from here."

Despite a part of him wishing to lie back down inside the tent, Taki found himself following her. "What're we doing?"

"Chores, obviously. You think I got my hands on fresh muslin just because I'm cute?"

"I, uh," Taki said and stopped. "I guess that makes sense. There must be many wounded who need those more than me."

"Lucky for you, I'm the master of greasy snacks. I give the quartermaster a plate of croquettes, and he gives me clean stuff right from the stores. Here, step in and let's get to work."

Hadassah drew aside a flap leading to one of the nearby mess tents and plopped on a bench. Nearby was a bucket of potatoes in various stages of peeling, as well as another bucket of skins. She handed Taki a peeling knife.

"Wait," Taki said, "are you doing what I think you're doing?"

"Join in," Hadassah said. She grabbed a potato and started to pry its eyes away. "I was actually doing this when I went to check on you. But if you're awake, then I'm putting you to work. Otherwise, you'll just end up pleasuring yourself or whatever it is that men do when they're alone in a tent."

"I wasn't going to do that!" Taki frowned, but sat down to peel anyway. "It's just weird. You swore over and over that you'd never touch a root vegetable again, so long as you lived."

"I may have, but your health is more important than some stupid oath. You're, like, one of my precious friends 'n' shit."

Taki's chest felt heavy, and his throat tightened. He set his peeler down and brought a grimy hand up to his eyes.

"Oy, oy!" Hadassah said. "Put those feelings into your peeling! Those latkes won't make themselves."

"Sorry," Taki said, willing himself to stop.

"It's okay. Anyway, you're probably wondering why I was picked to stay with you. You know, as opposed to your little girlfriend from Alfa.

Believe me, she definitely wanted to play surgeon. As in personal sex doctor—"

"I get it already," Taki said. He took his knife up again and started to work on a tuber. "Actually, it really hadn't crossed my mind to ask you."

"I'll explain anyway, because I'm just so awesome. You see, what happened to you happened to me a few times, back before I met the captain and before Mezeta enslaved us all. I overdid things, went far beyond my limit, and turned into a pierogi for a few days. So I know how to deal with what you have."

Taki raised an eyebrow. "Forgive my ignorance, Mikkelsen, but…what is it that you actually spend yourself on?"

"Rude much?" Hadassah kicked him in the shin. "I'm not just some layabout that eats bonbons and shits everywhere."

"I didn't mean that! I just don't really know much about you. I always thought you used your power to be a crack shot, but I could never figure out how."

Hadassah laughed. "I just like guns, is all. They go boom and make me happy."

"So how do you manifest?"

"I don't understand it completely, but I'm able to slow down the world around me. Even make things stop entirely if I really go all out."

"So you could dodge a bullet if you wished?"

"Or the Prince of Maladies. You should've seen the look on her face when I slugged her right in the gob."

Taki's jaw hung open. "That's…I didn't realize you were so strong."

"Can't do it for long, though. Which is where the rest of my story comes in, *if you'd stop interrupting me*. Well?"

Taki shook his head and clamped his lips shut with a finger.

"That's better. Anyway, it happened a few times to me when we were in a pinch. Draco was always the one who'd take care of me when I became a human croquette. And I'd be in a deep, deep sleep for a long time. That meant he'd have to feed me grain juice one drop at a time and clean up my messes. See, those were the days he was free to go wenching, so I know he missed out on spending his grad quite a few times. The men at the convalescence house were perverts, so Draco always stepped up to protect me from that. And no, before you ask, I *know* he never did anything gross. He was an honorable man, even if he was a sinner and easily bamboozled and—"

She quickly wiped a sleeve over her eyes.

"Mikkelsen," Taki said and reached for her, only to be swatted away.

"I'm fine," she said. "So there you have it. Glad you woke up, though. Washing you was a real pain in the ass. You're heavier than you look."

Taki set his freshly peeled potato on the pile. "Thank you for taking care of me."

"I'm just paying my debt, is all." She wiped at her eyes again and tried to resume her peeling, but her hands shook uncontrollably.

"Are you tired?" Taki asked. "I can do this alone. You should rest."

She waved a dismissive hand and tried to scowl, only to start tearing up herself. "Ah, fuck me, Natalis. I wish I hadn't been such a bitch the last time we talked. Was it *that* hard for me to say 'good luck' or even 'I hope you kill every last motherfucker?' I'm the worst. The absolute worst."

"I think he understood your feelings," Taki said. "You were worried for him. That much I could tell, and I'm pretty dense, as you said."

She looked up at him. "Tell me it wasn't too painful, Natalis. Even if you have to lie to me. I just want to hear it."

Taki bit his lip. "I can't say, but when he passed, he looked content. He was able to talk to me, too. He told me to tell you to take care of yourself. Those were his last words."

Hadassah lowered her head and was silent. Taki held still, afraid to breathe. He reached for her once more, but she swatted him off again.

"The nerve, Emreis," she whispered. "The absolute gall!"

Taki blinked. "Huh?"

"Treating me like a kid..." She slammed a fist on the table. "All right, Natalis. When's the last time you made me practice writing?"

"Uh, probably when we were heading to Xizhang. So, a year ago."

"We're going to make these latkes, and then after that, you're going to help me write. I'm going to write a book. A book that will make Draco Emreis immortal. Long after we're all dead, women of all countries will know what a...a presumptuous sinner he was!"

Taki swallowed back the doubt on the tip of his tongue. He knew Hadassah had little discipline for learning, and more than that, not much time. A promise made in a time of grief had less chance of fruition than most vows. But now was not the time to quash her fervor. Instead, he smiled and reached a hand out. "I'll do my best."

She took his hand in hers and smiled at Taki, genuinely, for the first time in the long time he'd known her. "I knew I could count on you. Now peel the rest of these while I find some quills."

* * * *

A day later, Karma arrived from the front on board a wagon train of wounded. By the time Taki made his way to his squadmate, he could already hear the man screaming and struggling in one of the treatment yurts. He lifted the flap with some trepidation, wondering if he'd regret walking into an amputation. To his surprise, however, he merely saw one of Chronicler's alchemists poking Karma in the arm with a tiny needle. Taki blinked in surprise.

"Harden the fuck up, honey," Hadassah said as she clamped down further on his shoulders to keep him from moving off the pallet. "You want Nata to see you screaming like a bitch?"

Sweat beaded on Karma's scalp, and he tried to twist away. "But they just *leave 'em in you!* Lots of tiny needles! That's not *natural! Help me, Taki!*"

"Are all you Argead men so weak willed?" Lucatiel snorted. She squatted on Karma's midsection with her heels grinding into his pelvis. "It's just acupuncture. It doesn't actually hurt."

"I hate needles! Is that so wrong?" Karma pleaded.

"It's wrong to be a grown man crying like a child and require the Prince of Maladies to sit on your lap," Hadassah said with a scowl. "I should beat you for moaning so shamelessly and gyrating your hips, you dirty strumpet."

"Oh my damn!" Karma whooped as another needle went in. "Just for the record, Dassa, I didn't ask her to sit on me. You're the one who thought of it."

"It's because I'm too light," Hadassah smirked.

Lucatiel glared at her. "Are you saying I'm fat?"

"Of course not, my Prince. You just have better muscles."

"That's true. You are a little too petite in general. Do you want me to show you how to bulk up?"

"I'd love if you did."

"Make sure you have plenty of grad to spare. You must eat at least twelve eggs a day on my regime."

"A whole dozen? Who could possibly stomach that? I'll be shitting lead!"

"It'll make your hair shinier and stronger."

Hadassah batted her lashes. "Will mine ever be like yours? Straight and black as night?"

"I would never wish for that," Lucatiel said. "I would smother babes in a nursery to have your beautiful, crimson curls."

"*Now* who's flirting?" Karma guffawed. He yelped again as another needle pierced him.

"Let's go out, my Prince. I'm through with this wuss," Hadassah sighed.

"Oh, Dassa, I thought you'd never ask," Lucatiel fawned.

"Just let me die already," Karma moaned.

Taki drew closer. "What happened to him?"

"He took a ball to the chest," Lucatiel said. "I think he was under the impression that I was in some sort of danger, so he dove in front of me."

"And now I wish I hadn't saved you after all," Karma sniffed.

"So why are you here?" Taki asked Lucatiel with a frown.

She shrugged. "I wanted to make sure he lived to regret his presumption. Also, he needs to see Master Chang here, not one of the regular sawbones. I'm leaving with the next convoy."

"Hey, Karma," Hadassah said. "How come you've never taken a bullet for me? Now I kind of want to shoot you so you can prove your commitment."

Karma rolled his eyes. "Are you serious? Natalis, this is exactly why we men are better off alone. I'm going my own way from now on."

"I'm just, uh, glad you're alive," Taki said with a shrug.

"All done with this part," the aged acupuncturist said. He wiped his hands. "Time for cupping. If one of you madams would help flip him over."

Karma started to sweat anew. "Not cupping! Anything but cupping! I'm healed, I swear. I feel like dancing!"

"Whatever," Hadassah said. "Roll over and take it like a woman."

Later on, after Taki had extricated himself from the yurt, he stood in the tent and surveyed his belongings. Most of the clothing and supplies he'd lost to the Templars had been disguises, thankfully. Most importantly, his coin-half was securely hung around his neck again. For the first time since his capture, he felt up to soldiering again. *Lucky for me*, he thought. If Karma was out of the fight, that meant the squads needed manpower more badly than before. The skin on Taki's arms and chest was still raw and red, but he no longer needed the bandages to prevent himself from leaking everywhere. Still, he decided to take a muslin roll and stuff it into his knapsack, next to a ball of seeded suet and a parcel of Hadassah's croquettes wrapped in paper. He tightened the straps on his brigandine and left the tent.

Just outside, he paused. Lucatiel squatted on a stump nearby, intently peering at him with her murderous blue eyes. Taki suppressed a shudder. "What do you want?" he said.

She frowned. "That's rude."

"Sorry," Taki said with a shrug. "I'm still unused to you. Is there something I might aid you with?"

Lucatiel pursed her lips. "I had a great amount of esteem for Emreis. I was sorry to see him go. You should know that."

"I appreciate it. And thanks for taking care of Gillette." Taki turned to head in another direction.

"That's not all!"

Taki stopped, the hairs on his neck rising. "Then what do you wish to say?"

"My brother, Aslatiel. What do you think of him?"

"I respect the man. He's a formidable warrior and a strong commander. What's your point?"

"Do you think he's different now? Since Irulan died?"

"I…" Taki paused. "I don't know. He was certainly miserable afterward, but now he's back to war. I'd say he's become whole again."

Lucatiel hopped off her stump. "But that's my point! He's *not* whole!"

"I couldn't say either way," Taki said, backing away. "I'll just take your word for it."

"Stop blowing me off," Lucatiel said. She moved to stand in Taki's way before he could meander by.

"Stop cornering me!"

"Wanna fight?" Lucatiel put up her fists.

Taki stumbled and almost fell on his behind. "No!"

"Why not? Punches are feelings. I want them to reach you."

"Your *feelings* are strong enough to kill me, von Halcon!"

"How the hell are we gonna become friends, then?"

Taki let out an incredulous laugh. "I didn't think you were interested."

Lucatiel's face reddened. "Well, I might be. You're stronger than you look, and my brother likes you a lot, which means that I should like you." She turned away and crossed her arms.

"Look," Taki said, "I'm not an expert on this by any means, but if I wanted to be friends with someone, I'd *talk* with her first. Not…exchange blows." He sighed and massaged his temples. "Why are you concerned for Sir Aslatiel? Has he done something strange?"

"Yes," Lucatiel said, and started to pace.

After a minute of silence, Taki let out an exasperated sigh. "I'm waiting."

"Don't rush me! I'm bad at explaining things."

That's obvious. Taki rubbed his eyes. "Take a breath and collect your thoughts first."

She strode up and grasped him by the collar. "Are you *sure* you don't just want me to beat it into you?"

"I'm damned sure," Taki said. "Start from the beginning."

"After Irulan died, you helped my brother out. And sure, he feels better and doesn't pine about her death like he did before. But now, he's different in another way. A way I don't like."

"What way?"

"He was always the most careful of commanders. Maybe too careful. He never wanted to see a single soldier die under his watch. But when we fought the chevalier column outside the forest, we'd lost half our people by the time we got to you."

"So? You lose men in battles. That's something any officer knows and expects."

"He didn't need to do that. He's better than that. Our companies were supposed to destroy the ambush and retreat to rejoin *Ba'gshnar*'s main column. But Aslatiel wanted to push forward after we routed the first group. Ordo Templars flanked us, and we barely held on. I killed their grandmaster. Somehow we got through them."

Taki shook his head. "I wouldn't be alive right now if he hadn't pushed all the way to the gate. I'd have lost the key-sword to that bastard Cassius, and we'd be right back where we started."

"That's not all," Lucatiel said. "Your brains turned to harspud so you didn't see what happened next. The Ursalans who didn't run away surrendered. Lots of wounded. Came out with their hands up and without arms. We killed them all."

"That's…" Taki's indignation died in his throat when he remembered the knife sunk in Lotte's back. "Surely there was a reason."

"There were a lot of reasons," Lucatiel said. "I'm not saying it wasn't just. But Aslatiel looked to be enjoying himself too much. When I asked him to hold back, he looked at me like he was going to kill me, too."

"Do you think he would have done it for real?"

"Don't be daft. Of course not!" Lucatiel sighed. "I'm not the only one who notices. The men are unhappy. We've lost a lot of people. *Ba'gshnar* promoted him, even still."

"What do you want me to do, then?"

"I want you to talk with him again. Tell him not to be so...so indifferent with his men. He listened to you last time, and not me."

Taki nodded. "I'll do my best. I owe him my life yet again, it seems."

"Damned right you do. Now pack your shit, because we're heading to the front. Also, do you have any food?"

By the time Taki was ready to depart the palisade, Lucatiel had already gotten her hands on both his suet and his croquettes. Taki had considered making her reimburse him for what she'd eaten but decided against it. He simply wanted to get the trip over with, for worry gnawed at his mind.

Lucatiel had mentioned what had happened to the surrendering soldiers but said nothing about the gray slaves that populated the inside. *I need to know what happened to the groom,* Taki thought as he chewed on a fingernail. But with only a memory of the man's tattoo and no other information to go on, such a task would be nigh impossible. He clenched his jaw. *I have to try anyway.*

"Don't think to leave without me," Hadassah said as she hurriedly pulled up on a stocky, gray donkey. "And yes, I know what I'm riding. They're better behaved and stronger than horses."

"You're just too lazy to learn to ride properly," Taki said.

"And you're an unappreciative little git," Hadassah said. "I made those croquettes for you to eat, not to feed my Prince on a date."

"It's really good, Dassa," Lucatiel said between bites. "Cook for me more often."

"Gladly," Hadassah purred.

"Why *are* you two so cozy with each other?" Taki sniffed.

"I've already told you," Lucatiel said. "Punches are feelings."

* * * *

Smells of petrichor and brimstone hung in the air. The former stronghold of the Ordo Arslan looked nothing like it had when Taki had assured its liberation. The Aegis was completely blackened with smoke and pocked with craters, and the roof of the castle had partially collapsed. Smoke still trailed toward the sky from its remains, though a permanent drizzle seemed to hang over the area. The chilly rain had already soaked Taki completely through to his smallclothes and coated everything in his vision with a drab, hazy sheen. The most striking sight, however, was the sheer number of bodies lying about.

The corpse field stretched as wide as Taki could see. Hulking Templars in shattered armor slumped in their death poses, turned into grotesque pincushions by broken ends of blades and spears. Strewn around the dead giants were men who'd met similar fates, splayed all over the muck. Shattered siege engines and mangled barricades formed their own twisted piles, some of which still smoldered and glowed. The blown-open shell of an armored reliquary was half sunk in the mud, its turret ripped clean off. And closer to the entrance were scaffolds, from which bodies swayed limply in a nonexistent breeze.

"God's mercy," Taki said. "What happened here?"

"An ass-whipping," Lucatiel said. "Two Ordos and at least a legion of infantry tried to take the archway back. It was four days of nonstop battle." She smiled. "That was the fun part."

"But why haven't the bodies been moved? Or at least piled and burned?"

"No time. *Ba'gshnar* wanted to siege Versailles before reinforcements arrived from Anglia and Hispania. They're only a month or two away, he says. We dealt with our dead and left the rest."

"What about the fools on the gallows?" Hadassah asked as they rode by.

Taki had been so preoccupied with getting to the arch for temporary respite from the rain that he'd paid the scaffolds no heed. Hadassah's question shook him out of his stupor, though, and he veered his horse closer to one of the bodies. He wiped the rain from his eyes and took a closer look. Then, he gasped. "Von Halcon! What the hell are thralls doing on the rope?"

Lucatiel blinked. "Why wouldn't they be? They're just some sort of zombie labor force."

Taki's stomach knotted, and he quickly trotted around to survey the bodies. Fortunately, none of them seemed to be the groom. "You don't understand. They're not mindless slaves but our people! One of them helped me escape. You could've executed him by accident, damn it!"

Lucatiel glared. "What are you going on about? It's impossible to talk with them. They either sit there and groan or try to strangle you."

"That's unbelievable," Taki said. "The man who helped me knew perfectly well who he was. They'd cut out his tongue, was all."

"Natalis," Hadassah said, "Luca speaks the truth. We tried to save these creatures at first, but it proved impossible. Even if they were our countrymen once, they're so far gone that killing 'em is a mercy."

Taki bit hard on his knuckles. "Even if that's the case, I know at least one of them is still human. That means more of them might be, too. I have to speak with the captain and Sir Aslatiel."

"You do that, Natalis," Lucatiel said. "For all our sakes."

The trio spent the next few days riding hard through scrubby hill country infested with knotted dead brambles and lacerating hedgerows. The Liberation Army had hacked, burned, and crushed a winding path through the brown wasteland, and the corpse-strewn aftermaths of skirmishes and harassing actions dotted the way. Adding to Taki's growing unease, the number of dead thralls only increased the deeper they went. Fortunately, none of the bodies were obviously that of the groom.

Crumbling spires and long-abandoned aqueducts dotted the countryside, while slivers of road meandered along valley floors and led into the skeletal remains of what Taki assumed had once been cities and towns. A gray sheen of decay had settled over what wasn't already overtaken by nature and, as they pressed further in, helped turn Taki's musings in a decidedly melancholic direction.

Finally one evening, Taki saw the Imperial standards fluttering limply in the twilight breeze. The army had set up its camp in and around what looked to be a massive cathedral whose walls barely held together. The smell of swamp water washed over the surrounds like a thick miasma, and Taki crinkled his nose in disgust.

A pair of sentries approached and held out their palms to signal a stop. One of them spoke: "Leutnant von Halcon, you have a summons."

"From who?" Lucatiel asked.

"The feldmarschall."

Lucatiel glanced at Taki and Hadassah. "I must go, then. You two should find your fellows."

"Let's find our captain," Hadassah said to Taki. "I need to show her you're not a turnip, or she'll fist me to death."

Taki nodded and dismounted. "Is it me, or are there fewer men around?"

"It's not just you," Hadassah said. She swung off her donkey and passed to reins to a nearby soldier. "Karma told me they've lost thousands getting here. Even the battle at the Aegis wasn't so bad, since we had the wall backing us up. But it's been a complete shit-show inside. Most of what they've fought doesn't even sound…human."

Taki frowned. "Then what have they been fighting?"

"How the hell would I know?" Hadassah shrugged. "I've just been taking care of you for the last two weeks straight. Actually, you should get off your horse and kowtow to me right now."

"I thought I was your precious friend," Taki said.

"Did I say something dumb like that? I must've been wasted at the time."

"I thought you couldn't partake."

"Washing a man will drive any woman to drink."

Taki chuckled. "With how much you talk about it, I swear you rather enjoyed it."

"I enjoy being a martyr," Hadassah said. "When I touch myself I think about all the times I made people feel shame and guilt. Now shut up, and let's find the captain."

Taki shuddered and fell silent.

The remnants of Tirefire the Lesser had encamped near a flying buttress that had long failed in its duty of bracing the roof and had plunged partway into the superstructure. Someone had attempted to make repairs a long time ago, studding the ruins with gigantic nails the height of a man. A ragged tarp suspended overhead shielded some sleeping pallets from the rain and the nonexistent sun. Embers from a nearly dead campfire smoldered within a ring of mold-covered rocks. Nearby, Lotte and Enilna squared off against each other in a furious, sparking clash.

Lotte stood rooted to the ground and pivoted her greatshield freely to deflect a flurry of attacks from the girl. Enilna's efforts to sidestep and reach around the edges of the shield with her rapier proved fruitless. With a frustrated growl, she feinted, drew back her leg, and aimed a kick straight at her opponent. Lotte swung her shield out in an unexpected parry and knocked Enilna onto her rear. Then, she swung her greatsword, two-handed, straight down at the girl's head. Before Taki could even think to shout, the weapon stopped before it would have splint Enilna like a log.

"What kind of idiocy possessed you to try and kick me?" Lotte asked. She slung her weapon over her back and offered a hand.

Enilna was wide-eyed but took the help up. "Uh, Luca does it to break an enemy guard."

"Lucatiel is like a myconid, but stronger and surlier," Lotte said with a smirk. "*She* can punch holes through steel all day, but *you* cannot. Don't use tactics that aren't suited for your build or power. Concentrate on your speed. You almost slipped in a few jabs here and there."

"Captain," Taki said with a grin. "We're reporting for duty."

Hadassah posed like a showman and grinned. "Look! I turned him from parsnip to human! Sort of!"

"Glad to have you back," Lotte said with a relieved-looking smile. "Both of you."

Enilna rushed over to Taki and caught him in a bear hug. "I thought you'd died, you turd!"

"I came back just to spite you," Taki said.

"Then go back to hell," Enilna said, though she didn't let him go.

"This isn't it?"

"I hate you," she said, and planted a soft but sloppy kiss on his lips.

Taki's cheeks reddened, and he suddenly felt self-conscious about the fact that Lotte and Hadassah were doubtless staring at the spectacle. He quickly extricated himself from her grasp. "I, uh, need to settle down here and do a few things first."

"Okay, but promise to find me later," Enilna said. "You owe me time with your face." She waved to Lotte and then headed away.

Taki looked sheepishly at his companions. "Sorry, I..."

"Natalis, that was a touch cold of you," Lotte said. "I thought you liked her."

Taki winced at his captain's teasing and Hadassah's effort to keep from bursting into laughter. "I'm a soldier, first and foremost."

"Aye, you are," Lotte said. "Come, take a rest for now. We're stuck in this place until we figure out how to overcome the shrieking tower."

Taki raised an eyebrow. "The what?"

"Ah, I forgot you've both been away," Lotte said, and tossed a nearby log onto the campfire. "With Gillette gone, I've been the only one here for a little while. How is the man?"

"Whiny as hell and tender as a babe, but he'll live," Hadassah said. "Swore he'd be on the next pony back here so long as he could skip out on more cupping."

"Good," Lotte said. "Were it me, I'd have let von Halcon take the bullet. The woman needs a humbling, badly."

"I don't know," Hadassah said. "I think getting shot would just make her stronger."

"Captain," Taki said. He settled on Karma's pallet and enjoyed the chance to stretch out his legs. "Where exactly are we? What is this...place? A swamp?"

"I think so," Lotte said. "No countryman of ours has ever set foot beyond the Aegis and lived to tell about it. So there are no maps to follow. The old man, the padishah—he's been leading us deeper and deeper in, and now we're just a stone's throw from the castle. He's clearly got some sort of esoteric knowledge that the rest of us don't, because this place is definitely not like anywhere we've been before. It's unlike Astarte or the Cantons. It's completely alien. It's filled with monsters and horrors the likes of which I've never even seen."

"Monsters?" Taki frowned. "As in chimerae? I thought this was the royal capital."

Lotte shook her head. "There are things here that look like no chimera we've ever seen. I'd rather fight ten of those Xizhang manticores than some of the beasts here."

"And what of the Ursalans? Have their commoners tried to kill us again?"

"That's the other thing. Besides some Templars here and there, we haven't seen peasants or infantry or even chevaliers. The only Ursalans we've seen have been those shambling thrall creatures—"

Taki's eyes widened. "Captain, you don't know this, but one of them helped me escape from the Ordo castle. He was a former Dominion man, and definitely not mindless, like everyone thinks."

"What happened to him?"

"They captured him before we took the gates. I need to try to find him, or he'll suffer a terrible fate because of me."

"Know you his name?"

Taki shook his head. "I know it'll be hard. I know nothing about this man, other than that he has a strange hex tattoo on his forehead. But I need to at least try."

"I've not seen anyone, thrall or otherwise, with such a mark," Lotte said. "So there may be some hope. We must aid our countrymen, especially those who've risked their lives for us."

"But if that guy had all his marbles, why don't any of the rest of 'em?" Hadassah asked.

"I don't know," Taki said. He raked his scalp with his fingers.

"Maybe he wasn't inside too long. Maybe the more time you spend here, the more weird you get," Hadassah said. "I feel gloomy as hell already."

"Perhaps," Lotte said, "if we take Versailles, then we'll be able to look for this man without too much interference. Problem is that I don't know if we'll be able to."

"Why not?"

"We forded the river with a hundred thousand, but this camp has a mere two hundred within. Most of my men are wounded and stricken with fever back in Morvan. We've got no siege engines because the roads are nonexistent, and monsters chip away at us every day." Lotte looked around to make sure no one was eavesdropping. "Personally, I don't know if we can win this. We might all be killed soon."

Taki sucked his teeth. "What does Sir Aslatiel think?"

"That's the problem," Lotte said. "I used to be able to discuss our strategy with him normally, but he's become obsessed, and nothing short of pressing forward will do. Lately, he's refused to see me and spends most of his time holed up in the old man's yurt."

"Ew," Hadassah said. "Are they fucking?"

"Probably not," Lotte said. "But the result is the same."

Lucatiel's words surfaced in Taki's memory. *I need to see him soon.* Overhead, the holey tarp hung undisturbed by wind and cast yet more gloom on the surroundings. A chill overtook him. He looked at the nearby firepit, held a palm out, and willed flame from the charred logs within the stones. Unsurprisingly, the new warmth did nothing for his goosebumps.

"So who's up in the tower shrieking at us to stop?" Hadassah asked. "Sounds sketchy as hell."

Lotte pointed north to a path leading up to a copse. "Past there is a path alongside a hill. Cross it, and we're in the streets of Versailles. There's a small keep with a belfry on it that looks over the path. Whenever we try to cross it, something within the tower casts a horrible light below and screams. Anyone who's caught for more than a few seconds in the light either dies on the spot, kills herself, or goes mad and starts trying to attack his fellows. That, and there are monstrous ape-things chucking spears at us all the while."

"Since when did they let giants and sirens into the Ursalan army?"

Lotte shrugged. "There have been more of these sorts of monstrosities the further we've gone in. I had thought the princesses were the worst of it. But now I'm not so sure what lives in the royal palace."

"Well, I'm back now," Hadassah said. "And there's nothing in this world that likes eating lead. Speaking of which, beg your leave, Captain."

"For what?"

"I promised Prince Luca I'd go hunting with her. Apparently there are many enormous creatures round these parts that need killing and eating."

"Try to bring back something *edible*," Lotte said. "And absolutely nothing that walks on two legs."

"My thanks, Captain!"

Hadassah skipped away with her rifle jauntily held over one shoulder. Meanwhile, Taki glanced up. Strangely, the sight of the massive white column shooting skyward had become less jarring the more time he'd spent traversing the lands. He'd almost forgotten to gawk at it, so omnipresent was the spire nowadays.

"I'm glad to see you again, Natalis," Lotte said. "It was lonely being here by myself."

Taki blinked and returned his attention to her. "Aye, Captain. I'm glad to be back, too."

"You should know that you've been mentioned in the dispatches back to the capital. Emreis got a posthumous citation for valor. His family, or what's left of it, will get some extra grad every year, too."

"He deserves it," Taki said. He drew his knees to his chest and stared intently at the newly kindled flames. "Captain, there was a tiger or some creature like it that was hidden in the grandmaster's room. I should've been more vigilant and killed it before—"

"Natalis," Lotte said, "say no more, and think no more on it. If you continue down this path, you'll end up enslaved to past regrets. I know this because I was the same. So too with every other commander who's lost men."

"With all due respect, Captain, that's easier said than done."

Lotte sidled up to him and rubbed his shoulder. "I know, but I had to say it. And I also think about Draco far too much for my own good."

"Does it ever go away? The regret?"

"Never. The only thing you can do is remain steadfast. Always tell yourself that *you did what you could.*"

Taki clenched his jaw. "I did what I could."

"Aye," Lotte said. "We all did."

Taki repeated it again, this time under his breath. Lotte had been right: though it was but one step away from blatant falsehood, the mantra was comforting in an odd way. *But what if I hadn't done everything I could?*

"Captain, is there truly no way to press on from here?"

Lotte shook her head. "Not without losing everything."

"I still need to find the man who helped me, and we all need to give Hecaton Mezeta her comeuppance," Taki said. "So I can't just give up now. I will talk with Sir Aslatiel and make him see reason. And if I cannot, then I will find some other way for us to win."

Lotte leaned over and rested her head on his shoulder. "Natalis, I'd say you were an idiot if I didn't know you better. Actually, I take it back—you *are* an idiot. But you're also special."

"Thanks, I think." Taki's hand found its way on top of hers. Their fingers interlinked. He inhaled deeply, enjoying her touch.

"You should go find her, Natalis."

"Huh? You want Mikkelsen to come back?"

"I didn't mean her, I meant Shpejtspate. She's been pining for you all this time, and I haven't been able to comfort her."

Taki squirmed. "She can wait a little longer. I've got my work cut out for me and...and maybe I wish to stay here for a moment, Captain."

"We can discuss strategy later."

"That's not what I meant." Taki met her eyes.

"Natalis, you shouldn't."

"Captain, there are differences between us, but they grow smaller every day. I'm telling you, again, I'm not who I was before. I like you. I want you."

"I'm too old."

"I don't care," Taki said. He inched closer and touched his lips to hers. Part of him expected Lotte to strike him, but instead, she grasped him by the back of his head and hungrily kissed him back. She pulled away after a few seconds, consternation on her face, but then dove in again, mashing her lips and tongue to his.

Taki's chest pounded as he undid the fastenings on her armor and jack, and grew elated when she offered no resistance but instead shifted her body to make the process easier. Finally, he pulled her smallclothes away and feasted on the sight of her, naked. Lotte glared at him for his, but nevertheless undid his lacings in turn. As they lay down on the ragged pallet together, her fingers passed over his chest before closing around the coin-half. He whispered a question in her ear. Her lips parted and started to form the word "yes," but then she abruptly let go and pushed him away.

"Stop. We can't go on." She rolled away and hurriedly covered herself.

Taki drew himself to his knees. "Why?"

"Because I'm still taking advantage of you," Lotte said. "And that'll never change. I wanted to use you. I've been thinking of using you, every day and night."

"But I want you too, Captain."

"Damn you, that's *not* what I meant! I wanted to make you give the coin-half to me."

Taki blinked and instinctively clutched at the fragment. "For what?"

"To make me feldmarschall, so I could force a withdrawal." Lotte wrung her hands. "Over the past two weeks I've lost hundreds under my command and haven't been able to do a damned thing about it. I've been thinking about that trinket of yours ever since you were wounded at the Aegis. If we'd done it, I'd have bent you to my will while you couldn't resist."

Taki clenched his jaw. His head still pounded with every pulsation of his heart. "That's...not an unworthy request. It sounds like we're doing poorly here, and—"

"And you just told me exactly why you couldn't give up here," Lotte said. "I'm sorry, Natalis. I acted badly, no matter the reason." She wiped at her eyes. "This is why you shouldn't be with me. I'm incorrigible. I'll never see you as an equal. Not on the battlefield, and certainly not in bed."

"Fine," Taki said as he punched the ground. "Then I'll take this as a lesson learned."

"Go find *her*, Natalis. She won't try to extort you. She's not a shitty excuse for a human being."

Taki tightened the laces on his leggings with a bit too much zeal and painfully cinched his waist. "I'm finding Sir Aslatiel first. I'll do something to break this stalemate or whatever we're in. And then, when we've either won or withdrawn, you and I are going to talk again, as man and woman."

Lotte was silent as Taki stormed away.

* * * *

Under the watchful eyes of trebizonds, Taki drew aside the flap of Aslatiel's tent and entered. What he saw inside, however, almost killed his new resolve. A soldier knelt, hunched over in front of Aslatiel with his hands in manacles and his back weeping blood from a flogging. Two spetsnaz from a unit unfamiliar to Taki stood at the man's sides, holding the chains connected to the shackles. Aslatiel himself stood with his arms crossed and his expression twisted with disdain.

"You are accused by your peers of cowardice," Aslatiel said to the man. "Do you have an explanation for this?"

The bloodied soldier looked up. To Taki's surprise, the man was middle aged and battle weathered, not a fresh recruit who'd spooked during his first battle. "Aslatiel—"

"Generalfeldmarschall to you, Hauptman."

"Yes, I apologize, Feldmarschall," the hauptman said through gritted teeth. "I'm already on my knees, so I'll just beg you again. Take a look around. We're wounded, outnumbered, and out of ammunition in a nest of horrors we never expected. We *must* withdraw, or we'll all end up dead for sure. Flog me if you wish, but you can't escape the truth."

Aslatiel shook his head. "We are compelled to take Versailles and end the Ursalan menace once and for all. Or do you doubt the authority and wisdom of our liege?"

The hauptman fixed Aslatiel with a glare. "*I do.* His Majesty is *destroying* the greatest army ever fielded in the history of the Imperium! And for what? A mad quest for something that might not even exist."

"His Majesty has brought us victory unimagined by his predecessors. It is only because of his power that we strike terror into the heart of the Sanctissimus Rex."

Taki took a tentative step backward. *Perhaps this isn't the best time.*

"Hold there, Sir Taki," Aslatiel snapped. "I want you to see this. One of my officers, a man I trusted, now seeks to render your suffering worthless and spit on the sacrifice of Master Emreis."

"Feldmarschall," the hauptman said, "we should withdraw to the Morvan camp and secure the southern border from the Iberians. Then—"

"I'll give you one last chance to redeem your honor," Aslatiel said. "Take your company and charge the pass. Bring the tower down for His Majesty, and I'll make sure you have a comfortable retirement."

"That's futile and you know it!"

Aslatiel bared his teeth. "Either die in battle or die by my hand!"

"I won't sacrifice my men like that! Godrot you, Aslatiel! How many must die to make up for *her*?"

Aslatiel drew his pistol from its holster, pressed the muzzle against the hauptman's forehead, and pulled the trigger. Taki cursed and instinctively leapt back from the spray of gore. The hauptman slumped face first on the ground. Casually, Aslatiel put the weapon away and gestured to his adjutants to remove the body.

"S-sir Aslatiel," Taki began, trying to keep his teeth from chattering. "That was…"

"Necessary," Aslatiel said. "We walk a thin line between final victory and crushing defeat. Unity, not discord, is what's needed for us to triumph. One day, you might lead the padishah's army. Learn from this example, brutal as it is."

Taki bowed his head and glanced at the flecks of pink that still studded the rug under his feet. "My captain told me about our situation."

"She has my utmost respect, but she can be overly pessimistic. I hope she has not sent you to argue with me."

Considering what just happened, I wouldn't even if she'd sent me to do so. Taki shook his head. "I wanted to see how you and everyone else were doing. And show you that I'm ready to fight."

"Good," Aslatiel said with a smile. "I was worried. There have been others like you who've never woken up. I don't know what I'd have done if you'd died. And you have my condolences about Master Emreis. He was a gentleman and a scholar who paid the ultimate price for the Imperium. I couldn't have asked for a finer soldier in my service."

Taki's chest tightened. "Thanks. There have been a lot of people who've died for me, lately." He wrung his hands and started to pace. "Sometimes I think if I'd just perish, maybe no one else would have to suffer for me. Hah."

Aslatiel clapped a hand on Taki's shoulder. "Sometimes, lives must be spent for the greater good. Master Emreis, Mikhail, and…even Irulan knew that and wouldn't have wanted any other fate. I too sometimes wish I'd shared Irulan's fate. But all I can do now is make sure her sacrifice means something."

Taki closed his eyes and resisted the irrational urge to flee, shout in anger, and burst into tears all at once. None of those would do any good. The only thing to do was press forward. "What would you have me do, my general?"

"Rest for now," Aslatiel said. "I will go to *Ba'gshnar* for counsel soon and think of a way to continue our advance. Keep your faith."

"Aye," Taki said. He stepped back, bowed, and lurched out of the tent flap. The moment the stink of twilight swamp air hit his nostrils, he was overcome with the urge to vomit. The trebizonds stared at him quizzically as he scrambled away, but they remained silent.

After he'd finished retching over the side of a nearby log, he felt a tap on his shoulder. He wiped his lips and turned his head to fix a bleary-eyed stare at Enilna.

"You're breaking your promise," she said, and planted her hands on her hips. "Instead of coming to me, you go hobnob with the feldmarschall and now you're puking? What are you guys, drinking buddies? You're stealing bullets from our children's mouths, deadbeat!"

Taki's jaw hung open. "What? What in the fuck?"

"Maybe you had some brain damage after all. Your sense of humor's even shittier than before."

"I wasn't aware I was the entertainment," Taki said. "Actually, I'm supposedly higher ranked than you."

"Not for long," Enilna said. "Look, I'm a fahnenjunker now! Aslatiel—er, General von Halcon—signed my commission stuff himself."

"Congratulations," Taki said. "You're the regiment's new gopher."

"And you still stink like a thousand unwashed assholes. Did you sleep in those same clothes all this time?"

Taki sighed. "I heard you really wanted to play surgeon on me. I'd glad you didn't, otherwise I'd be dead."

"I'd have only molested you a little," Enilna said. "Anyway, it's all good. I'm glad Dassa got some time to mourn, too."

Taki looked back over the collection of fetid pools nearby. "Why in blazes did we pick a swamp to camp in?"

"The chimeras stay away from this place for some reason," Enilna said. "That and there's that crazy tower nearby that fries your brains if you approach it."

"I've never heard of such insanity," Taki said. "What's even up there?"

Enilna pursed her lips and winked conspiratorially. "Wanna find out?"

Taki frowned. "What do you mean?"

"We've been stuck here with nothing to do, so I went exploring."

"Are you even allowed to do that?"

"Probably not, but Aslatiel hasn't really been around to tell me no."

Christ, Taki thought. *I just saw him execute a man for defying orders.*

"Are you listening? There's a little cave I found that you can squeeze through. There's a built-up tunnel on the other side that seems to go toward the tower. I haven't explored further, though."

"Why not?"

Enilna rolled her eyes. "Because it's *scary,* and I didn't want to go alone."

"Have you told anyone about this?"

"I was going to tell Aslatiel, but his men turned me away."

Taki glanced around for eavesdroppers. "Perhaps best to keep it between us for now."

"If you say so," Enilna said. "Will you join me or not?"

"Let's go," Taki said.

The path Enilna led them along soon had Taki up to his knees in brackish water that reeked of decay. His stomach sank with every step. Quicksand and mud would suck him into a horrific death by suffocation, and that was discounting the very real possibility of predators lurking just beneath the surface. A few times, he'd sworn something had nibbled at his toes and had barely willed himself not to panic. Eventually, they stopped in front of what seemed to be the ruined corner of a fallen sentry tower.

"It's here," Enilna said. She gingerly pushed aside a clump of dangling vines with her knife to reveal a small, barely man-sized hole in the masonry. "Don't worry, I brought torches this time."

Taki peered in and took a deep breath through his nostrils. He didn't get a head rush or feel nauseated—the air inside wasn't likely to kill them. "How'd you find this place, anyway?"

"Hunting these," Enilna said, and held a writhing, clacking creature up to Taki's face.

He let out a yelp and fell backward into the muck. The mud was enough to cushion his behind from harm, though. "What the hell?"

"Sorry!" Enilna lowered what Taki now realized was a crab whose body was the size of a man's head. "Bad joke of mine."

"I'll say," Taki muttered, and got to his feet. Now his brigandine was covered in muck, as were his blade and Herstal. He would have to disassemble the gun and scrape filth from every crevice to make sure it didn't just explode next time he fired it. "Christ, where'd you find that thing? I thought crabs only lived in the sea, not swamps."

"They're all over the place, but I know the spots where they gather to *rut*," Enilna said.

"Dare I ask why?"

"Oh, don't give me that look. I gather them because they're edible. In fact, boiled in water they're super tasty. With suet—or better yet, *butter*—they're heavenly. I'll cook you some when we get back to camp, though we've got no butter."

Taki eyed the crab suspiciously, even more so when it reached for him with a snapping claw. He'd seen the insides of the creatures before, after birds had lifted them from the shoals and dropped them on rocks to burst the shells. The smell had been the same revolting shade of asafetida then as it was now. "I'll pass on that."

"Don't be so delicate," Enilna said. "If I can't find reach your stupid heart through your loins, I'll do it through your stomach."

Taki crossed his arms. "You're assuming a lot, you know. It's not like you're my wife or anything."

"No, we're not married. But nearly all of the senior army commanders *are*. So are the heads of the Administration and the Frauenbildungkorps. Basically, get hitched or stay a small fry."

"Is that why you're talking about marriage all of a sudden? Are you itching for power now?"

Enilna laughed. "Of course I am. It's nice that I like you, though. Many people don't have that luxury."

"What makes you think I'd agree to tie the knot in the first place?"

"I thought you liked me too."

"I do," Taki said, "but things are complicated."

Enilna tossed the crab aside, making a splash and disturbing the silt. Her teasing smile had been replaced with something devoid of mirth. "Complicated. I see. It must be difficult, having to choose from that vast harem of yours."

"That's not what I meant," Taki said.

"Fine, fine. What you meant to say is that you still think you'll somehow make your way into Lotte's britches."

"Leave her out of this."

"Hit a nerve, didn't I? Are you mad? Think about how I feel, then. Think about how you've treated me."

"Damn it, I don't understand why we're arguing! I thought we were going to explore this tunnel or whatever you found!"

Enilna glared at him in a way that looked as if she were holding back tears, and then she turned away. "I thought you were just a little dense. Now I see the truth. You're just an asshole who takes people for granted. Leave. I've got dinner to catch."

Taki sucked his teeth and threw up his hands. *Whatever. Screw her moody self. I've got to clean my gun, anyway.* He'd just started sloshing away when the water in front of him shook and frothed. Before he could collect his thoughts, a claw—like the one he'd just seen but a dozen times larger—shot out of the water, followed by an equally monstrous body. Taki wiped the splattered muck from his face.

"C-crab," he stammered. "Big! Crab!"

Taki lurched back just in time to avoid a swipe of the creature's slime-covered spikes and tried to scurry away. The mucky bottom gripped at his hands and feet, and he struggled to gain traction. He felt Enilna's hand grasp the back of his jerkin and yank him upright. The gigantic crab reared back and swung its claws down at the pair.

"The tunnel!" Enilna screamed.

The claw slammed into the water and sent up a blinding, muddy splash. Taki's hand somehow found Enilna's, and they sprinted, albeit slowly and unbearably, toward the opening. He pulled with all his might and thrust her into the darkness before leaping in himself.

Taki heard an unnerving crunch when he hit solid ground, but he retained some primordial urge to tuck in and throw himself into a roll. His consciousness washed white. Purple streaks shot across his vision, and pain wracked him with convulsions. In his fading vision, he saw the tips of a claw thrust toward him and wildly thrash about, but he ceased to care when he passed out.

5

"You dead? If you don't open your eyes, I'll start biting."

Taki blinked his eyes open and saw Enilna's face hovering over his. Something warm pressed against his chest; he realized it was her hand suffusing him with her prana. She quickly withdrew it, though, once he started to move. Groggy and sore, Taki sat up and glanced around the dank murkiness. Only the feeble light of a small torch kept complete darkness at bay.

"We're screwed, aren't we?"

"Don't be so negative," Enilna chided. "We haven't been turned into poo, and that's the important part."

"Did you know those things got so big?"

Enilna shook her head. "First time I've seen one. God, if only we'd had Lucatiel with us. We'd have been able to feed the entire camp. Imagine how much meat's in one of those claws!"

"There you go, thinking with your stomach again," Taki said. He cracked an involuntary smile.

"There are worse parts to think with," Enilna said. "And I'm definitely going to hunt that thing down and cook it when we're through here."

"Maybe it was justified," Taki said. "How many of its brothers and sisters have you consumed?"

"Not enough, that's for sure."

Taki patted at his waist. Reassuringly, he still had his kriegsmesser, even if the Herstal was too gummed up to use. "Can we get out of here?"

"I lost the rope and hook. We have to go toward the tower."

Taki licked a fingertip and held it in the air. "Cold air's coming toward us. So, forward then?"

"Aye. Fair warning, though. I just poked around a bit in here, didn't look through the entire thing. So protect your ass from grief."

"I'm years ahead of you," Taki said with a smirk. "Just make sure we don't fall down any holes."

They silently treaded through a dank, gently graded corridor. A central channel ran in the middle, but without any water running through it. Strangely—for Taki had figured the corridor to have been a drainage effort—it was lined at regular intervals with statuary. When he'd peered closely at one, he'd been repulsed by what he'd seen. They appeared to be men wearing robes, but the faces had been rendered in a way that seemed vicious and thoroughly alien.

In the silent darkness, it was hard to tell how much time had passed—probably many bells, but without sunlight there was no way to judge. Eventually, their way was blocked by an iron door set into an elaborately wrought grating. Beyond that, a cavernous hall seemed to stretch out farther than he could see.

"Okay, this is weird," Enilna said. "It wasn't locked when I came here before."

Taki tugged at the door, but it didn't budge. He shook his head. "Do you want to turn around? Wait for the others to rescue us?"

"I didn't tell anyone we'd be here," Enilna said. "It could be days before they come looking for us. I'll starve at this rate."

"Then we have no choice but to force through. Stand back," Taki said. He raised an arm and willed his power to form. "*Plei Khala!*"

A churning vortex of swirling, sparking air formed in front of his outstretched palm and shot toward the iron grating. When it struck the metal, the grating bowed inward with a piercing squeal and ripped off its moorings entirely to slam into the ground with a resounding clang.

Enilna clapped her hands over her ears and winced. "Ow! What's your deal? I was going to just pick the thing!"

Taki crossed his arms. "No, we needed firepower."

"Sounds an awful lot like Lucatiel." Enilna frowned. "Don't tell me she's part of your damned harem, too."

"You don't have to worry about her," Taki said. "I don't like insane women, no matter how comely."

Enilna's lips opened for a retort, but she stopped. After a silent moment, she whispered, "Uh, something's coming."

Taki clenched his jaw. She was right. From farther on than he could see, he heard shuffling feet and metal clanking on stone. Strangely, there were none of the usual curses or small talk he associated with any gathering of soldiers. "Snuff the torch!"

"Then we'll be blind!"

"I've got light," Taki said, and summoned a small, flickering flame that danced right above his palm. He glanced around, desperate to find a hiding place. Fortunately, the same sort of statuary from the corridor also decorated the chamber, mounted atop pedestals of copper-flecked granite. Enilna hesitated but then tossed her torch down the corridor and rushed over to where Taki crouched beside the pedestal. The two held their breaths and waited.

Dim, undulating light spilled their way. Taki stole a glance from around his cover. Three adversaries approached. Two were tall and wrapped head to toe in what seemed like oily rags, with ungainly, long limbs and a loping gait. In their hands were lanterns and the ends of chain leashes that led to the central figure.

As unnerving as the two flankers were, the being they restrained made Taki's gorge rise the highest. It was as tall as the tallest Templar Taki had ever dealt with, but unlike those fearsome knights, this one wore no armor or even clothing. Its exposed flesh was a patchwork of bulbous, ill-fitting parts lashed together with oozing suture lines. In place of a face was a mishmash of weeping crevices that only vaguely resembled a mouth and slits for a nose. The eyes glowed an unsettling, shimmering red.

"Hold still," Enilna said. She braced her forearms on one of Taki's shoulders and aimed her pistol.

Taki's eyes widened. "What the hell are *you* doing?"

"We need firepower, remember?" Enilna squeezed her trigger, and the flash and pressure forced Taki's eyes shut.

Almost immediately, he heard a groan and the sound of something massive collapsing on stones. When he opened his eyes and blinked the purple floaters away, he saw the giant face down on the ground with its handlers shrieking in raspy, incomprehensible tongues.

"Dude, take 'em out!" Enilna shouted, and drew her rapier. She took a bounding leap toward the closest rag-creature and drove the blade right through its chest while tackling it to the ground.

Taki drew his kriegsmesser and charged the second. It dropped the length of chain and quickly pulled out what looked like a corroded, wickedly curved dagger. Taki pirouetted out of the way of a jab and slashed his enemy from its shoulder all the way to its groin. Sticky liquid splashed on his face and started to tingle unpleasantly. The rag-creature reeled and screeched. Taki pressed the attack with a backhanded swing and caught it across what he surmised was the throat. The creature collapsed with a gurgling rattle. Taki panted and wiped the sticky vileness from his face.

"What's wrong with you?" He glared accusingly at Enilna. "We could've let them pass."

"I was *not* going to be caught from behind by *that thing*," Enilna said. She flicked the blood from her weapon and sheathed it. "Besides, they were all begging for death."

"Lucky that your shot didn't just piss it off," Taki said. He decided against poking the large body with his foot. "What are they?"

"Hell if I know. But the big one, he's as tall as a Templar would be, don't you think?"

"I've only seen one with the helm off, and he…" Taki clenched involuntarily at the memory of Cassius. "He looked human. Sort of."

"Tell me the story sometime, when we're out of here." Enilna glanced around. "Shit, the torch! It's probably ruined now."

"Don't worry," Taki said. He blew gently on the flame hovering above his palm, and it grew in intensity. Then, he pushed up with his hand and snapped his fingers. The flame now hovered over his shoulder.

"Nice. You've gotten better at the whole spewing fire thing."

"Thanks," Taki said. "Not *everything* ends with me burning my hair off or falling asleep for a fortnight."

"You'd be insufferable that way. So where next?"

"I thought you're the one who'd explored the place."

"I only went up to that door." Enilna laughed nervously. "I, uh, got too scared to go on."

"No shame in that," Taki said.

She smiled. "I'm glad you think so. Others might've called me a coward."

"A coward? For not wishing to die alone in some dark shithole?"

"Oh, Natalis, I might be convinced to like you again." Enilna grinned. "When push comes to shove, you're pretty sane."

Taki sighed. "I'm sorry for earlier. It's just that my captain was the first woman who liked me back. And to be honest, I still desire her. But perhaps we aren't a good fit, and there are too many differences between us. So, if you still feel the same way about me when this is all over, we can talk about…"

"I'm sorry too," Enilna said, and smiled gently at him. "It wasn't right of me to hound you like that. We're not old, after all. We can take our time."

"There's a piece of…sinew in your hair." Taki reached to her hairline and gently lifted away the drying piece of gore. His lips drew closer to hers, and she closed her eyes and tilted her chin back. Without thinking overmuch about it, Taki leaned in and kissed her.

Enilna cupped his face in her hands and returned his hunger equally. "You know," she whispered, "we're *actually* alone now."

"You really want to do it? Here? Surrounded by dead monsters and covered in blood and smells?"

"Ew, of course not! I just wanted to make out a little."

Taki chuckled. Filthy and sodden as he was, he still felt her warmth and the contours of her body under her jerkin. Caressing and tasting her filled his mind with enough of a pleasant fog to drown out the fact of where they were and what they'd just endured. Most importantly, there was absolutely no chance for interruption. And no possibility that he was being used.

Enilna gasped.

Taki tensed and stepped away. "What's wrong? Am I hurting you?"

"The huge thing!" She pointed past him.

"I'm   not   that—"

"No! *The body!* It moved!"

"How? It's dead!" Taki turned his head and almost pissed himself.

The patchwork monstrosity groaned and shuddered and pulled itself to its knees. With one hand, it tried to push itself to standing; with the other, it pressed at a bleeding hole on its forehead.

Enilna grabbed Taki's hand. "Run!"

They sprinted across the grand hall, only to find their way blocked by another set of doors. Taki jammed a shoulder against one of the ornately graven wooden slabs and strained with all his might. "Dammit! Won't budge!"

Enilna kicked at them. "Probably doesn't open from this side!"

"Then what the hell do we do?"

"Duck!"

Instinctively, Taki dove out of the way just in time to avoid being tackled by a bull rush. Right where he'd just been, the patchwork creature barreled headfirst into the doors. What had been immovable to Taki bent and warped like the lowest grade of ancient plastic under the creature's onslaught and then broke. Light flooded the hall, and Taki threw an arm over his eyes in a vain attempt to shield them before he tumbled awkwardly away.

Just as he'd collected some semblance of his senses and gotten back to his feet, he heard a rasping, pained roar. He brought his kriegsmesser up to face the threat.

Enilna clasped his arm. "Taki, look! We're at the surface again!"

Beyond the shattered doorway lay a windswept stone terrace, strewn with the remains of the gilt oaken slabs. Unlike where they'd been in the swamp, the air carried an evergreen chill to the senses, and the wind was anything but stagnant.

"The creature," Taki said with a gasp. "What happened to it?"

"Look." Enilna pointed to a freshly destroyed section of stone railing at the edge of the terrace. She bounded ahead to inspect it.

With trepidation, Taki followed her to the edge, peered down, and immediately wished he hadn't. The terrace was perched over a great expanse of trees many hundreds of meters below, giving him the overpowering, horrific urge to toss himself over. Worse, hanging by fingertips just under the lip of the ruined stones, was the creature. It swayed in the air, snarled at Taki, and tried in vain to swipe at him with its free hand.

Enilna drew her gun. "Should we?"

Taki shook his head. "Leave it. Let's just try to get back to camp."

"What's gotten into you? Don't tell me it's an honorable streak?"

"No, nothing like that. Just…were it me hanging like that, if I were to die anyway, I'd prefer to not be kicked down."

Enilna holstered the pistol and backed away. "If you insist. I've got only one round left, anyway. Where to now?"

Taki chewed at a thumbnail. "I've no idea where we are. But is that the tower you all were talking about?" He pointed at the red-bricked dome of a belfry that rose nearby. Most of it was blocked from view by the sloping hilltop they'd just emerged from.

"Whoa, you're right," Enilna said. "Just be glad we can't actually see the bell chamber from here. Whatever's in there is what fries your brains."

"I find that implausible," Taki said. "There's no chimera that does anything of the sort, and we've seen some of the weirder ones."

"I still feel bad about the Weeping Lady of Lucerne. The poor titan was just depressed over her worthless man, and we went in and killed her."

"She—it—tried to turn you into jam," Taki reminded her. "What choice did we have but to fight?"

"I know, but the coolest friendships begin with a fight," Enilna said with a sigh.

"Let's get a move on. Captain said the tower blocks the army's advance. So there's got to be some sort of path leading from the tower back to camp."

"Are you saying we should go toward that?"

"Aye, but we'll be discreet. You're almost out of ammunition, and my gun's still jammed."

"Hey, you're the leutnant here," Enilna said.

Painstakingly, they picked their way through the ruins set into the hillside. It became clear to Taki that the entire area was no more than a series of unwieldy additions on top of prior additions, no matter how grandiose the builders had wanted their creations to be. In an odd way he found it comforting: the Cloud Temple had been built on the same principle. The air even bore a similar, omnipresent chill, and small veins of ice were frozen between gaps in the cobbles. Periodically, Taki ran into the same sort of rag-wrapped men they'd encountered in the darkness. It was easy to sneak past them, for most of the creatures seemed inattentive or even comatose at their posts.

"I hate to be a bother," Enilna said, "but I really am thirsty. Can we rest for a moment?"

"Aye," Taki said. He licked his chapped, dry lips with an almost equally dry tongue. Enilna's question couldn't have come at a worse time, for now he was reminded of the fact that since entering the tunnels, none of them had eaten or drunk anything. "Let's stop a while in that chapel-looking building there. There might be some basins or chalices there. We can scrape some of the ice up and melt it. No food, I'm afraid. Von Halcon ate it all."

"You really need to watch yourself around her. She'll eat people if she's hungry enough," Enilna said.

Before long, they'd managed to create a small fire kindled with the remains of smashed-up pews. Over the blaze, Taki had set an offering basin on a trivet and filled it with the meager shavings they'd managed to eke from centuries-old ice frozen deep into the stones outside. Despite all the effort it had taken to fill the basin with the delicate fluff, the result was only a few spoonfuls of water.

"Drink up," Taki said. He took the basin off the trivet and offered it to Enilna.

"It's so little." Enilna sniffled. She tipped the basin back and took a swig and then gave it back to Taki.

"You didn't finish," he said.

"Course I didn't. You need this too."

"I'm fine, really."

"Don't give me that machismo crap. I can tell you're thirsting. Listen to your wife or lose your life."

"That's a new one," Taki said, but smiled anyway. He put his lips to the golden vessel and finished off the dregs. Though only a few drops made it down his throat, he felt instantly better.

"I made it up just now," Enilna said. "I'm really good at this."

"You're a true poet."

"You're just making fun of me."

"Maybe."

"Stupid boy," Enilna said with a yawn. She lay on her back with her arms crossed behind her head.

"I'll take first watch," Taki said.

"Mm, feed me people," Enilna murmured, and quickly passed out.

Taki idly tossed a shattered chair leg onto the fire. The only advantage to being in a desiccated place was that everything made of wood was rapturously flammable. He gazed for a while at Enilna's features while the girl slept. *I take it back. She's quite beautiful after all.* Unconsciously, he fiddled with his coin-half. Remembering what had happened with Lotte made bitterness seep into the back of his throat. It was impossible to say if she'd been genuine with her confession. Either way, she was right. Perhaps there was no future between them after all. Perhaps it was time to move on and embrace what lay before him.

He stretched out to give his aching back some respite. The chapel's ceiling bore the flaking remains of murals whose details had long degraded to incomprehensible swirls. Perhaps when new, they might have been beautiful, but like the rest of the faded world, they were only ghostly reminders of an increasingly implausible past. *A ring surrounding the world. A spire to heaven. Maybe it's all bunk in the end,* Taki mused. Despite the fact that he was stretched out on a freezing stone floor in the middle of a ruined settlement deep behind enemy lines, he was overtaken with a powerful urge to sleep. He rubbed at his eyes and rolled over on his side. *I shouldn't wake her yet. She needs rest,* Taki thought as he gazed at Enilna. Strangely, he couldn't hear the crackling of the fire anymore but instead heard a pleasant, lulling drone.

A sliver of something shiny and translucent, as if silk had turned to liquid, seemed to stretch from the ceiling to the floor. Taki raised an eyebrow but couldn't find the strength or will to react otherwise. Several more strands of the same substance slid down from above, swaying gently in a new breeze that doused the flames of the little campfire. Someone—womanly in shape but with impossibly long and graceful limbs—descended down the tangle of lovely strands, coiling and uncoiling them round her limbs as she effortlessly slid her way down to the ground. Even when her feet finally touched the ground, she seemed weightless. Taki tried to sit up but found that his limbs no longer obeyed his commands.

The woman glided up to him, knelt, and cradled his head in her lap. Besides a pair of thin, demurely smiling lips and a pert, pointed chin, the rest of her features were obscured by a veiled helm. *But I've seen that face before,* Taki realized with growing but impotent panic. She gently slipped her fingers under Taki's chin and tipped it back. Then, she drew a glinting, bladed hook and set it against his throat. He felt her press; his neck started to burn.

"Get off him, bitch!" Enilna said, and blasted the intruder right in her faceplate. The woman flew across the room and slammed into a row of unbroken pews, reducing them to splinters.

Taki felt energy and will rushing back to his body and leapt to his feet. He held out a palm and opened his gates. "I thought you were asleep."

Enilna flipped her slide release and holstered her now-empty Colt. "I was, but the humming woke me up."

"Humming?"

"Yeah, it's super annoying, like when you're trying to doze off and Elsa keeps clearing her throat every few seconds, Irulan won't stop rolling and thrashing, and Luca's obviously pleasuring herself and doing a shitty job of keeping quiet. There's just no excuse! If I can be *dead silent* when I do it, so can *she.*"

Taki looked over at the pile of broken pews. "I, uh, didn't want to know *any* of that. But you have my thanks. That was an Ursalan princess who nearly offed us just now. I'm going to burn her, just to be safe."

"A princess? I thought they just turned into giant bees with guns where their lady parts should be."

"The one you saw in Astarte, yes. Another tortured me for a while when I was imprisoned in the Teufeslbrucke. She was more like this one. They can do something to your mind. Make you unable to move." He edged forward and started to incant *pyr.*

"Strange. All I felt was pissed off." Enilna made a fist and grinned. "I'm such a badass!"

"Don't get cocky," Taki said, and blasted a fireball off just as the princess shot up from the pile. The splinters exploded into flames, but the princess had already evaded the blast. She ran up a nearby column, pushed off it, and dove at Taki with a set of twin hooks to slash at him.

Enilna grasped the back of Taki's jerkin and wrenched him back just in time to prevent his decapitation. In the same motion, she ripped his

Herstal from his waist and opened fire. The princess wheeled away and started to flit between the columns.

"Why'd you do that? You could've blown your hand off!" Taki flailed and caught his bearings again.

"I had to take a gamble," Enilna snarled. "Now stop bitching and help me fight this thing!"

The princess swooped at Enilna with her twin knives and aimed a savage series of slashes at the girl. Enilna hopped and rolled, parried with her rapier, and jabbed the point into her attacker's thigh. Black blood splattered on the rough cobbles, and the princess pirouetted away with an unearthly screech.

Taki opened more of his gates and sent a blast of fire at the princess when she went in for another attack on Enilna. Part of the gossamer surrounding the creature's body caught aflame. In response, the princess made a flicking motion at him. Taki raised his arms to block and felt something punch into the meat of his forearm and splatter his own blood on his face. He cursed, sucked his teeth, and glanced down at his wound. Impaled in him was a long, hand-length needle the thickness of his small finger. Instinctively, he yanked it away. Not a second later, it burst into fragments that ricocheted off the stones and lodged in the soft parts of his armor.

"Careful!" he yelled in Enilna's direction. "Don't let her needle you!"

Though his left hand felt tingly now, he could still move it well enough. Binding the wound would have to wait. He opened more gates and shot an orb of compressed air at the princess's back, tossing her off balance. Enilna followed up with a riposte and caught the princess right in the chest. Strangely, the blow only seemed to push the princess away instead of penetrate through her.

"Damn," Enilna huffed. "Thing has tough bones for being so thin."

Taki eyed the chapel door. "Then we should run."

As he started for the entrance, a guttural roar assailed his ears. Through the only exit they had charged the misshapen, patchwork creature he'd left hanging of the ledge.

"Wonderful!" Enilna threw up her hands. "Hope you're *real happy*, Taki!"

"I didn't—" Taki clenched his jaw.

To his surprise, the princess ignored the two humans and instead charged directly at the patchwork monster. Her knives were a blur as she opened up innumerable gouges and rents all over its body. The monster, however, seemed unfazed as it grabbed the princess with both its hands, slammed her across its knee three times, and then smashed her on the floor. Taki looked over at Enilna in horror and then looked up at the area behind the chapel's altar.

"Behind us," he shouted in realization. "There's a ladder up! Climb!"

Enilna wheeled and sprinted toward it and was already halfway up by the time Taki started his ascent. The patchwork creature rose from where it crouched over the twisted remains of the princess and made its lumbering, loping advance. Taki clenched his buttocks and climbed with all his strength. Enilna looked at him from atop a small landing and shouted something he couldn't understand.

Something wrapped around his ankle with crushing force and yanked at him. Only sheer force of will kept Taki from letting go of the rungs. He shot a glance down and saw the patchwork creature at the base of the ladder, leering up at him with its red, glowing eyes. Gunfire cracked above him, and he felt bullets zipping by his head. Small, red craters blossomed on the creature's shoulders. The injuries didn't seem to blunt its efforts, though, and Taki's fingers started to slip. He looked up at Enilna, who'd just run out of ammunition and gazed on him in horror and realization. *Oh, fuck it,* he thought.

"I love you!"

The creature's grip suddenly slackened, and Taki was free again. He shot a hurried glance down at the creature, only to see the princess behind it. She'd plunged both her hook knives into the patchwork creature's back and was slowly pulling them apart. Crimson sprayed from the wound and drenched the burnt gossamer and pale skin. Her veiled helm had been knocked away some time ago. Now Taki could see that instead of human eyes, hers were fist-sized, multifaceted orbs that glinted darkly in the meager light. The creature convulsed, groaned, and collapsed on top of the princess. Taki tore his gaze away from the sight and scrambled up.

Enilna pulled him over the edge of the landing, and they both collapsed in a heap. Taki wrapped his arms around her, and they held each other in stunned, fearful silence. After a long time, Enilna spoke.

"So, uh…did you mean it, or did you think you were dead anyway and wanted to sound cool?"

Taki swallowed on a dry throat. "Can it be both?"

Enilna wiped at her eyes. "I guess it can. Those are some lame last words, though."

"What was wrong with them?"

"I'd have said something like 'I just wanted a pony!' or 'Not in the groin!'"

"Those…are really not cool at all."

Enilna laughed. "I'm glad you're alive. Guess I'll take what I can get."

Taki glanced around. The landing they rested on was a narrow space that led to stairs heading up. Though he disliked the prospect of treading such cramped quarters, he was still unwilling to chance going back down the ladder. The patchwork creature had made a comeback twice already, and he was loath to give it a third chance. "Up we go," he said.

Carefully, and without even Taki's light to illuminate their path, the duo felt their way up the stairs until they came to the top of what looked like a gatehouse. *Reminds me of my first battle,* Taki mused. *What I'd give to have everyone here with me…even Hecaton Mezeta.* At the far end of the chamber and just before a large, open viewport was a man-high lever without any ornamentation, set in front of a rusting, hulking gear that emerged partway from a slot in the floor. With sword in hand, Taki strode toward the lever and started to examine it.

"Oh no," Enilna whispered.

Taki raised an eyebrow at her. "What?"

"Look right outside." She pointed. "That's the tower. You know, the one that fries people's brains. And, there's a…a thing in it."

Taki walked up to the window. Sure enough, no more than perhaps a dozen meters away was the massive, red-brick-domed belfry that he'd seen earlier from below. It was easily as wide as twenty men stacked head to toe, and its bell chamber was wide open save for a pentad of arched support columns to bear the weight. Inside, in the center of the chamber, was an otherworldly hunk of flesh. As if a human's body had been ripped inside out and mashed into a ball, the thing was varying shades of pink and crimson and festooned with pulsating arteries and veins that penetrated the surface with their tributaries. At the top of the grotesque mass rested a pair of lidless eyes; slowly, they rotated to face Taki and stare at him.

"Get down!" Enilna shouted. A moment later, the room was bathed in searing golden light.

Taki screamed and raked at his scalp with his nails. His eyes were squeezed shut, but the inside of his head might as well have been a quenching pool for hot irons. In the most distant parts of his perception, he felt his bladder go. Thousands of tiny razors cut away at his skin, intentionally seeking the most sensitive parts to rake over. He thought he heard Enilna shrieking in agony but couldn't care less. Blood sprayed form his nose, and he felt his eyes bulge out of their orbits. Blindly, he flailed around for his sword.

His fingers wrapped around a handle. He'd press his sword against his neck and pull as hard as he could. Release was moments away. He yanked at it with all his might. *Sever the arteries. Bleed out in less than a second...*

The world rumbled. Bells clanged. The end was coming. If it didn't, he'd demand his milligrad back. Sweet, sweet death was his right.

Just as abruptly as it had started, the golden light vanished along with the agony. The chamber fell into darkness, and dust poured in through the viewport to cover Taki with a thick layer of gray. Where his tears had streaked his face were now rigid clay whiskers. He groggily pulled himself to his hands and knees. He would've vomited, save for the fact that his stomach contents were already all over the stones. *This is death*, he thought. *It's gotta be.* He struggled to his feet. *Shit. This must be purgatory. Well, I couldn't expect to go straight to heaven. I'm a tainted Polaris, after all. Still better than hell, at least.*

"Taki..."

He turned to see Enilna flopped on the ground. She beckoned to him, and he shuffled over.

"Taki, there's a problem."

"Enilna, it's fine," he said. "We're finally dead. It's over."

"No, no." She shook her head. "I'm about half sure we're alive. More important, I shat myself, and I don't want you to see it. But I need you to help me up. So, uh, lend me your arm but don't look at me. Actually, don't even look vaguely in my direction."

Taki squatted and stretched out an arm while turning his head. "Okay."

"Thanks." Enilna tugged herself to her knees.

"Are you sure we aren't dead? It's pretty peaceful here."

"I'm sure. See, I'm supposed to get seventy-two hot virgins when I die in battle. There's only one in front of me."

Taki scowled. "You can help *yourself* up."

"But I called you hot!"

Taki tottered over to the viewport and coughed furiously. By now, things were becoming less opaque. He vainly tried to wave the dust away. "Wasn't there a tower right here?"

"Huh? There should've been," Enilna said. She sidled up next to him. "What the hell? It's gone."

Taki craned his neck for a better view. Where the tower and the horror inside it had been, there was now a gaping crater in the earth that billowed dust like the last spurts of a spent geyser. He looked back at the lever he'd been inspecting earlier. It had been pulled back. He thought for a moment, and the realization hit him. "I think we might've destroyed it by accident."

Enilna shook her head. "No, no! We can't afford to pay for that! Look, Natalis, the most important thing now is to keep our story simple and never ever deviate. Repeat after me: the tower was *already gone* when we arrived, and…" She slapped herself. "What am I saying? Taki! Do you know what we've done?"

"Committed a crime and lied to cover it up?"

"Better than crimes!" She took him by the shoulders and shook him wildly. "We've just taken out the last thing that kept us out of Versailles! We're basically heroes! Now they can't flog us for dereliction of duty! I'm gonna take a bath for a week straight! *Then I'm gonna get a pony!*"

6

Chronicler shifted incessantly on the battle throne of the padishah. The terrain was uneven, and one of the support legs sank into the soft loam more than the others, giving him a lopsided appearance. Aslatiel, who stood at attention next to his master, knelt and received an ornate wooden box, which he opened to reveal two thickly proportioned but well-crafted brass medallions depicting the Imperial seal. Aslatiel bowed to Chronicler and then came up to Taki and Enilna, who fidgeted on their knees. Though the sun beat down on everyone and made the humid heat of the swamp unbearable, they were both dressed in full brigandine with tabard and wore ermine-trimmed cloaks.

"For valor and self-sacrifice that are the utmost of Imperial virtues, I, Generalfeldmarschall Aslatiel von Halcon, name Leutnant Taki Natalis and Fahnenjunker Enilna Shpejtspate as Paragons of the Way. They are shining examples of the highest ideals of our people."

He walked forward and hung one of the heavy plates around Taki's neck and then did the same for Enilna.

"There have only been twenty of these ever given in the history of the Osterbrand Imperium. Wear them with pride. *Uukhai!*"

The massed soldiers behind them returned the battle cry, and the hairs on the back of Taki's neck shot up. Chronicler rose from his throne with a grimace. He strode past the two new Paragons, giving them a glancing pat on their shoulders.

"Long have you suffered, my subjects," he said. "And long must you have doubted. But now we are on the verge of securing our people's future forever. You may wonder how it is that we will destroy the Ursalan menace with so many wounded, no siege engines, and few supplies. I will give you my answer now."

Chronicler raised a foot, held it in the air, and then stomped the earth. The air around him seemed to fold and thicken. Simultaneously, a corona of force shot out to bowl over those near to him and sway those farthest from him. The ground rumbled and shook, leading to panicked cries from the assembled.

"I have heard disparaging remarks of late. There are whispers that the Padishah sends men to die for him but will not raise a finger to help in the effort. But I have not been indolent. I have been preparing myself for the most important task entrusted to this vessel during this lifetime. When we take Versailles, fear not and go with glory beating in your hearts. I am joining the fight with my full power. I will take my rightful place at the head of the army. And I will bring us victory."

The cheer that went up, along with the celebratory gunfire from the crowd, made Taki need to cover his ears. Chronicler waved his hand to silence them. "Make yourselves ready for battle, my dear host. We will not delay a second longer. Ursala falls by the morrow."

* * * *

Taki let out a happy shout when he saw Karma saunter up to Tirefire's campsite.

"Hey, Natalis," Karma said with a jaunty grin. "Congratulations on the medal. Is it brass?"

"I think so," Taki said. He took the chain off and passed the medal to Karma. "It's certainly heavy enough to be. I don't think I'll wear it when I do battle."

"Damn," Karma said as he weighed the medal with his palm. "That *is* a lot of weight. This must've taken at least a hundred rounds of Luger casings to make. Maybe more, considering the purity. Probably why they don't give out a lot of 'em." He passed it back to Taki.

"How're your wounds, Gillette?"

"Holding together nicely," Karma said. "Though I didn't expect it. Who'd have thought that needles would do the trick? Medicine's come a long way from what it used to be."

"You mean when the army surgeon knits you together with fresh catgut right after scratching his balls?"

"Don't forget wiping his ass with the same hand, too."

"You sure you'll be okay to fight, though?" Taki said.

Karma made his typical, inscrutable smile. "Don't worry, I'm fine. You, on the other hand, have been through a lot. You should leave more of the heavy lifting to your friends, you know. Two suicide missions in a single month makes you look like a brownnoser."

"Actually, this last thing wasn't really planned." Taki shrugged. "It just kind of happened. With my luck, I'll probably wind up in the Rex's digestive tract or something of the sort."

"The truth is," Hadassah said, "he went out to catch crabs with his lover, fell down a hole like a lazy strumpet, and then blew up a perfectly good castle by accident. He owes *millions* of rounds in damages." She turned to Karma and planted a kiss on his cheek. "Cleaning my guns right now. Find me later."

Karma winked and swatted Hadassah on the rear as she dashed away. "Speaking of which, Natalis, how's your woman?"

Taki reddened. "We're not really lovers or anything. Or at least, we haven't gone that far yet."

"Come on," Karma said.

"I speak true."

"Okay…" Karma rubbed his hands together and scrunched his brow. "I'm sorry I haven't been more observant. The acupuncturist in Morvan is actually a pretty cool guy when he's not trying to stick you or suck away your vital essences. His people have spent *thousands of years* coming up with cures for your condition. A few poultices, some cupping, and you'll be able to perform just like normal. Maybe better than normal! I'll introduce you two. Normally he doesn't offer those services to any old asshole, but we've become good friends."

Taki laughed. "Gillette, I'm not impotent. Actually, I'm a bit insulted you'd conclude that, but it's fine. I've decided not to worry about it anymore. Enilna and I are taking our time and doing what comes naturally. If we don't couple for a while, then we just don't couple for a while."

"Natalis, there's a godrotting *war* on. That means everyone's getting it on with everyone else. Save for you two."

"Not like we haven't tried and been rudely interrupted."

"Mea culpa and touché." Karma bowed with exaggerated flourish. "So I take it you've gotten over your first, fizzled-out love? I mean, our captain?"

Taki glanced over at Lotte, who was in an animated discussion with her subleutnants. "I…yes. I think I'm over her, finally."

"You two almost rutted, but something weird happened."

"How do you—I mean, Christ, Gillette!"

Karma laughed. "I just guessed, but seems like I hit the mark. You haven't lost the coin-half, right?"

Taki glared and shook his head. "Still on me."

"If I were you, I'd have long requested my promotion to general, an immediate discharge with the accompanying pension, and a retirement dacha next to hot springs frequented by maidens."

"I can't do that. There's someone I want to save. And we still need to get Mezeta."

"Ah, I heard about your business with that thrall. The hex tattoo is placed when the Ursalans don't want to completely strip the poor bastard of will or intelligence. The afflicted can do tasks that require a finer hand, such as taking care of animals and the like."

Taki's eyes widened. "Gillette! How the hell do you know this?"

"Don't forget, my mother is the basileus of the Dominion," Karma said. "I learned this stuff when I was a kid."

"Why didn't you say anything?"

"You never asked," Karma said.

Taki angrily gripped him by his collar but quickly relented. "Sorry...I've no right to be angry at you. I assumed you'd be just as clueless as the others, and I was wrong. So is there any way I might find the man who helped me?"

"The mark is actually pretty rare. Usually, the Ursalans will only give such a privilege to those who've been distinguished in battle. Sounds like your hoplite fits the bill. And no, I haven't come across him or his body."

"Gillette," Taki said, "they chose to capture him rather than execute him on the spot. What do they intend to do with him?"

"I can't say exactly." Karma shook his head. "They'll probably let a young princess feed on him, is my guess. The girls gain power faster when drinking from a person with some...uh, spunk."

Taki let out a pained sigh. "I know it's crazy, but that's a relief. Means he hasn't just been killed. I lasted a long time, so perhaps he can, too. We just have to find where the princesses are and kill them all."

"You kind of sound like a psychopath, you know that?"

"Oh, I'm glad things ended up this way." Taki took out his medal and kissed it. "Now I can repay the debt."

Karma smiled and clapped Taki on the shoulder. "So be it. I'll be there fighting alongside you. Besides, I've got to dole out some payback for ol' Draco and drink some more wine for him at the victory feast. First, though, I've got to find the old lady, or I'll be sorry. See you in the abattoir, Natalis."

"Aye," Taki said. "Last one there's a rotten harspud."

An Imperial herald approached and knelt. "Paragon, the feldmarschall requests your presence."

Taki blinked. "Okay."

"Shall I escort you, Paragon?"

"No, that's quite all right. I know the way."

Taki glanced at the sky. There were only a few hours in the day left to begin the march. Why would Aslatiel waste his time? *Not my place to question him, though.*

By now, the camp was abuzz with activity. The impending assault had rekindled spirits, and their numbers had been increased by reinforcements. Both recovered wounded as well as newly arrived veterans from the northern theaters had swelled the ranks, and now the legions were back to a passable two thousand. Still, the army remained a far cry from the massive juggernaut that had forded the Rhone.

The trebizonds bowed deeply to Taki and held open the tent flap for him. A smile crept over his face at the sight—respect and recognition were an intoxicating combination. Aslatiel looked up from his strategy table.

"Paragon, you honor us. Please, come closer."

Chronicler, who stood next to Aslatiel, gave Taki a nod, as did Lucatiel. Surprisingly, her expression wasn't suffused with its usual mix of snark and murderousness. Enilna had shed her ermine-trimmed cloak, and the fancy tabard was nowhere to be seen. She took Taki's arm in hers when he approached.

"What's this about?" Taki said.

Aslatiel motioned to the map. "With *Ba'gshnar* at the front, there is nothing stopping us now. You, Sir Taki, were responsible for getting us through the Aegis and also for toppling the tower. The Imperium owes you an incalculable debt."

"Hey," Enilna said. "I did stuff, too!"

Aslatiel patted her head. "Aye, you have. This is why I called both of you here."

Enilna beamed. "Very good! I always welcome more praise. And you can pat my head too, whenever you want."

"Forgive me, then, because I did not call you for an accolade. Rather, there is one more task I must order you to complete."

"Of course," Taki said. "I—we—will do whatever it takes to defeat our enemy."

"I knew you would," Aslatiel said. "Today, you both will leave the camp and head back to Morvan and then from there to Vistula and Nova Muscova. A hussar company will assure your security during the journey."

"Wait." Taki blinked. "Why the Imperial capital? What does that have to do with our battle here?"

Aslatiel placed a hand on Taki's shoulder. "During this campaign, you've shown valor that even I cannot hope to match. The same goes for Enilna. As Paragon of the Way, you are a shining beacon of hope for the Imperium—an example of patriotism and self-sacrifice that our citizens can actually touch and hear and see. The last Paragon I knew saved my life once. The mere *sight* of him prevented me from deserting and abandoning my duty to the nation. That is the power you two now wield."

"Then why are we being sent away? Why should I not give courage to the troops here? Where it's most needed?"

"Because your luck is going to run out," Aslatiel said with a shake of his head. "We're looking at a bloody battle coming up. All it takes is a stray bullet or random knife in the back, and we've lost a priceless national asset. So instead of needlessly risking your lives, the Imperium demands you serve a greater purpose as a leader of our people."

"How? By...by giving rousing speeches and attending functions and shaking hands?"

Aslatiel nodded. "Exactly that."

Taki rubbed at his cheek. A wave of vertigo assailed him where he stood, but he held his footing, if only barely. "What if I say I can't?"

"I'm afraid you don't have a choice," Aslatiel said. "It's for your own good, and for the good of the Imperium. And you *swore* to serve the Imperium."

"I'm sorry, Sir Aslatiel," Taki said. "But I can't do as you wish. One of the thralls in the Ordo Arslan—a man of the Dominion—aided my escape and even helped me fight my way to the keystone. He was captured, and I think he might be in Versailles. He's probably being tortured, if not prepared for execution. I cannot abandon him to his fate. I must join the assault. After Ursala falls, I'll do whatever you ask me to. I'll put down my blade forever if need be."

"Damn it, Natalis." Aslatiel took Taki firmly by the shoulders. "Think for a moment. I'm giving you security, fame, and riches. Isn't that what you've always wanted? Isn't that why you agreed to stay in the army?"

"Aren't you listening? I need to find my friend!"

"You and I both know he's dead. Even if the Templars didn't just execute him on the spot, there's no way he hasn't been killed by now. There's no happy reunion waiting for you, Sir Taki. I'm sorry. I promise you I'll do everything I can to find his remains and make sure he is honored as a hero and his family provided for."

Taki bared his teeth. "I'm having a hard time believing your promises, Sir Aslatiel. Remember when you swore to find Hecaton Mezeta? And then reneged to our faces? How do I know I can trust you? I can't! And for that reason, I need to make my own way and fulfill my own obligations."

"I don't understand you at all. I give you everything, and you defy me. Why?"

"Don't you remember lecturing me in Kosovo? You're the one who taught me that there are more important things than comfort and safety. That *principle* should guide my actions."

"We have no time for this. You will leave immediately."

Enilna placed a hand on Taki's forearm. "Taki, listen to him. Let's just go now. You can argue with me on the way, if you must…"

Taki wrested his arm away from her. "No. You are free to do what he wishes, but I will not."

Aslatiel's expression darkened. "Don't make me force you, Natalis."

"What're you gonna do?" Taki puffed his chest out. "Shoot me?"

"If I must." Aslatiel drew his pistol and let it hang at his side.

"Please!" Enilna said, and stepped in between the two men. Tears formed at the corners of her eyes. "Please don't do this, Taki. Listen to Aslatiel! He's the feldmarschall, for fuck's sake!" Her voice cracked. "Would you be acting like this if…if Lotte had given the order?"

"Shpejtspate, step away," Aslatiel said. "And Natalis, I've made myself very clear. If you disobey my direct order, I have the right to put you to death. Even Paragons are not above the law, and we now have *more than one*."

Taki glared. "You're not going to change my mind."

Aslatiel drew the hammer back on his pistol and jammed the muzzle between Taki's eyes.

"Brother," Lucatiel said. "Please, stay your hand. You're overheated right now. Let me—"

Aslatiel wheeled around and smacked her face with his palm. "Silence!"

"I'm not above the law, but *this* is," Taki said, and reached under his armor. He brought out the coin-half and thrust it in Chronicler's direction. "Your Majesty, I'm staying and finding that thrall, and then you'll take us to wherever Mezeta is. Now, honor your end of the pact."

Chronicler's face was inscrutable.

Taki's hand started to tremor. It was all he could do to keep his knees from turning to jelly. He wanted to shrink under Chronicler's gaze. *Focus on something else. Focus on the offering.* He stared at the golden coin-half with all his might and blurred the old man's features out.

Chronicler finally let out a belly laugh and pushed Aslatiel's gun hand down. "Keep it, young Natalis. 'Twould be a grave dishonor for me to extract remittance for such an earnest and selfless request. Aslatiel, my boy, who are we to deny a young warrior his desire? He is, after all, a Paragon of our people."

Cold rage washed over Aslatiel's face. A moment later, though, he holstered the gun and bowed deeply to the padishah. "*I obey,* Your Majesty. Sister, escort our Paragons to their companies."

Taki let out a ragged breath as Lucatiel grasped his wrist and yanked him away and out of the tent. When the stinking swamp air hit Taki's nostrils, he felt not nausea but relief. He'd have started chewing on a nail but for Lucatiel's iron grip.

"Enilna, go," Lucatiel said.

"Where?"

"I don't care. Just go!"

"Aye!"

"I should rejoin my unit," Taki volunteered. "The assault's in less than a bell."

"No," Lucatiel said. "Come with me."

Without letting Taki go, Lucatiel pulled Taki away from Aslatiel's tent, past several assembled platoons readying for inspection, and finally into one of the impromptu sparring rings that dotted a dry rise in the land. The rest of the army was embroiled in final preparations for the attack, and thus they were alone.

"You and me are gonna have a little talk," Lucatiel said. "Put up your dukes."

"What?" Taki barely had time to look confused before Lucatiel's fist crashed into his face. Stars exploded in his vision, and he reeled back and only barely managed to avoid falling on his ass. "Shit! What was that for?"

"I *told you* to defend yourself," Lucatiel said. "Anyway, remember when I called you a manlet and said you had noodle arms?"

Taki gingerly probed at his nose. It didn't feel broken. He saw Lucatiel advance. When she took another swing at him, he ducked out of the way and hunched over with his fists in front of his face. "I remember! But why are you punching me?"

"Because I was wrong about you," Lucatiel said. "I disparaged you without truly getting to know you!" Her foot lashed out and caught Taki in the flank.

He collapsed to one knee, overcome by pain and nausea. "Normal people don't apologize like this!"

"I want to make sure you understand me," Lucatiel said, and followed up with a haymaker to Taki's face. "Look, I thought you all were losers and screwballs when we met. Well, except for your captain. But getting to know you all makes me realize that maybe *I'm* the one with issues. Hey, why aren't you punching back?"

Taki rolled over and tried to get to his feet. "You haven't given me a chance!"

Lucatiel offered a hand up, which Taki took. She pointed to her chin. "Fine, fine. I'll give you a free shot."

Taki looked at her incredulously but then drew his arm back and smashed her right where she'd pointed.

Lucatiel reeled back and pressed a hand to her jaw. "Ow! Good…that's more like it."

"This is stupid! I'm leaving."

"You're not allowed! But if you're going to be such a whiner, I guess we can drop this farce. You're not exactly making this fun for anyone."

"Get to the point," Taki said. He rubbed at his tender jaw. "You didn't drag me here just to say sorry for calling me names."

"What do you think of Aslatiel now?"

Taki sighed. "You were right. He's changed. I feel like I don't know him anymore. Or maybe I was under a false impression all along."

"He was wrong to threaten you like that," Lucatiel said. "As his sister, I…I apologize."

Taki spat red-tinged spittle to the ground and looked up at her. Where he'd struck her, there was nary a mark. But Aslatiel's palm had left a reddish welt on her cheek. "That's horseshit! How are you at fault? He treated you *horribly*!"

"He can treat me as unfairly as he wishes. That is my burden and my right. But the same does not apply to you, or Enilna, or any others in the unit or under his command. A general must be firm but also *evenhanded*. That was how Ashoka Atreus was."

"Who's Ashoka Atreus?"

"The Paragon Aslatiel spoke of, the one who saved his life. General Atreus was our first commander, after *Ba'gshnar*. He was a great man, and I thought my brother would take after him. But with Irulan gone, I don't know anymore." Lucatiel squatted and traced in the dirt with a finger. "The real reason I called you here was to beg a favor. And it has to do with Aslatiel."

Taki spat again and snorted. "Attacking me is a hell of a way to beg. So what do you want?"

"You can still compel *Ba'gshnar* to do what you wish. If Aslatiel is about to make another mistake like he did to you, then I want him"—Lucatiel's voice wavered—"stripped of his power and thrown out of the army."

"What? You really want your brother humiliated and disgraced?" Taki shook his head.

Lucatiel stood and wrung her hands. "I promise you won't suffer his wrath. I will take all responsibility. I will make sure Aslatiel knows I am to blame."

"Why? Why would you do this to yourselves?"

"Because my sweet, honorable brother is *losing his soul!* I can't let that happen to him. I love him too much. I'll suffer anything if it means he regains his old self."

Taki stepped back. "We both know he'll never forgive me. And he'll never forgive you."

"We still have to do what's right."

"That's a hell of a request," Taki said. "I don't know if I can promise anything."

Lucatiel wiped at her eyes. "I know, and I'll understand if you wish for something else. I shouldn't rely on you to fix his problems. It should be my responsibility. But please, think on my words should the time come."

"Fine," Taki said, and ran his fingers through his hair. "I'll consider what you said. Can I go now?"

"One more question," Lucatiel said, and stuck her hand out. "Can we be friends?"

Taki looked down at her hand and then up at her face. Then, he reached out and shook. "Sure."

Lucatiel beamed. "Good! That makes five!"

"Beg pardon," Taki said. "Five of what?"

"Oh, people I've made friends with in my life."

"I should get going now." Taki bowed and edged away. "S-see you in battle!"

"Wait! Don't you want to hang out more?" Lucatiel drew one of her pistols. "Shoot at some bricks together?"

"No, I really can't!"

Taki departed at a half jog that turned into a full run when he was sure that Lucatiel was out of earshot or eyesight. By the time he finally returned to the squad's little grotto, he was out of breath.

"Natalis?" Lotte pointed. "What happened to your face?"

"Huh?" Taki put a hand to his cheek, only to find it noticeably swollen. "Nothing. Just had a talk with the Prince of Maladies, is all."

"Do have a care," Lotte said with a roll of her eyes. "We're right about to march! Is our ammunition ready?"

"Aye, I—"

"Prince Luca did that to you?" Hadassah said. "Why? What could you possibly offer her that I can't? I thought I was her bestie!"

"Don't worry, I won't usurp you," Taki said as he brushed by her. He squatted and opened the unit's purser's chest. Inside, gleaming milligrad rested tightly packed in battle-blackened clips. "Everyone load up if you haven't already, and then take another portion in your pockets. This is a fight for our future."

He reached in and took two extra magazines for his Herstal and shoved them into free loops on his belt.

Lotte reached into the box and retrieved some clips for her pistol, which she shoved into her bandolier. "Do you really think you'll find your friend?"

"Aye. I'm damned sure. I've staked everything on it." Taki reached into a wooden, straw-lined crate beside him and pulled out an oil-black, first-class relic rifle that would have made the Temple's archangels envious. He slapped a magazine in, pulled back on the charging knob, and let it rock forward with a loud clack. "Now, let's take down this bullshit nightmare kingdom once and for all."

* * * *

The Liberation Army had now fought for four bells, and the sky was rent with streaks of crimson, encroaching twilight. A storm of brimstone assailed Taki's senses. The hot, swirling tide shot its way up his nostrils, clawed at his eyes, and plugged his ears. At the front of Lotte's phalanx, he fought for his life, shoulder to shoulder with the others.

Blocking the tercio's advance over a stone overpass above the burning streets of Versailles was a seething abomination resembling a mound of corpses drenched with tar. It lashed out with whiplike protrusions at the pikes that held it at bay, snapping some of the shafts but also earning the blobby abomination jagged rents in its oily membranes. Through the widening tears, bloated corpses spilled out and broke apart where they hit the cobblestone plaza. Inured to the sight by adrenaline, the pikemen shuffled ahead and punched steel deeper into the beast. With a final, disgusting shudder, the horror liquefied completely and was no more.

The men had barely let out a collective victory cry when a wave of moaning thralls lurched forth with axes and staves. Sharpened steel points tore through disintegrating chain mail and decayed leather and stopped the assault in its tracks. Taki thrust his kriegsmesser into one of the shambling attackers. It screeched and pushed its way up to the weapon's hilt before falling over and slipping off the bloody blade. Taki glanced at the fallen slave's face. *Not him, thank God.*

They were now a mere few hundred paces from the gates of the royal palace—the fortress-cathedral of the Sanctissimus Rex. Once, the soaring battlements and buttressed spires had been the highest structures in all Ursala, but now they were dwarfed by the spire that rose from inside the impenetrable walls and stretched upward to pierce the blue-black sky. A rumbling in the castle's direction made Taki squint ahead.

"The gates!" Hadassah exclaimed. "They're opening up! What the hell?"

Like the opening of a fanged maw, the bone-white slab that blocked entry at the end of the castle bridge rose amid a maelstrom of dust and smoke. From the blackness within, a thick mass of armored fighters swarmed out to form a column that shambled full tilt toward the tercio. Leading the charge were figures in glittering, bulbous plate, wielding enormous hammers. The fluted look of the armor made Taki think of advancing onions, and were it not for their weapons he'd have thought the sight humorous.

Next to where Taki stood, Lotte hefted the company's battle standard and thrust the flag forward. "Pikes maintain formation and above all, hold your ground! Guns, fire volleys at will!"

Taki barely had time to clap his hands over his ears before the loosely assembled musketeers raised their guns and let off an earsplitting, smoky chorus. The ground in front of the Ursalan column erupted in a shower of stone chips and dust that quickly swept back and left writhing bodies in its wake. This seemed to do little to thin out the enemy ranks, however.

The foremost of the bulbous attackers took a running leap. Ivory-feathered wings shot out from its back and started to flap with inhuman speed. The winged creature rose in an arc, sailed through the air, and then started its descent. Taki glanced at Lotte, whose eyes widened in a look of realization. Her hand shot out and pushed Taki on the shoulder, hard enough to throw him to the ground.

Something crashed to the ground nearby, sending a shock wave that flung Taki farther away. He hurriedly scrambled to his knees and gawked in horror at the sight. The winged knight crouched not a meter away and lifted its hammer off the splattered remains of a pikeman. It was almost immediately assailed by a thicket of spear points, but with a single sweep of its hammer sent broken pikes and men flying.

A blur shot through the phalanx, and Karma burst into the fray with his twin swords sweeping a deadly arc. The winged knight brought its hammer up with surprising speed, however, and Karma's blades bit deeply into the hammer's metal-embossed shaft. The knight punched out with a gauntleted fist to smash Karma's torso and send him crashing into a gaggle of pikemen. Then, it raised its weapon for another swing. Taki raised a palm. *Not enough time for a strong sutra, but if I can just distract it...*

Before Taki could send off a burst, the winged knight abandoned its swing and stepped backward to block a blow. Lotte marched toward it with her greatsword raised and struck out with the gigantic weapon again and again, forcing the knight to take more steps backward. The knight flapped its wings, leapt meters back, and then spun around in an upswing to catch Lotte in the flank while she lunged.

The hammer's shaft caught the edge of her sword, and with a skull-piercing sound, shattered into fragments. Simultaneously, Lotte drove her point toward the winged knight's chest. It slipped into a gap in the armor and punched cleanly out the other side to send gobs of blackened crimson splattering everywhere. She wrenched back on her blade, and the winged knight collapsed onto a pair of stubby knees. Then, she drew her thrusting sword and drove it through the creature's eyeslit before kicking it over. The hushed tercio let out a throaty hurrah.

"Back to your positions!" Lotte roared. "We're about to be overrun!"

Taki turned his attention back to the front. True to Lotte's warning, the front of the swarm was less than a hundred paces away. The pikemen shouted and hastily tried to resume their places in the square. *Shit*, Taki thought. *Won't be enough!*

The wave of shrieking bodies hit the front of the weakened pike phalanx and shattered the line. Taki barely managed to lift his blade to run a thrall through the gut before it bowled him over. The desiccated fighter rasped something unintelligible, drew a short dagger, and punched it into Taki's chest. Taki's eyes widened in panic, but to his surprise he only felt pressure where there should have been burning agony. The pressure eased up quickly, however, when the thrall's grip slackened on the dagger and it ceased to move. Taki blinked, grasped the dagger by its hilt, and pulled. With no small amount of resistance, it broke free and clattered to the ground. He looked at the rent in his surcoat, anticipating blood. Instead, his Paragon medal gleamed back at him.

Taki tore his eyes away from the sight just in time to catch another thrall standing above him, about to bring an axe down on his face. He jerked his head sideways, and the axe fractured the cobblestones. Sharp pain lanced across the side of his head, and he felt warm wetness trickle down his scalp. The thrall raised its axe again, only to have the end of a bayonet erupt from its mouth.

Against expectations, the thrall lurched forward and spun around to face its new attacker. With one fluid motion, Hadassah shifted her hold on her rifle and smashed its buttstock into the thrall's head.

Taki shrugged the body off, scrambled to his feet, and wiped rotten-smelling brain matter from his face. "Thanks," he said, and reclaimed his sword.

"Piss on everything," Hadassah snarled. "Where's our backup? Where's the old man? He's supposed to be at the front! Instead he just disappears once the fighting gets tough!"

"I'm sure—" Taki looked around, bile rising in his throat. "I don't know! What's important is that we hold the line!"

"Against that?" Hadassah pointed. The bridge was now packed so densely with Ursalan fighters that not a bare patch of ground could be seen. "Face it, dude. Aslatiel left us to die! I love his sister, but *fuck that guy!*"

Taki clenched his jaw and scanned his surroundings. The phalanx was wavering fast. Two other winged knights had forced Lotte to her knees with a barrage of hammer blows. *We should retreat. This is unwinnable...*

A throbbing, basso drone above caught his attention. Taki looked up and gasped. Bearing down on him was a massive ovoid shape shrouded in smoke. Slowly, he recognized the contours of an Imperial zeppelin. *The Lyudmila,* he realized. The airship tipped its nose up just as Taki feared it would crash into the phalanx, and from its gondola fell a shower of smoking cylinders that Taki realized were bombs.

"Dassa! Get down!"

He leapt and bowled her over. Orbs of white flame erupted and grew across the entire length of the bridge like blossoming peonies in procession, and all was drenched in white light and overbearing pressure.

When Taki finally opened his eyes again, he found himself nearly unable to, for his lids felt swollen. His mouth felt stuffed with cotton. The world spun crazily on its axis. He felt like vomiting but swallowed the bile back, somehow. He felt blindly around for a handhold and settled on something surprisingly soft.

"Shit, Natalis!" Hadassah said. "You mind letting go of my tit? Or must I seek damages?"

Taki wrenched his hand back. Hadassah was beside and partially under him. Her face was covered in dust and soot and dried blood, but her eyes bore a clear, accusatory look.

"Sorry," he said, and rolled away to ease the pressure off her. "I didn't mean to."

"Yeah, I've heard that excuse before." Hadassah pulled herself to her hands and knees. "'I was just trying to save you from that explosion!' and 'This happens all the time in those drawings of people with the big eyes!'"

"But there *was* an explosion!" Taki objected. "Look at the bridge! They're…they're all dead! Ha!"

He pointed. Where there had been a swarming mass of rabid enemies, there were now piles of shattered bodies and parts strewn about in shallow craters. Whatever forces had survived wheeled around drunkenly, hemorrhaging all the while. Overhead, the *Lyudmila* circled the spire.

Taki brought up a fist to rejoice, but another thought overtook him. "Captain!"

He spun around, trying to locate her. His eyes focused on two twisted but still bulbous forms lying nearby. Then, he saw a glint of silvery armor. He bounded clumsily over to it and found a gauntlet sticking out from under a pile of thrall bodies. With fear nibbling at his heart, he pulled.

"Damn you, Natalis, lemme help too," Hadassah said.

"And me three," Karma said, joining in.

Taki pulled again, redoubling his efforts. Slowly, the pile shifted, and Lotte slid out from under it. Her armor was rent with gouges and dents, and she was missing her helm. She coughed, rolled on her side, and vomited. Taki crouched near her and tried to hold her hair back, but she swatted him away.

"I'm not a godrotting maiden," she huffed, and wiped at her mouth. "And neither are you, so stop trying to help me while I puke!"

"Sorry, Captain," Taki said. "You okay?"

"No," she said, and got to her feet. "The formation's gone to hell. We can't fight like this."

Taki nodded, though reluctantly. Of the two hundred they'd commanded, only a dozen or so were still in fighting shape. Some had died, and most were too wounded to press on.

A horn sounded behind him. The remains of Tirefire the Lesser turned their heads to see another column approach. This time, the arrivals were Imperials. At the head of the troop, Chronicler and Aslatiel rode in on tired-looking chargers. Lucatiel, Elsa, and Enilna walked behind, along with a handful of niqab-veiled attendants of the Imperial Cult. Everyone was streaked with soot and grime, and most of the foot soldiers looked ragged and bloody. Aslatiel rode up to where Taki stood and dismounted.

"Where were you?" Lotte demanded.

"Stopping you from getting flanked," Aslatiel said. "You didn't know it, but there was a horde of creatures trying to ascend the piles. We destroyed them, though with much effort and many lives lost."

"Then I owe you thanks. But my company's destroyed all the same. I can't make my survivors go any further."

"Indeed," Chronicler said. "They served valorously. We, however, will push forth and claim the Rex's head. And, when the opportunity presents, ascend the spire. Will you join us?"

Lotte shook her head. "I have already ordered my men withdraw to camp."

"Do what you will," Chronicler said. "Aslatiel, have the airship descend and take the wounded back to camp. Use your starspeaker."

A cross between a roar and a wail lanced right through Taki's skull and forced his eyes wide open. From somewhere above the gates shot a beam of pure white light that streaked over the bridge and pierced the *Lyudmila* from fore to stern. Flames belched out from the nose cone, only to be sucked back in and spewed out as a fiery lance from the rudder. A moment later, the massive, canvas-wrapped envelope imploded on itself and lit the darkening sky orange. Like a moth with wings aflame, it drifted slowly down and crashed amid the pilings. Hellfire and smoke rose from below and lapped at the edges of the bridge.

Aslatiel's face contorted in rage, and he held his sword in the air. "Storm the castle and kill everything inside!"

"Stop!" Chronicler grabbed Aslatiel's sword by the blade and wrested it from his protégé's hand. "Look at the palace! *Look!*"

Right over the opened gates, something loomed. It was a massive creature, probably thirty meters from end to end, and roughly human-shaped save for its lanky, spindly limbs and massive, oblong head. Its skin was a mess of disorganized scales and nappy tendrils of fur, and its hands and feet were more like a monkey's than any man's, or would have been if monkeys had possessed hooked claws. Those same claws anchored it to the palace walls by punching deeply into the stone façade. It twisted the oversized head around, as if to scan the surroundings. Set deep within a mass of pulsating sulci and gyri was a large, rheumy eye.

"Gillette," Taki whispered, "you're familiar with chimerae. What the hell is that?"

Karma squinted. "Not certain, since they're supposed to be extinct. But I think it's a *Caenorhabditis*. Big, ugly, and can shred you like a sodden cabbage. Also, it shoots godrotting spears of lightning out of its eye."

Taki looked back at the massive chimera, and a wave of nausea passed over him as he realized that the creature's gaze was firmly fixed on the company. The creature arched its back, and white arcs of current leapt from the ground and into its malformed face. Then, it fired again.

I'm going to die, flashed through Taki's mind. The white light barreled toward him as he instinctively thrust an arm up to cover his face. He resolved, however, not to turn away. He'd face his death like a soldier. Being obliterated by a ray of pure energy wouldn't be so bad: simply a moment of heat and then an eternity among the faithful in the kingdom of heaven.

Yet ascension never came. Taki slowly lowered his arm. In front of the company, Chronicler stood solidly, shrouded by thick smoke and with his outer layers burnt off and his hair singed. He shot a wink back at Taki. "Young Natalis, be not so quick to embrace death. I'd be insulted to have you snub my gift!"

Before Taki could reply, Chronicler pushed off the stones into a leap, leaving a crater where he'd once stood. The old man's form rocketed toward the chimera, which tried to swipe at the incoming enemy with a clawed hand. The creature missed, and Chronicler barreled into its bulbous head fist first before they both pitched off the side of the bridge and into the flames below.

"*Ba'gshnar!*" Lucatiel screamed. She started to run toward the edge, only for Aslatiel to restrain her.

"Stop, dear sister. *Ba'gshnar* will triumph, or he will die honorably. We have no right to interfere with his destiny. We must press on."

"But I can help him! The drop is only a hundred meters!"

"No. We press on to the palace. Don't let his sacrifice be in vain. Now follow your godrotting orders!"

Lucatiel turned on him with tears in her eyes. "We swore to serve him!"

Aslatiel drew his hand back to slap her.

Taki's feet moved, and before he could comprehend the gravity of his own actions, he was already at Aslatiel's flank, with the feldmarschall's wrist firmly restrained.

"Stay your hand, Sir Aslatiel! It does not become a general to strike a subordinate!" Taki gritted his teeth and tried to root himself to the ground. Touching a superior officer in anger had meant death in the Dominion Army. The Imperial Army was no different, save for possibly the sort of torture that might be inflicted on the offender first.

"Natalis," Aslatiel said softly, "this is the second time you've been insubordinate. If you value your life, make sure there is not a third." He wrenched his hand away from Taki and strode away to address the company. "His Majesty has cleared the way! Advance!"

Taki glanced at Lucatiel. "Are you okay?"

She glared back at him. "Don't expect my thanks. You took a stupid risk opposing my brother without *Ba'gshnar* around." The corners of her mouth relaxed. "Be careful in there. I don't want to lose a friend."

"Aye, I will be," Taki said. "And more than ever, I will consider what you asked me for earlier."

Lucatiel dashed off to mount her horse without acknowledging him.

"This will end badly, especially if the old man's gone," Lotte said, as she checked the fittings on her armor. "Attacking the royal household with less than two hundred tired and wounded men will lead to disaster."

"Should we fuck off, then?" Hadassah asked quietly. "Aslatiel can't fuck us if he can't see us."

Lotte glanced at Taki. "Natalis, what say you?"

"I..." Taki bit his tongue. On one hand, his exhaustion made a compelling argument for withdrawal, but on the other hand, the groom was still nowhere to be found. The palace was the last place he could look. "I made a promise to find someone. If it pleases you, Captain, I wish to fight on."

"It does not please me, but I will allow you," Lotte said. "And...I will join you."

Hadassah let out a groan. "Nata, you idiot. You're forcing my hand here."

"And I promised Draco I'd loot the treasury for both of us," Karma said with a wink. "I've got my honor to maintain."

Taki beamed at his companions. "Thank you. Thank you all."

Lotte cleared her throat. "This might be our last battle. We should pray. We haven't done so in God knows how long."

"Now that you mention it, wasn't Draco our chaplain?" Karma asked.

"Aye."

"So who among us should do the benediction?"

"I guess I will," Hadassah said. "All you potato-brains kneel."

She closed her eyes and pressed her palms together. "Almighty Yahweh or Tengri or Mohammed or whatever, we unworthy who've been bequeathed your holy boomsticks humbly beg your blessing while we blast away the plague of brutals. Please don't let us get killed in a really embarrassing way, especially not like how His Majesty Niketas was done in by Taki on the shitter. The gun is good. *Yaupdedeodid* and amen."

Taki resisted the urge to correct the butchered invocation. Instead, he clapped his palms together and grinned. "Amen."

7

Taki unsheathed his kriegsmesser and gritted his teeth as he sprinted with the column. He thrust a palm forward and concentrated his power. A blast of freezing air would deflect arrows and bolts, though there was no stopping milligrad. Next to him, Lotte bared the flat of her greatsword to shield herself. They crossed the threshold. *Here it comes!*

"Hold!" Lucatiel shouted. "There are no soldiers here."

Taki lowered his palm. He stood in a grand antechamber with a sweeping staircase that led to an ornate door of what looked like solid gold. He'd expected barricades, gunfire, or a shield wall, but instead all he saw were thralls on their knees. Instead of swords or spears in their hands, they carried rags. Strangely, they seemed to pay the invading troops no mind but rather scrubbed the filthy tiled floor with single-minded intensity.

"What is this?" Taki muttered.

"Bind them," Lucatiel ordered the soldiers. "And watch your flanks!"

"More slaves," Lotte said. She stepped up to one of the thralls, who wore the tattered remains of a servant's frock, and hoisted her—for the features were preserved enough to show that she had once been a woman—by the scruff. "Look at the forehead. Isn't that the tattoo you wanted to find?"

Taki gasped. Emblazoned on the woman's forehead was a red hexagon. "'Tis."

"The man who helped you could be here. You should inspect them before they're carted away."

"Aye, Captain. Thank you," Taki said, and made his way to where the tied-up thralls were being pushed into a huddle. They offered no resistance, merely staring at their own feet where they stood. Most of them looked nothing like the groom had, being too tall, too short, or the wrong build. Taki inspected a few of the men's faces, but none of them matched. *Damn it. Gillette was right—he's probably being fed to some princess right now, but I have no idea where the creatures are.*

Aslatiel clapped a hand on Taki's shoulder. "Do you see him? The groom who aided you?"

Taki shook his head.

"Unfortunate," Aslatiel said. "But if it is meant to be, you two will reunite. We must press on, in the meantime."

"Aye, Feldmarschall." Taki tried not to meet Aslatiel's gaze.

"Sir Taki, I know this is not the right time, but I...apologize for my behavior earlier. It was uncouth, and you were right to chastise me. I still have much to learn about my position, it seems."

"Sir Aslatiel, if you wish to apologize to anyone, say sorry to your sister. I didn't think you were the type to strike your own family."

Aslatiel looked defeated for a moment. "I wasn't. Not until Irulan...I've let my emotions betray my honor. But once this battle is over, and once we rule Ursala under the Way, I'll be a general worthy of your respect."

Taki gave a half smile. "I hope so. I'll be pleased to serve you when that happens."

"Then let's move on," Aslatiel said, and extended his hand. "We have a king to dethrone."

"Aye, let's go," Taki said.

At the top of the stair, a gang of soldiers set on the golden doors with an improvised ram fashioned from a broken column. With every thunderous crash against the unyielding metal, the column cracked a little bit more, until it finally broke to pieces. One of the soldiers teetered backward and nearly fell before Lucatiel caught him by the jerkin and righted him. She patted him on the shoulder in reply to his breathless thanks and gestured to make room. Lucatiel inhaled, closed her eyes, and drew back an arm. Then, she stamped her foot and drove her fist against the metal.

With a gut-churning crunch, the stone framing the golden doors buckled and shattered, throwing off a downpour of dust. The entire assembly swayed to and fro and then finally fell away from Lucatiel to let out a titanic clang when it hit the ground. She turned to Aslatiel and gave him a jaunty wave while the rest of the soldiers cheered.

With Taki in tow, Aslatiel marched up the dusty path, where he clapped Lucatiel on her shoulders. "Sister, how many times have I told you to mind your energy? You'll be snoozing any moment now."

"I want this battle to end, brother," Lucatiel said. "The sooner it does, the sooner we can look for *Ba'gshnar*. Together."

"Aye, Luca, we will. But no more spectacle, for now."

Lucatiel nodded. "Brother, what of the thralls?"

Aslatiel turned to the men and made a chopping motion with his hand. "Kill them."

Taki's jaw dropped in disbelief as he heard the sounds of metal cleaving flesh below. He twisted his head around a moment later, only to see Aslatiel's company slash, stab, and crush the dozens of bound slaves who'd been herded into a corner.

"Sir Aslatiel, what's the meaning of this?" he hissed. "They were unarmed! This is against the Way!"

Aslatiel shot him a cold-eyed glare. "The Way applies to *humans*."

"Damn it, they *are* humans! The tattoo on their foreheads means they're still able to think!"

"Enough nonsense. They're just withered husks, and liable to stab my men in the back."

"These ones are different."

"I don't have the time or patience to argue with you," Aslatiel said, and brushed Taki aside.

Taki stumbled but regained his footing. *You really have changed. Didn't you chide me once for blindly following an unjust path?*

Lotte grasped Taki by the arm and whispered in his ear, "Natalis, whatever you're going to say, keep it to yourself. We have a bigger problem now. Look!"

Past where Lucatiel had breached the doors was a columned rotunda with a domed ceiling so high as to be entirely shrouded in darkness. Flickering torches set into each column provided meager and shifty light. The dust from earlier had settled in the meantime and now revealed a figure resting in the center on bent knee. At first glance, it appeared to be an armored Templar, but as it stood, Taki realized that it was in fact much taller than any Templar he'd seen, at least three times the size of Siridar Cassius. Its armor, brass-colored and tarnished, gave off the impression of a spiny carapace, and the helm was topped with two thin, swooping horns akin to antennae. In its hands was a massive pole hammer whose head shimmered with malign energy.

"Holy shit, is that the Rex?" Hadassah said.

"Nay," Lotte said. "That's Crown Princess Phillippa. We have to get through her first."

"No one stands in our way," Aslatiel said. "Alfa Gruppe, Tirefire the Lesser, I command you to kill that thing. The Rex waits beyond."

Taki tore his attention away from the killings he'd just witnessed. Once again, he'd been party to something heinous. Too slow on the uptake to realize what would happen, and too powerless to prevent it. Bitterness rose in his throat and choked him. *Taki, you godrotting fool. You thought the Imperium was some sort of mythical land of justice and virtue, when it's really just another king expanding his lands and crushing everyone in the way. You thought Sir Aslatiel was a hero who could do no wrong. You thought he listened to you, valued your counsel, considered you a…a friend. But you're just a feeble pawn to him and his country in the end. The Imperium's not your home. You're just an exile and a regicide and a fuckup.*

Slowly, he advanced with his kriegsmesser out and one hand ready to channel. The combined squads had spread out in a semicircle around Crown Princess Phillippa, who remained silent but warily shifted her footing as those surrounding her made probing steps back and forth. Behind Phillippa was an archway, through which Taki could barely make out the shape of a large throne set on a high dais. Someone—or something—sat in it, but he was unable to determine more than that. When Phillippa drew closer to the arch, however, she suddenly turned and swung her pole hammer.

Taki flinched but quickly realized that her swing hadn't been intended for him—or for any of her enemies, for that matter. Instead, the weighted end of the pole hammer crashed into a large, lion-head boss set into the wall near the archway. From the top of the archway, a solid portcullis started to descend.

"She means to cut us off!" Aslatiel shouted. "Get through that door before it closes!"

Before Taki could calculate his chances of making it to the door, Phillippa charged him. Faster than he'd thought possible in her massive carapace, she pirouetted, sending the pole hammer into a deadly sweep. *Don't block! Don't run! Roll!*

Prana surged through him, and he leapt toward the oncoming blow. The shaft of the pole hammer passed a mere hand's breadth under him and barely clipped the toes of his boots as he tucked his knees under his chest. He hit the floor, bounded to his feet, and bolted blindly in whatever direction he thought would get him away from the armored horror. Something ahead of him was closing, so he threw himself into a slide and passed under the obstacle right before it would have crushed him to paste.

Just as quickly as it had begun, the adrenaline haze subsided. Taki's breathing slowed; his vision became clearer. He blinked, amazed at the fact that he was still alive. *How the hell did I survive that?*

Enilna's face popped into his field of vision from above. "Taki! Are you okay? I think we're the only ones who got through."

Taki sat upright and jerked his head around in a panic while he tried to scrabble to his feet. "Where are the others?"

"They didn't make it here," Enilna said and pointed to a now-blocked-off archway. "Probably still fighting that armored thing." She rapped the hilt of her rapier against the portcullis. "This gate is *solid*. Can't hear anything from the other side. God, I hope no one's...squished under that."

"Christ," Taki said. "I need to get back to the captain."

"Nice to see you, too," Enilna said, and crossed her arms. "Geez, Taki. Aren't you at least happy to see me again?"

"I am, but..." Taki cleared his throat. "It's just that a lot of things are happening right now. I've nearly died more times than I can count. And Sir Aslatiel is..."

"I heard you arguing. Why *are* you so upset over some thralls? None of them were the one who helped you, and they'll betray you at the first opportunity."

"The ones with hexes can *think*. They're prisoners—your and my people! They're not mindless. And he killed them, just like that."

"Aslatiel did what he thought best for all of us," Enilna said. She exhaled slowly. "Have you ever thought you're the one being unreasonable?"

"I speak the truth."

"Even if you're correct, that doesn't mean you're right."

"That's a load of bullpocky."

"Damn you, Taki. Why do you have to be so stubborn? Aren't you and Aslatiel friends?"

Taki frowned. "I thought so, once. But now I'm not so sure. We started out enemies, and perhaps that is how we shall end."

"You wouldn't betray him, would you? You wouldn't turn traitor..."

"I'm a godrotting kingslayer. I'm already a traitor."

Enilna cupped his face in her hands and fixed an intense gaze on him. "Just so we're clear on this, *I love you*, Taki Natalis. I want to be your first. Marry you. Have your children. But I also owe Aslatiel my life, and for that he will always be my commander. So if I ever have to choose between you and him, I will choose him. Please consider that if the time ever comes."

"I think I love you, too," Taki said. "But my mind is already made up."

He stepped away to break off the embrace. Enilna's hands fell to her sides, and she stood dejectedly for a few beats. Then, she forced a smile.

"So, now that we're through the gate, what the hell are we supposed to do here?"

"I think that has something to do with it," Taki said, and pointed at the shadowed throne.

"Oh God! Is that…"

"Probably. I just wonder why it is that we've not been attacked yet."

Enilna rubbed her chin. "Strange. He's not talking or doing anything. You'd expect a king to like, throw a temper tantrum because we haven't prostrated ourselves to his divine grace or some shit."

"We need to investigate," Taki said, and readied his blade at a low guard. "Watch our backs, will you?"

"Aye."

Together, they tentatively advanced up the carpeted steps toward the throne. The chamber was a surprisingly narrow space—almost claustrophobic compared to what Taki had imagined the inner recesses of Ursalan power to look like. Unlike in Phillippa's arena, however, there were no torches to be found. Instead, all illumination came from what seemed to be dimly glowing red orbs, strung high above like luminescent beads. The other noticeable difference between the rest of Ursala and the throne room was that it was extremely, uncomfortably warm. Taki set foot on the dais and inched closer to the throne.

As if a chunk of malachite had been partially melted and then reformed in the rough approximation of an oversized chair, the seat of Ursalan royalty was almost haphazard in its appearance, unlike the sleek brass throne of the Argead Basileioi. Alien-looking protrusions warped its contours, and it seemed as if it would get up by itself at any moment and slime away. Leaning against one of the armrests was an enormous greatsword of onyx. But it was the man slouched on the throne itself who made Taki's eyes widen. The man was still clad in thrall's rags, but his face, along with the hexagon tattoo, was unmistakable. The only difference from earlier was that now he wore a golden circlet on his head.

"You!" Taki lowered his sword. "Do you remember me? You helped me escape the Ordo Arslan! I've been looking for you all this time! I thought they'd torture you and…what the hell are you doing sitting on…" His hands shook.

"Taki, isn't it obvious?" Enilna asked, shaking her head. "This is the Sanctissimus Rex of Ursala." She leveled her rapier at the groom. "Aren't you?"

The groom—the Sanctissimus Rex—cracked a smile. "Yes, I am indeed. And yes, I remember you, young Taki Natalis. I don't forget easily."

Taki fell to his knees. *This can't be real. This is a joke or an illusion. Why would the enemy king ever help me? For what purpose?* His blade hit the floor and sent up sparks. He looked back up at the Rex. "How can you speak? I thought your tongue had been cut out. I saw the stump."

The Rex laughed. "Do you think I'm so feeble that I can't simply make one anew if it pleases me? I am the holy emperor of all Ursala. I created the first Templars from *corpses*. I control life itself."

"Hold on," Enilna said. "If you're so powerful that you can just grow body parts at will, why do you look like a scrubby wastrel? Shouldn't you look more buff? Handsomer?"

"Girl, I have lived for a very long time. I have gone far beyond the need for things that only appeal to silly women. Flowing locks. Quivering pectorals. A girthy penis. Bah, it's all high-maintenance tripe. I prefer my original form, with all of its imperfections."

"Why the farce?" Taki growled. "If you're the lord of all Ursala, why did you help me? You must've known who I was and what I wanted. Why did you help me destroy your own wall?"

"Young man, the simple answer is that I was using you. The Ordo grandmasters would never have assented to any plan that involved compromising the integrity of the Aegis, so I had to rely on an outsider to carry out my task. You happened to be there, and when I realized you had the key-sword, I acted to help us both."

"That doesn't answer his question," Enilna said. "Why'd you poke a hole in your own wall? That's like stabbing yourself in the back, don't you think?"

"Without that breach, I'd never have been able to entice my brother so far into my domain. You see, I've wanted to sort some things out with him for a very, very long time. Once I crush him for good, then there truly will be peace and harmony in this world."

"So you're willing to let us trash your kingdom and kill all your friends in the process?" Enilna rolled her eyes. "That's *retarded!* Taki, this guy's an idiot. No wonder he's sitting here all shriveled up on his lumpy throne in the dark. Doesn't even have a queen, because no woman would tolerate this kind of bullshit. Let's just capture him and get the door open so we can help our friends."

"Wait, Enilna." Taki held a hand up. "Who's this brother of yours, Your Majesty?"

"Ah, forgive me for being unclear. My brother is the one you know as your padishah."

Enilna started. *"Ba'gshnar?* The hell? I didn't know he had any family."

The Rex waved a hand. "That man from the Blue Sky Land is not who I mean when I talk about my brother. The one called Chronicler is merely a vessel that my brother has co-opted for the ability to wage war on the front lines. I actually feel a bit sorry for Chronicler. I doubt he knew what he was getting into."

Taki felt a head rush and fell to one knee. "I don't understand. What do you mean 'vessel'? Who the hell is your brother, if not Chronicler? And who—no, *what*—the hell are you?"

The Rex shifted in his throne. "That story will take some time to tell, but if you wish, I will give you the entire truth."

"Give me the truth," Taki said.

"Taki, we shouldn't delay," Enilna said, glancing anxiously toward the door.

"I trust my companions to take care of themselves," Taki said. "And I'm tired of being used yet again. I want to hear what the Rex has to say. It's the least he can do in recompense."

"Very well. Young Natalis, I will start with a question. Are you a student of history?"

"I've read books, yes."

"Tell me, then," the Rex said, "how many great empires like mine or my brother's have started with noble intentions only to fall into corruption and savagery?"

Taki ground his teeth. "Many. But that's what happens to every endeavor of man."

"Correct. So how have Ursala and Osterbrand lasted for so long, while every other power has failed? Give a competent man absolute power and his kingdom will prosper, but eventually he will die. His heirs will always fight over the land and drive it into ruin. The same goes for their children and their children's children. This is why the concept of absolute empire is completely unsustainable. Except for mine. And my brother's. So how do you think we both overcame this little problem?"

It sounds ridiculous, but...compared to the things I've seen so far... Taki shifted his grasp on his blade. "Neither of you died in the first place."

The Rex clapped his hands. "Perfect marks for young Natalis! I didn't think you'd come to the conclusion so quickly. And to think stupid Cassius wanted to chop you into spare Templar parts. No, you're far better than that."

"Taki," Enilna said, "you don't really think this asshole's lived for centuries, do you? Are you sure you weren't hit on the head by that crown princess?"

"Oh, but I have, girl. My brother and I have lived for nearly a millennium. We've seen the fall of mankind; in fact, we're two of the people who caused it in the first place. Your ilk are all our descendants, though pathetic shadows in comparison."

"Demons caused the Fall," Taki muttered. "That means you're…"

The Rex flashed a rictus tinged with malice. "Do you get it now? I'm a demon. And so is your beloved Padishah."

"Ridiculous," Enilna growled. "*Ba'gshnar* is not a demon!"

"Silly girl, are you deaf? My brother has merely taken hold of Chronicler, as he has taken hold of every vessel he's used over the past nine hundred years. I envy him, you know. While I am confined to one body, my brother can switch them as he pleases. All he has to do is get some poor sap to kill the previous vessel."

The Rex pushed himself off his throne and stood in front of it. "I dare say, when Chronicler outlives his usefulness, my brother might very well desire you to be his next host, Taki Natalis. But not to worry. It will all be moot soon enough. I will take care of the problem that is my brother, and then you and all your companions will serve me."

"What makes you think *any* of us will serve you?" Taki asked.

"I will need able servants to replace those whom you've culled. I will make you grandmaster of the Ordo Arslan if you enjoy killing. Or primate of Astarte if you desire carnal pleasure. Or basileus of the Dominion if you feel any attachment to your old nation. You will be able to crush anyone who's wronged you. All I ask is that you swear allegiance to me. You're already on bent knee. The rest will follow."

"Just, *no*," Enilna said incredulously. "I've had enough. Taki, I'm going to tie him up right now. And gag him. Don't squirm, old man. It'll just hurt more."

She brought out a length of rope and tromped up to the Rex, but as she reached for one of his arms, she froze midmotion.

"How annoying," the Rex said. "If you wish, I'll make her more docile. It's a simple process. A few bits of tissue excised from her frontal lobes, and she'll meekly assent to whatever you want to do with her. Now, Taki Natalis, I want your answer."

Taki bowed his head and fought off another wave of nausea. Enilna was fully at the Rex's mercy, but if the old man was truly a demon of the old world, then there was nothing Taki could do to force her free. And something told him that the old man would easily sniff out a lie. He got to his feet and leveled his sword. "I cannot swear loyalty to you, Your Majesty. My trust and my faith have been abused by far worthier men than you, and to tell you the truth, I'm sick of it all. Why should I exchange one duplicitous master for another? No sum of grad, no title, is worth the loss of my dignity. Now release my companion and defend yourself if you see fit. I intend to capture or kill you before I leave this place."

The Rex looked crestfallen for a moment but then shrugged and picked up the onyx greatsword leaning against the throne. "What a waste. You risked so much, only to lose your head. But I suppose that is the way of things. At least you might die with some sense of fulfillment." He pointed a palm at Taki with his free hand.

Taki prepared to dodge a sutra but instead felt his limbs go numb. His sword clattered to the marble flooring, and he sank to his knees. Only force of will prevented him from slumping over and crashing face first to the stone. He screamed at his arms to move again, but they remained dead at his sides. His prana was locked in place, unable to go where he needed it. *I've been used by assholes all my life, and it's finally caught up to me. I don't deserve better.*

"I told you," the Rex said. He lined his greatsword's edge up against Taki's neck and then drew it back for a decapitating strike. "I can control life itself. Take this lesson to the underworld. Great men don't play fair."

"No," someone said from behind the Rex. "They don't."

The Rex's chest exploded in crimson as a fist crashed through it from the back and exited out the front. Inside the clenched fist, a sclerotic, beating heart squeezed jets of blood from torn arteries to splash all over Taki's face. Fingers closed around the disembodied organ, and then the fist wrenched back. The Rex wheeled on his attacker.

"Hello, brother," Chronicler said. "It is good to see you again after so long a time."

The Rex tried to speak but only managed a rasping gurgle. He collapsed to his knees and then slumped to his side and did not move again.

Almost instantly, Taki felt his strength return in time to prevent himself from falling completely to his face. He vomited clear bile and groaned as he tried to push himself to his feet.

"Natalis," Chronicler said.

Taki looked up and saw Chronicler standing over him with a hand extended. He'd obviously been in a fight, as his leggings were mostly in tatters and his bare torso boasted a large, diagonal gash running from shoulder to navel. His gray, bedraggled hair was damp with blood and sweat, and he smelled of burnt powder. Taki hesitated but then took Chronicler's hand and stood. Nearby, Enilna lay on her side, unconscious but breathing.

"Is he dead?" Taki stared at the Rex's body.

"Aye. He's dead. I had to wait until just the right moment to remove his heart with one strike. Had I been unsuccessful, or had he shifted its location within his body, we would not be speaking right now. But yes, he's finally joined the rest of his brethren." Chronicler wiped at Taki's face with a pair of fingers. "Perchance, did you ingest any of his heart blood?"

Taki sought out the characteristic taste of iron in his mouth, but it was so dry as to make tasting anything impossible. "I can't tell. What if I have?"

"I don't know, myself," Chronicler said. "You may very well die in agony in a few days. But…now is not the time for gloom. I have defeated the Sanctissimus Rex. It took nine hundred years to position myself for the perfect strike, but I finally did it!"

"So what he said was true," Taki murmured.

"I heard your exchange. He spoke without deceit."

"So…what happened to the original Chronicler? The one who I faced at the Hot Gates?"

"Still here, young basang." Chronicler laughed. "Think of this latest venture as a rare joint partnership. I enjoy the Padishah's knowledge of all secrets of this world, and I also enjoy the power of the greatest warrior to ever walk the earth. We will have full need of both our assets when it comes time to invade my homeland. The people of the islands closest to hell will put up a resistance that makes all Ursala seem pliant in comparison."

"Then what now? My friends and I have fought all this way and gotten you the victory you wished for. How will we reach Hecaton Mezeta? How do we ascend to this Ring of yours that supposedly circles our world and yet we've never seen in the heavens? Don't tell me it was another lie."

Chronicler opened the fingers of a blood-encrusted fist. Sitting in the palm was the Rex's heart. It was about the size of a fully mature walnut and emanated a subtle, shimmering glow from small rents on its exterior and from the torn ends where the great vessels had once attached. To Taki's horror, it still beat a regular rhythm.

"To activate the spire takes a great deal of energy," Chronicler said as he walked toward the throne. "Normally, to even turn on the lights would require the sacrifice of a hundred thousand human lives, but a demon's essence gives a far better return on investment. My brother sought to lure me here so he could kill me and power his contraption. Now, I will use him."

He held the heart out before the throne and then squeezed his fingers to crush it. Light spilled out and filled the room before a loosely coalescent orb of shimmering energy rose quickly from Chronicler's open hand and floated upward. As it raced upward, the softly glowing red beacons from earlier flashed brilliant white to illuminate the inside of a cylindrical shaft that stretched upward, seemingly to infinity. The shaft hummed with a force that Taki felt from his scalp to his toes.

"Is this…" Taki craned his neck in a vain attempt to determine if there was a ceiling at the end of the shaft. "Is this the inside of the spire? Is this real?"

"It is indeed," Chronicler said. "And now that we've turned it on, we should open that gate and welcome your friends in."

As soon as Chronicler spoke, the solid portcullis blocking the archway rose. Taki rushed down the stairs and out the archway. The rotunda's interior was in shambles. Its columns were broken, and the immaculate tile floor was a moonscape of gouges and craters. In the center, Crown Princess Phillippa lay prone amid the twisted remains of her armor. Flames licked the corpse and sent up thick, acrid-smelling smoke that formed a menacing black cloud overhead.

"Natalis, report!" Lotte and Aslatiel shouted at the same time.

Taki saluted reflexively. "The Sanctissimus Rex is dead! The Padishah lives!"

"*Ba'gshnar!*" Lucatiel gasped. "You're alive! Thank…everything!"

Chronicler emerged into the rotunda, carrying Enilna slung across his arms. "Indeed I am, Lucatiel. And we are victorious. We may now take the fight to the Blue Sky Land."

"It is good to see you alive, Your Majesty," Aslatiel said, and knelt. "I knew you'd prevail."

"You need never doubt me," Chronicler said. "Now, we must make preparations for the Ursalan occupation."

Aslatiel bowed. "I have already dispatched envoys to the peerage of Anglia and Iberia. With the Rex perished, they will either surrender to us in exchange for keeping their titles or keep resisting as isolated enclaves. I will need the veteran reserves from Silesia to keep the pressure up, though. Anglia will be a thorny patch for us."

Taki marched up to Lotte. "I saw it, Captain. The spire is real. It lit up when the padishah crushed the rex's heart. We can get to Hecaton Mezeta now!"

"Natalis, you're not making a lot of sense. Are you wounded?"

"No, thank God. How about you?"

"Only a few scratches," Lotte said. "Unlike these two, who stayed a fair distance away and didn't break a sweat."

"Hey," Hadassah griped. "I did my part. I got Her Majesty right in the eye!"

"And I set her on fire," Karma said.

"After she was already dead!"

Taki glanced around and did a tally in his head. "Where's Rana?"

"The Crown Princess got in a lucky blow," Karma said. "Elsa took it in the knee. It was a bad wound. Bone sticking out. Even if she doesn't lose the leg, she'll never fight again."

"Shit." Taki ran a hand through his hair. "There's always a price, isn't there?"

Lotte clapped a hand on Taki's shoulder. "Always."

"Where is she now?"

"The men are taking her back to camp. I doubt…I doubt we'll see her again for a long while."

Nearby, a pair of Imperial Cult attendants speedily wrapped Chronicler's wounds in liniment-soaked bandages and replaced his tatters with a padded caftan, over which they fastened a jerkin and leggings of lamellar steel. Over his shoulders went a cloak of ermine as befit the Padishah; atop his head, a peaked flap hat of fox fur. On his belt, a large, gold-engraved scimitar crusted with jewels.

Like a steppe warlord, Taki thought, as Chronicler waved off the attendants and then clapped his hands for attention.

"It is time for the ascension. I intend to take the Blue Sky Land for the Imperium and will be in the vanguard yet again. I leave the newly conquered lands of Ursala in the hands of my subordinates and the feldmarschall. May Tengri watch over us all." He turned to walk through the archway.

"Your Majesty!" Taki said. "What of your promise? To take *us* with you to find Hecaton Mezeta?"

"Hold your tongue in His Majesty's presence," Aslatiel snapped.

Chronicler shook his head. "Of course, I would never purposefully renege on a promise. But I warn you that your group will find nothing but death where I am headed. The horrors you've faced here are nothing compared to the power and wrath of my people. Your ilk are little more than bugs to them. For your sake, Natalis, and the sake of your friends, I would leave here now and enjoy long and happy lives as heroes of the Imperium."

"And do not forget that you swore to me to serve as Paragon after this battle," Aslatiel said. "Now fulfill your obligation."

"And what if that's not what he wants?" Lotte said. "What of *your* promises to us, Sir Aslatiel? We have not fought all this way for the sake of your glory. We have our own honor to uphold!"

Aslatiel drew his sword. "Captain Satou, I have endured your insubordination willingly up to this point, but not anymore. Under my authority as feldmarschall, I place you all under arrest. Those who serve the padishah, place Tirefire the Lesser in irons and escort them to the brig. We will discuss your punishment later."

Hadassah drew her pistol and aimed it at Aslatiel. "Dude, what the fuck? We win your war, and you send us to jail?"

Karma followed her in quick succession, while Lucatiel whipped her pistols out of their holsters and leveled them at the squad. Lotte tightened her grip on her greatsword and held it at the ready.

Holy Christ, why does it always come to this? Taki thought, but nevertheless pulled out his Herstal and leveled it at Lucatiel.

"Your Majesty, I apologize for this," Aslatiel said through clenched teeth. "I should have never trusted their ilk back in the Dominion. Do not worry, though. They will die here."

Chronicler shook his head. "You all make and break your promises too easily. Resolve your differences expeditiously, or I will take matters into my own hands."

Taki glanced over at Lucatiel, who met his gaze. Though her expression was tense, her lips moved. He recognized what she was saying. *I guess I might as well use it before the old man kills us all.* He slowly reached below the collar of his jerkin and pulled out the golden coin-half. "Your Majesty, I request a boon."

"Well, Natalis?" Chronicler's expression was immutable. "What do you ask of me? I will fulfill it without hesitation."

"Sir Aslatiel is no longer fit to serve you as feldmarschall. The honorable man I once admired more than anyone else in the world died during the attack on Chalon-sur-Saone, along with his love, the Lady Irulan." Taki rubbed at his eyes with a sleeve and continued. "There is a man in front of me who only sees through a mask of vengeance, commands through fear and violence, and values not the lives of his loyal followers. For the good of the Imperium, I ask you to strip him of his command!"

Aslatiel went pale for a second but then hardened his expression. "*Ba'gshnar* will never do such a thing."

Chronicler sighed. "A promise is a promise, my boy." He gestured to a trio of halberdiers nearby. "Strip Aslatiel von Halcon's mark of office and detain him. A civilian should not be present in this place."

"*Ba'gshnar!* You can't be serious!" Aslatiel tried to storm up to Chronicler, only to have a halberdier step in front of him and push him back. The second halberdiers wrenched one of Aslatiel's arms back while another stepped on the back of his knee and forced him to kneel. "Let me pass, you bastards! What the fuck are you doing? Do *not* touch my chain!" He reached for his blade, and the air around him distorted with the telltale signs of gathering prana.

"Brother, stop. This is for your own good," Lucatiel said, and pistol-whipped him across the scalp.

Aslatiel groaned in pain and his prana dissipated. He fixed an accusatory grimace at her. "It was you, wasn't it? You made Natalis do this. Why? How have I wronged you? I am your honored brother, for fuck's sake!"

A tear slid down Lucatiel's face. "Remove him," she ordered the halberdiers.

Aslatiel let out an anguished roar as the halberdiers dragged him by his arms, across the ruined floor and out of the rotunda.

"Your wish has been granted, Natalis," Chronicler said, and took the coin-half from Taki.

Taki all but ignored him and went over to Lucatiel, whose knees wobbled as she tried to stand at attention. "I—"

"Thank you, Taki," Lucatiel whispered. "I'll make sure he doesn't try revenge on you or your companions. I'm sorry. I need to go now." She squeezed him awkwardly on the arm, turned, and shuffled away.

"Taki," Hadassah said. "That was actually pretty manly of you. I'm impressed."

Lotte wiped the sweat away from her brow. "So, Padishah, will you also honor our request? Or must we see more anguish today?"

Chronicler nodded. "The spire may accept two people. Obviously, I will be one of them. Decide among yourself who else will go."

"Can I go?" Hadassah asked brightly. "I want to try moon cheese!"

Chronicler extended a finger and started to tap her on the forehead. Hadassah's brows furrowed in confusion, but after a few taps from Chronicler's fingertip, she blinked.

"Old man, what the hell are you doing? Stop it!"

"For your own good, you should not go," Chronicler said.

"And why the hell not?"

Chronicler stopped tapping her, and she stopped blinking. "Because…you are an idiot."

Hadassah rubbed her forehead; she parted her lips for a response, only to have Karma clap a hand over her mouth.

"Dassa, he's right and you know it. Besides, I have no intention of getting my balls torn off by space bees or whatever the hell kind of eldritch horrors live up there, because there's no way that shit was ever intended to be witnessed by man!"

"I wish to go," Taki said. "I need to see this through to the end. I need to find my own way."

"Natalis, are you sure?" Lotte said. "You have…you have a place in the Imperium, unlike us. And frankly, I don't trust the padishah to watch your back. I should be the one to go. I have the most history with Mezeta. I should be the one to deliver her justice."

"Nay, Captain. 'Tis something I want, even with all the danger. I want a chance to forge my own destiny rather than be directed by others. Besides, I doubt Sir Aslatiel will ever forgive me for what I've done. I don't fancy spending the rest of my life looking over my shoulder."

Lotte clenched her jaw. "I should order you to stand down."

Taki stroked the side of her face with his fingertips. "But you won't. Because if I stay here with you, I'll never find my truth. I'll miss you, Captain, but I promise you I'll return."

"Then that'll be my order," Lotte said. "Return to me alive, or I'll kill you."

"Aye," Taki said, and kissed her.

"And now I see how it is," Enilna said.

Taki broke off the kiss and whipped his head over to where he'd heard her. Enilna stood, supported by the two cult attendants. On her face were tears and fury.

"I heard everything. You betrayed Aslatiel. You betrayed me."

"Enilna, I—" Taki started to say.

"Don't. This is what you decided. You broke my damned heart, Taki Natalis. Get out of my sight before I do something I'll regret."

Taki looked down at his feet. "I'm sorry." Then, he walked over to the archway where Chronicler waited. He brushed by the old man and walked up the stairs, determined not to look back.

8

Taki's eyelids fluttered, irritated by the warmth of a ray of sunlight that pierced through a ruined roof above him. A breeze close to the earth swept ash and grit through his hair and into his ears and nostrils, and he was taken with the urge to sneeze. The release never came, and instead the burning in his sinuses made his eyes water. Irritated, he lifted his head and took in his surroundings.

He was on his back, buried up to his chest in a shallow pit filled with sand, broken pottery, and long-spent embers. Sheltering him were the remnants of a stone cottage of amateurish construction that barely supported a scorched, still-smoking thatched roof. Slowly, and with his whole body aching, Taki pushed himself up and out of the pit and stumbled outside.

Around him was a grassy plain that might have once been pasture or fields left fallow but now was charred to barren ground. Whatever fires had caused such a catastrophe had long been extinguished, but not before wreaking damage as far as he could see. Taki looked back at the hovel he'd emerged from and flinched as it finally buckled and collapsed.

It came to him slowly that he should check his own supplies and armaments. He looked down at his waist and patted at his pouches. The kriegsmesser and Herstal were still sheathed at his hip, along with a spare magazine for his pistol. His armor still reeked of sulfur from the fight on the royal bridge, but it was intact. Most importantly, he didn't feel as if he'd been wounded. However, Taki was still totally alone. *Chronicler...*

He squatted and surveyed the expanse. The old man was nowhere to be seen and hadn't left any tracks leading from the cottage. That is, if he'd even been there in the first place. Taki scraped between his gums and cheeks with a finger and spat in a vain attempt to expel the accumulated grit. *Did it even work? Where the hell am I? Where's everyone else?*

The last thing he remembered was walking up to the throne of the Sanctissimus Rex alongside Chronicler. The old man had sat on the throne, and the entire dais had started to rise up the shaft. At first, the movement had been slow, but it had quickly picked up speed until everything had become an incomprehensible blur. Unbearable pressure had assaulted him from all sides, and then nothingness.

"Think I've been had yet again, you old bastard," Taki muttered, and rose to his feet. Far away from where he was, to the east—or at least what he thought was east based on the sun—was what looked like a mountain range. Where there were mountains, there were usually rivers, and where there were rivers, there would be people.

The thought made him again check his arms. If he were still in Ursala, he'd have to be careful. Word of the Rex's death wouldn't have even left the confines of the Aegis, let alone be accepted by the populace at this rate. And given how rabidly the Ursalan peasantry had defended their regime, he could expect a knife in the gut as surely as the rising of the sun. His fingers strayed to the griffin emblazoned on a patch sewn to his gambeson. *Better not to.* Usually, it was a bad idea to remove one's heraldry, even behind enemy lines. An unbound warrior wandering the countryside was at best a highwayman and at worst a spy to be hideously and painfully executed. If it came down to defending himself, he'd just have to run.

First, however, Taki needed to eat. Since the attack on Versailles, he hadn't even taken a sip from his waterskin, let alone filled his belly. And now that the excitement of the last few hours was past him, he was feeling hollow and ravenous. Another look around him confirmed that there was nothing to provide sustenance where he stood and no means to prepare anything should he manage to down passing game. He needed to move, and quickly. For now, water would have to do.

"Shit!"

The skin was empty. Incredulous, Taki turned it over in his hands and saw the hole. Probably an errant spear thrust had done it, and he hadn't noticed a thing. With a growl, Taki hurled the useless vessel in the air and then squatted with his face buried in his hands. He'd risked it all to come out with nothing—actually, less than nothing. The groom had turned out to be an enemy, Aslatiel would certainly seek vengeance, and Enilna's affection had been replaced by hatred—and they'd never even tumbled together, either. And for all that, neither Taki nor his friends were any closer to finding Hecaton Mezeta. Once again he was a patsy, and once again he'd been deceived, thrown in the midden, and left to rot. Taki was so useless that Chronicler hadn't even bothered to kill him. He let out a long, despairing scream, and his body heaved while he let out tearless sobs.

Perhaps it was better to just die here after all, in this blasted wasteland in the middle of nowhere. Taki reached to his side and unholstered his gun. He pressed the muzzle against the side of his head and rested his finger on the trigger. If the stories were true, perhaps he'd at least get to hang in the afterlife with Draco. He closed his eyes.

Shit, Lotte. He'd made a promise to her to come back alive. He eased his finger off the trigger. Of all the people left out there, she'd be the only one glad to see him alive again. *How godrotting inconvenient,* he thought to himself, and spat more grit to the dirt.

He resentfully plodded over to where the waterskin had landed and picked it up. He'd be able to repair it once he got his hands on waxed thread and an awl. He looked blearily over at the mountain range and started to walk.

* * * *

When the sun touched the horizon, Taki finally set foot on a road. He'd made his way out of the charred lands and for the last bell or two had stumbled through what seemed to be pasture. Still, he had not come across any other living things, save for some strangely proportioned birds that flew overhead. Now, he was running out of time. The pain in his midsection was unbearable, and his head pounded from thirst. More than a few times he'd considered shedding some armor or a weapon to lighten his load. At this point, even a pack of roving bandits would have been a welcome sight.

In the distance, something moved skyward; Taki squinted at it. *Smoke,* he realized. And smoke meant people. Even if those people were Ursalan soldiers ready to execute him, he'd be able to at least ask them for a sip of water beforehand. With every muscle in his body burning in protest, he trudged down the road in the direction of the smoke column.

When he crested a rise in the road, he finally saw it: a large, circular tent like the one Chronicler had once used as his quarters back in Morvan. Thick smoke rose from a vent hole on its highest peak, and around it was a mob of tethered horses, goats, and what Taki recognized as yaks. But most importantly, there was a strong smell of roasting meat. With his heart pounding in anticipation, Taki shuffled his way toward the yurt and found its entrance.

The inside was as smoky and dimly lit as Chronicler's had been, and seemingly just as cavernous. Over a large central fire pit roasted slabs of meat resting on an iron grating, along with bubbling cauldrons whose contents Taki could only guess at. Melting fat dripped from the hunks of meat and provoked gouts of flame from the coals underneath. A squat, leathery-faced couple with muscular arms tended to the cookery and turned the slabs with their bare hands.

Around the cookfire were low-set tables, all occupied by men and women wrapped in hides and wearing the same style of Cossack hat that Chronicler had sported. Dozens of simultaneous conversations created a nearly deafening hum shot through with boisterous shouts and what Taki could only guess were some sort of expletive. As far as he could tell, everyone was also armed with knives at their waists and large sabers slung across their backs.

Strange. Don't sound like Ursalans, or Imperials, or Argeads, Taki thought. Rather, the snatches and dipthongs he heard reminded him more of his foray into Xizhang than anywhere else. *Did I end up in the eastern reaches?* Stabbing pain assailed his stomach again, however, and he dropped further inquiry.

"I need a drink," Taki said breathlessly to the couple tending the fire. "I don't care what it is. And food, like that meat over there."

The man looked up at Taki with a quizzical glare.

"Dahin helj ugnuu uu?"

"Water! Food!"

"Ta haanaa irsan be."

Taki clenched his jaw. This was getting him nowhere. In desperation, he started to mime the motions for eating and drinking.

The man shrugged and muttered something to the woman. She shushed him, picked up a cleaver, and deftly sliced a few rounds of sizzling meat from a nearby haunch into a wooden trencher. Next, she lifted a clay bowl off a stack and ladled out a murky substance from a nearby trough. She passed these to Taki and waved him off.

Near delirious with relief, Taki hustled over to the closest empty table he could find and set his prizes down. He looked at the bowl, and his eyes widened in recognition at the smell. *Pocha! I hate pocha,* he thought before setting the bowl to his lips and draining its contents in one gulp. Then, he set on the meat. Fresh off the grill, it was hot enough to burn his palate, but he cared not and devoured it quickly, and then meticulously sucked all of the grease off his fingers. Finally, he took his trencher and licked it entirely clean.

Once he felt whole again, it was time for exhaustion to attack. He set the trencher down, folded his arms on the table, and set his forehead down. He'd have to think of what to do next, but for now, sleep beckoned.

Someone nudged his shoulder, and Taki stirred a bit and mumbled incomprehensibly. The nudging stopped, and he started to drift back to sleep. A second later, he sat bolt upright after receiving a sharp cuff on the back of the head. He rubbed his aching scalp and twisted his head with an indignant glare, only to find the woman of the cooking pair looming over him with her arms crossed and a cleaver hanging ready at her side.

"Oh," Taki said. "Right, sorry." In his haste to eat and drink and sleep, he hadn't paid anyone for his meal. He smiled contritely and reached into one of the pouches at his waist to retrieve a round of Luger milligrad. Even the most ambrosial tavern fare wasn't worth an entire round of Luger, but it was better to receive change than offer too little. The cook let out an exasperated sigh and reached for the cartridge.

"It's on me," a man said, and dropped a tarnished-looking coin into the cook's hand. She snorted in approval and then walked away.

Taki blinked in surprise and stared at his benefactor as the man took a seat at the table. Though dressed like the other patrons, the man boasted a different set of features than everyone else. His hair was dirty-blond in an undercut, and his eyes were gray.

"Grad isn't worth as much here as it is back home," the man said. "You weren't going to get any change for it, anyway."

"I thank you," Taki said. Much as he wished to embrace the new arrival for speaking a tongue he could understand, rashness of that sort would only lead to folly. "May I know your name, good sir? So I can give you recompense later?"

"Ringo Trevelyan, formerly of Astarte. And you?"

Astarte...an Ursalan. Shit. Taki maintained his smile. "Giles of Rouen."

Ringo's eyes narrowed. "Master Giles, worry not about the coin but repay me with your time. Tell me—how goes the war? Have the Imperial dogs breached Sanct Gotthard, or have we held them off?"

Taki swallowed. "It goes badly, Master Ringo. The Osterbrands took the Teufelsbrucke. Last I heard, they've set sights on crossing the Rhone."

"God help us," Ringo said. "Are the Templars too busy buggering each other?"

"'Tis distressing, indeed," Taki said, fidgeting on his cushion. *I'd better not tell him the whole thing. Might just upset him more. And I still need to figure out where the hell I am.*

"The primate of Astarte," Ringo said. "By chance, does he…still live?"

"Aye."

Raw, almost feral joy crossed Ringo's face for a moment. "Master Giles, you know not how much this pleases me." He waved over to the cooks. "This demands a celebration. My treat! *Arkhi,* on the double!"

The cleaver woman brought over a small wooden tray with two drinking bowls and a clay carafe filled with pungent-smelling clear liquor. Ringo poured two bowls and set one down in front of Taki.

"To what shall we drink?" Taki asked, as he lifted the bowl.

"To His Holiness the Rex, of course."

Taki placed the bowl against his lips and suppressed the urge to shudder, both from the taste of the liquor and from Ringo's mention of the Rex. "Aye, to His Holiness."

"And," Ringo said with a toothy smile, "to the end of Hecaton Kheiris Mezeta."

Taki spewed a fine mist of *arkhi* all over Ringo's face. A moment later, he flushed hard with embarrassment, and his heart raced in panic. *"I beg your pardon, sir!"* He clumsily tried to daub at Ringo's face with a sleeve.

Ringo glared. "I've never been toasted like that, Master Giles. At least not by any man who wished to live."

"I humbly apologize," Taki said. "I was just taken aback by the mention you made."

"What do you know of Hecaton Mezeta?" Ringo's eyes narrowed. "Do you seek her too?"

Taki nodded.

"Who hired you to kill her? Was it the primate? The Dominion?"

"No," Taki said. "I've not been hired by anyone. I might not even need to kill her. But she owes me and my fellows a great debt and must be compelled to pay."

"Mezeta owes a lot of debts. But I didn't think anyone else was mad enough to journey all the way here to collect. Where are your fellows? How did you come here?"

Taki slowly lowered his free hand to rest near his pistol. He'd have to tread carefully. "We're here and there. Problem is that we're not familiar with this demesne and lost our maps and sextants in a mishap. How far are we from Versailles, Master Ringo?"

Ringo raised an eyebrow. "Versailles? Did you crack your skull open, man? Versailles is on the other side of the godrotting world. This is the Blue Sky Land, in the Islands Closest to Hell…"

The Blue Sky Land! Taki nearly leapt to his feet. If Ringo could be trusted, it meant Chronicler hadn't reneged on the promise after all. And if Ringo was hot in pursuit of Hecaton Mezeta, it meant that Taki's search was nearing its end. His scalp tingled, and his lips drew back in an involuntary smile.

"Say," Ringo began. He tipped his bowl back and drained it. "Where'd you make landfall? At Galden Tsereng?"

"Yes, it was a terrible journey," Taki said.

Ringo's blade was out and pressed against Taki's throat in the blink of an eye. "Enough with the farce. Who the hell are you, *really?*"

Taki clenched his jaw and slowly closed his fingers around the Herstal's grip. "I told you, Master Ringo, I'm just Giles—"

"Put your godrotting hands on the table."

Taki ground his teeth and reluctantly complied. *I need to distract him, somehow.*

As if he'd read Taki's mind, Ringo leaned in closer and grabbed Taki by the collar. "Why do you wear the Griffin of Sevastopol? And don't give me any shite about taking it off a dead Imperial."

Should've taken the fucking patch off. Taki's heart pounded in this throat.

"Fine, I'll come clean. Just be easy, man. My name's not Giles. I'm not from Rouen."

"I figured that," Ringo snarled. "Spit the truth out."

"I'm Taki Natalis, of the Argead Dominion. I was once a Polaris."

"And now you're spetsnaz."

"Yes. I am." Taki swallowed. "So what're you going to do? Kill me?"

"I should. I've lost many brothers to your ilk."

"Then why haven't you done it already?"

Ringo let go of Taki's collar. "Because we both want to get Mezeta. And you and I also know that we're not going to succeed alone. So I want you to meet someone. Try to screw me, and I'll nail your guts to a tree."

Taki let out a quavering breath. "So where do we go from here?"

"Come with me," Ringo said, and tossed another coin on the liquor tray. "We'll have to share my horse."

* * * *

141

The moon shone full overhead and cast a pale glow over the land. Ringo's chestnut mare cantered slowly over the rutted road. Taki shifted for the umpteenth time on the rug that had been laid over the mare's back. His rear end ached from the lack of a saddle, and also from the muzzle of the pistol jammed against the small of his back.

"We're coming up to a fork," Taki said.

"Right," Ringo said.

"You want me to go right?"

"No, left!"

"Then why'd you say right?"

Ringo sighed. "I was acknowledging you, damn it. I was being *polite*. Go left."

"You've been holding a gun to me for two bells. How's that polite?"

"Decorum runs in every Ursalan's blood. That is a quality you Imperials lack."

"I told you, Sir Ringo, I served the Dominion once. I know about chivalry."

"Not like *I* do."

Taki frowned. "What ordo did you serve?"

"I squired under the Ordo Anglia for Grandmaster Siddhartha *himself*. Princess Valeria dubbed me at sixteen. I swore on her garter that I would bring her twenty Imperial heads."

"So do you serve the Ordo Anglia, still?"

"My heart shall always belong to Anglia and Her Majesty."

"So is that a yes or a no?"

Ringo was silent.

Taki's lips thinned to a smirk. "You're a knight-errant, aren't you?"

"I…I'm no less honorable for it. Many knights take leave of their ordo in search of enlightenment. The ordos guard the keeps and collect the tolls, but 'tis we, the knights-errant, who truly defend our people."

"Really," Taki said. "When you say 'defend,' do you really mean 'wander around in packs and commit theft and murder' on whatever peasants you happen to come across?"

"You've got a lot of gall for someone with steel to his back," Ringo said. "How dare you insult the honor of mine brethren?"

"I've traveled Ursala before," Taki said. "I came across a group of rogue chevaliers from Rouen. They imposed on a defenseless homestead and brutalized its people."

"And what were *you* doing at that homestead?"

"I was there to steal provisions. But I wasn't there to set on the women and abuse the men."

"So you skulked around while this supposedly happened."

"No." Taki spat off the side. "I killed the bastards."

Ringo cursed. "If what you say is true, then they got what they deserved for straying from the virtues."

"Weren't they your brethren?"

"Do you think we knights turn a blind eye to each other's misdeeds? Nay, Master Taki, we hold each other to a higher standard than any others. Even a grandmaster must face the judgment of his brothers from time to time."

"So what have you been doing with your time, Sir Ringo? Saving damsels and fighting chimera?"

"You could say that."

"How much will you earn for killing Mezeta?"

Ringo chuckled. "A lot, though the exact amount I'd rather not say."

"Ah," Taki said. "So the truth is that you're a bounty hunter."

"No worse than you, Imperial debt collector."

Taki tugged at the reins. "Where are we going, anyway?"

"Tsam."

"What kind of place is Tsam?"

Ringo rolled his eyes. "You know absolutely *nothing* about these lands, do you?"

"I don't."

"How the bloody hell did you even get here? Did you fall out of the godrotting sky?"

Taki laughed. "You're going to hate me for this, but I think I might have."

"You bastard. Is everything handed to you on a silver platter by angels?" Ringo shook hard enough for Taki to feel. "I spent *six months* at sea to get here. Six months losing my guts all over my boots with every step. Six months crammed in a relic without sails, beaten by storms every night. Six months eating nothing but slimy, disgusting *fish*. And when we finally made landfall, what did I find? A land of hide-wrapped savages babbling a blasphemous, incomprehensible tongue. They drink rotten milk and call it nectar. Their idea of faith is some pagan idolatry that communes with demons from hell. My grad is worth so little that I can't even afford a damned saddle. But did I give up? Nay. I learned their sinful tongue and their sinful customs. I saved up enough to get myself a horse and even willed myself to like the godrotting pocha. I suffered to get here, Master Taki, while you just waltzed in on a lark. So yes, I hate you for that. Just like I hate this place. God, I can't wait to have some samosas when I get back to Anglia. Then, I'll make sure these islands burn."

A relic without sails? Taki's ears burned at the mention. He turned his head.

"You mentioned a vessel, Sir Ringo. I've been told that no ship can survive the storms east of Imperial Goryeo. So how did you come here?"

Ringo chuckled with a hint of malice. "No ship could've survived that, but I didn't come in on one. I rode aboard the Dominion *Ooss*."

Taki started and tried to pivot, only for Ringo to poke him harder with the muzzle.

"I told you, no sudden movements," Ringo said. "Next time, I pull the trigger."

"Sir Ringo, did you say the *Ooss*? Surely you jest!"

"Are you mad?" Ringo purred. "Are you furious that *I,* Sir Ringo Trevelyan, defiled your holiest temple and slaughtered your priests to get it?"

Taki blinked. "No, I don't really care about that, but—"

"What?" Ringo sounded confused. "What do you mean, you don't care?"

"I said I don't care about the *Ooss*. It has very little to do with me—"

Ringo grimaced. "How can you just let such blasphemy go?"

"Will you stop interrupting me already? If you sailed aboard the *Ooss*, then you've also sailed with Hecaton Mezeta! Don't deny it!" Taki's voice nearly cracked from excitement. "Tell me where she is, Sir Ringo! I beg you *tell me now!*"

"Y-you heathen," Ringo spat. "Is nothing sacred to your kind? What's your problem?"

"The problem is that you keep answering my questions with questions! Now tell me where Mezeta is!"

"I don't know!"

Taki's face fell. "Then what're we doing?"

Ringo rubbed at his temples with his free hand. "We're…we're meeting up with my partner in Tsam. She's got information on Mezeta's last known whereabouts."

"Why didn't you just stay near her when you got off the *Ooss*?"

"I came with three others. One, we'll meet soon. I quarreled with the remaining two, who convinced Mezeta that I was plotting to get rid of her. So Mezeta expelled me from her party. My partner left of her own accord to join me."

Taki scratched his chin. "To be fair, your former companions weren't lying. Who were these others?"

"Chevaliers, like me. Knights-errant. And believe you me, they also plotted against her as well. We all received the same offer."

"And let me guess," Taki said. "The prize increases the fewer men there are to claim it."

"Aye. Which is why I must strike at her before they can hatch whatever cockamamie scheme they've devised."

"How about your partner? Won't she be entitled to a share of the prize? Do you plan to eliminate her, too?"

Ringo was silent for a moment. "Perhaps. It's complicated. And stop interrogating me, damn you. It's supposed to be the other way around!"

"Sorry," Taki said with an involuntary snicker. For all of the chevalier's bluster, it was apparent that he was also starved for conversation. *Something I might be able to exploit.* "One more question. Where's the God Hand?"

"I said stop it!" Ringo was silent for a few beats but then relented. "Mezeta has it."

"Now that," Taki said, "is a real disaster."

Sensing that Ringo would be unwilling to divulge more for the time being, Taki pressed the man no further for the rest of their ride. With the passing of another bell, the indigo night gave way to seedlings of pink that peeked their way up from the black horizon and then blossomed orange that spilled over the land. Shortly after, Taki caught sight of a massive stone curtain wall as the horse crested a ridge.

"The fortress of Tsam," Ringo said. "Just a little bit longer, and we'll be inside. You can trade in some of your grad for Birchen coin. You'll get a far better rate than if you just bartered with peasants. I'll...I'll help you with the process."

"Thank you," Taki said.

"Don't forget, Master Taki. I'm a knight. 'Tis my duty to provide succor, even to mine own prisoners."

The dirt road gradually widened and flattened as they approached the gates, and they shared space with an increasing number of travelers. Most appeared to be merchants on carts pulled by donkeys or yaks, but more than a few riders thundered by, dressed in what Taki recognized unequivocally as military armor. Their standards were nothing that he recognized from the continental forces, further confirming that he was indeed in an entirely foreign land. The realization tempered his ire at Chronicler, but only a small amount.

In front of a pair of massive wooden gates, Taki's heart sped up as a pair of guards in scale armor approached. Each was armed with a wickedly pointed, gleaming halberd. They spoke with Ringo in their strange language, and Ringo responded in kind. After much hemming and hawing, the guards waved them on through the gates.

Taki strained his neck, simultaneously entranced and repulsed by giant carvings of four beasts that stared down at him while he passed under them. Was this what Ringo had meant when he'd talked of the islanders communing with demons? He'd barely had time to wonder before he emerged into a busy square paved with tightly fitted stones. Hawkers' cries filled the air, along with ululations that Taki figured were calls to prayer. Not a long distance away was the keep itself. A deep-green stack of quadrangles with whitewashed wooden walls, it reminded Taki of the Potala that he'd visited in Xizhang.

The smell of spices and roasting meat made him salivate and reminded him of his slowly growing hunger. He'd also need to take up Ringo's offer or mount up increasing debt. Ringo grunted for them to veer onto a nearby side street lined with what Taki realized were moneychangers.

Everywhere in the world, they're the same, Taki thought to himself. The men and women all sat cross-legged before low-set tables mounted with scales and weights of varying sizes. Taki could not read the script on the banners flying over the stalls, but he surmised that they touted the accuracy of the weights involved and the purity of whatever metal they used for coin.

"We'll use this one," Ringo said. "Get off."

Taki did as he was told and squatted with Ringo in front of one of the tables. Opposite them was a stocky, round-faced woman who chewed on the end of a long pipe that she periodically refreshed with pinches of sweet-smelling tobacco. She motioned with a hand to them.

"Uh, what should I do?" Taki fidgeted. "Show her my grad?"

"Aye, though don't give up your entire stock. I haven't seen much useable ammunition in my time here, and what I've come across is little better than the dirty shite we'd turn our noses up to at home."

"How about reloads?"

"Haven't found any. But go through the old woman here, and a Luger will get you enough to eat for a week, so long as you aren't averse to pocha and jerky for every meal. You can earn more later, if you're willing to break some heads."

Taki furrowed his brow in thought and thumbed four of the gleaming pistol rounds into his hand. "I'll exchange these."

The moneychanger took the rounds, plopped them on her scale, and let it level out. Then, she swiped them into a pouch and dispensed eight thick, dull-colored coins onto the table in a stack. These she pushed over at Taki.

Taki looked over at Ringo. "Does this look fine to you?"

"Aye, 'tis fair. Though you'll want to break up at least one of 'em into silvers. People will look at you funny if you try to pay for a bean cake with steel."

"Can you ask her for me?"

"*Nadad baga heregtei baina,*" Ringo said, and pushed two of the thicker discs back to the moneychanger. She took them back and then pushed over two stacks of small silver coins with square holes in their centers.

"Thank you," Taki said, and deposited the heavy currency into his belt pouch. "And thanks for your aid, Sir Ringo."

"'Twas nothing. Now come with me. We'll walk the rest of the way, as it's only a short distance to the flophouse."

Taki nodded, and they left the moneychangers' lane. The thought of running crossed his mind, but if he did, then where would he even go? Ringo was the only other expatriate he'd met so far, and furthermore, he'd been in contact with Hecaton Mezeta. *Plus, I don't think he's really interested in killing me,* Taki noted. Of all the people he'd anticipated traveling with, an Ursalan chevalier had been the least likely possibility.

A few minutes later, and in a decidedly poorer section of town, Ringo stopped in front of a ramshackle multistory whose foundation had crumbled partway and now leaned into the building next to it like a wounded soldier on the battlefield.

"Wait a moment," Ringo said, and pushed past Taki to the door at ground level. He knocked on it with an obviously coded beat, and it opened inward. He turned back to Taki. "Okay, go in first. No sudden movements, or she'll definitely gut you."

"Is this your partner we're about to meet?"

"Aye. And I didn't tell her I'm bringing company, so..."

As Taki passed the threshold, the delectable smell of mutton soup and fresh bread warmed his senses and made his insides spasm with hunger. He stepped in quickly, hunger overwhelming caution. Right away, his sword arm was twisted painfully into a joint lock and someone shoved a gun barrel against the back of his head. Before Taki could react, his attacker hustled him toward the stove and shoved his face toward a bubbling cauldron. His face stopped just short of the boiling soup, and he let out a scream of terror, echoed by Ringo.

"Shut the fuck up and identify yourself," a woman hissed. "Damn you, dearest, were you taken hostage by this imbecile?"

"Samara, please!" Ringo squeaked. "He's not an enemy! I mean, he is to *me*, but maybe not to you...what I mean to say is that he's also looking for Mezeta."

"That just means he's dangerous! Hope you like headcheese!"

"Please wait!" Taki blubbered. "I mean you no harm! I'm from the Imperium! Alfa Gruppe spetsnaz! I wear the griffin over my heart!"

Samara wrenched Taki back, and he fell on his behind.

"Thank y—"

She kicked Taki in the chest, and his back slammed on the packed-dirt floor. Then she put a knee on his solar plexus and leaned all her weight on it. "You picked the wrong unit to fake being a part of. Alfa is for badasses, not for little shits like you."

Taki barely managed to choke the words out. "Look at what's around my neck. I'm a Paragon, for fuck's sake! If that doesn't convince you then I don't know what will!"

Samara reached under Taki's armor and pulled out the heavy brass medallion. Then, she leaned over and bit it. Her expression softened. "How disappointing. I really wanted to kill a fool today." She eased off Taki's chest.

Coughing and sputtering, Taki rolled over onto his side and tried to catch his breath. To his surprise, Ringo did nothing but cringe in the corner near the entrance.

"Husband," Samara said and snapped her fingers at him. "Set the table with an extra place for our guest. Use the good trenchers, please. I got my hands on some greens at the market. Give yourself an extra portion."

"I'm not a rabbit," Ringo pouted.

"You'll eat them, *and you'll like them,*" Samara warned him, and then nudged Taki with her foot. "And you, stop lollygagging on the floor. You haven't even introduced yourself. Is this really what they're letting into Alfa these days? Is Aslatiel that desperate for bodies?"

"S-sorry, milady..." Taki got up to his knees. "I'm Taki Natalis. Leutnant in Alfa. Company Tirefire the Lesser under Captain Lotte Satou. I presume you also serve the padishah?"

"Aye," Samara said, as she started to ladle soup into wooden bowls. "Vympel Gruppe. You don't need to know more. How's Irulan?"

Taki bowed his head. "She died in battle after we crossed the Rhone."

Samara sucked her teeth and shook her head. "Dumb bitch. Well, eat up. I'm sure we've got a lot to talk about."

Taki eased into one of the chairs and stared at the soup in front of him. Just a moment earlier he'd have died a horrible death thanks to the stuff, but he was hungry and the mutton smelled heavenly, so he dug in. Ringo was already consumed with eating and dipped large chunks of sour-smelling bread into his bowl to clean it. A pile of braised greens on a nearby trencher went untouched.

"Say 'ah,' dearest," Samara said, and pinched Ringo's nose with her fingers. Then, she shoved a spoonful of greens into his mouth. He resentfully chewed them but did not complain.

"Beg pardon, but I have to ask," Taki said. "Why're you two acting like you're...married?"

"Because we *are*," Samara said with surprising indignation. "In fact, we're coming up on our anniversary."

"But Sir Ringo's an Ursalan chevalier. You're sworn enemies. How did this happen?"

"Against my better judgment," Ringo muttered, earning himself a pinch on the arm from Samara.

"It's a long story, Natalis," Samara said. "One I'll tell some other time if I get to like you. But yes, Ringo is my husband in the eyes of Ursalan knightly custom and Imperial common law. And before you ask, the marriage has been consummated. Many, *many* times."

"Samara, dammit," Ringo whined. He sighed and turned to Taki. "Speaking of my homeland, you owe me the truth. How *really* goes the war?"

At least he's not waving his piece at me anymore, Taki thought. He inched his chair closer to where Samara was. "It's over. The Imperium has taken Versailles."

"Liar!" Ringo slammed the table and stood upright.

"I tell the truth, Sir Ringo!"

"The Aegis is impenetrable!"

"Our forces broke through to the south. We provoked the Ordo Arslan to sally forth and then slipped into the castle to retrieve the key to the Queen's Right. Then, we toppled the gates."

Ringo sank back down into his chair.

"And His Holy Majesty?"

"Killed in battle," Taki said. "By Padishah Chronicler the First."

"Fie! Fie upon it all!" Ringo said, and buried his face in his hands.

Samara rose from her seat and draped an arm around Ringo's shoulders as he heaved. She rubbed his back and kissed his scalp. Taki raised an eyebrow at the sight. Comfort to the enemy was the last thing he'd have expected from a fellow spetsnaz.

"Did I hear you right?" Samara asked. "*Ba'gshnar* is the padishah now?"

"Yes, milady," Taki said. "After we took the Sanct Gotthard pass, Chronicler announced that the previous padishah had abdicated, and that he'd taken the mantle. He then led the army across Ursala and took Versailles before coming here."

Samara whistled appreciatively. "*Ba'gshnar* has always been a supreme warrior. I guess it was inevitable that he'd take over. And to have brought Ursala to its knees at the same time? Say, Natalis, were you ever selected to train with him? I don't recall ever seeing your face around the bihara."

"Nay, milady. I was recruited to the service by Sir Aslatiel. I was a Polaris of the Argead Dominion before that."

"Aslatiel must've seen something in you that I frankly don't see," Samara said. "No offense intended."

"None taken," Taki said, and looked down at his feet.

"So how did you come here? Have we found a way past the Goryeo storm wall?"

"The what?"

Samara rolled her eyes. "How ignorant are you?"

"Very," Taki said. "Please, go easy on me. I have no idea how I actually arrived here. One moment I was in the spire of Versailles, and the next, I was buried up to my chest in sand in a hellscape. I didn't sail here like you two."

"Fine," Samara said. "As an Argead, you wouldn't have known this. The reason the Imperium hasn't tried to expand east across the sea is because when you get about three days east of the tip of the peninsula, it quickly becomes impossible to travel further. There's an ongoing storm that'll tear any ship apart, and the creatures that live beneath will finish off what's left. No one's found a way around it, and it's been raging nonstop for centuries on end. This cluster of islands is on the other side. We're probably the first Imperials ever to set foot here."

Taki let out a slow breath. "Sir Ringo told me that you lot stole the *Ooss*. I had no idea it could still sail."

"Neither did I," Samara said. "But your people made a fine vessel. It allowed us to go under the waves and avoid the storms. And being all metal, it saved us from quite a few hungry sea creatures. You're probably pissed about all the blasphemy, eh?"

"I'd have never been allowed near it," Taki said. "So it doesn't matter to me."

"For the best, then. Where's the rest of Alfa? Did they arrive with you, or will they come later?"

Taki shook his head. "Everyone else is back in Versailles. It's just me."

"Ugh." Samara rolled her eyes. "The homeland faces the greatest threat to its existence in a century, and I get a *kid* as backup. Thanks. Thanks a lot."

"Now I'm taking offense. What threat are you babbling about?"

Samara crossed her arms. "There was a woman who came with us to these lands. Actually, she's the one—"

"Hecaton Kheiris Mezeta," Taki said, cutting Samara short. "I know. I actually came in search of her specifically. Is she the threat?"

Samara looked surprised. "Aye. Since she arrived, she's already conquered most of the native kingdoms. She gallivants around with the crowns of murdered kings atop her head and leads a swelling army of her people, the 'twice born.' Soon, she'll have the entirety of the Islands Closest to Hell under her thumb. And it's no guess where she intends to aim her wrath, next."

"The Imperium," Taki said with a groan. "But why?"

"I'm not sure, but I suspect it has something to do with *Ba'gshnar*. Soon after we'd left on our journey, she received word of his coronation as padishah. Are you familiar with her mannerisms?"

"I am," Taki said. "I served under her for a long time. When I was a Polaris."

"Then you know what she looks like when she's enraged. That's what I saw that day. I hope you're not about to ask why I haven't tried to kill her yet."

"I know exactly why," Taki said. "And frankly, I was under no illusions that I'd be able to do a damned thing to her."

"So why did you come? And hell, why did you come alone?"

"I didn't," Taki said. "That is, I thought someone else had come along with me."

"Who?"

"Chronicler."

Samara rose from her crouch next to Ringo and grabbed Taki by the shoulders. "He's here?"

"I don't know! He ascended the same…contraption as I did to get here. But I woke up alone. I have no idea if he made it or why I ended up where I did."

"When did you arrive?"

"Sometime yesterday."

"That explains it," Samara said. "The astrologers have been going batshit for weeks with all the omens popping up. The shamans are just as bad. Why, not more than a fortnight ago, both groups had a huge brawl. The last few days have been particularly bad."

"Omens? What omens?"

"Standard stuff. Mostly lights dancing in the sky and animals dying left and right, but the night before you came, two comets descended to earth and destroyed some pretty large tracts of land. One landed near where Ringo was traveling, and the other obliterated a forest near the Western Ban."

Taki's eyes went wide. "When I came to, the land around me was blasted and charred. That means Chronicler…"

"Might've made it here, too," Samara said, and started to pace. "It's ridiculous to think that you and he somehow fell out of the sky riding comets, but given that you're sitting here in front of me…best not to ponder it overmuch. Be glad, Natalis. Your story gives me hope. If *Ba'gshnar* is here, then perhaps we have a chance against Mezeta after all."

"So what should we do now?"

Samara tapped her fingers on the wooden table. "Tell me, Natalis, did you part with her on good terms?"

Taki's expression darkened. "My company served her well and brought her glory. In return, she had us humiliated and singled out for punishment for years. Finally, she stole our pensions and had us ejected from the Cloud Temple. If Sir Aslatiel hadn't come to recruit me, we'd have starved or fallen into banditry."

"She must've *really* liked you," Samara said with a smirk. "I think you might have an in. Someone that Ringo and I don't have."

"An in? To where?"

"Mezeta's army, of course. A pack of ridiculously powerful thugs who've taken over the old Kvara city. Locals call it the Ring, by the by. Anyway, the old hag's put out a call for strong adventurers to join her for conquest and pillage, and all you have to do is get on her good side. Since she's already fond of you, it'll be easy for you to get into her inner circle."

Taki rolled his eyes. "Why the hell would I ever want to do such a thing? I came here as her enemy. The last thing I wish to do is serve her again."

"You're not there to serve her. You'll be acting as a spy. Ringo and I will go out and find *Ba'gshnar* and alert him of Mezeta's plans. Once he hears of the threat she poses, I'm sure he'll aid us in taking her down. You just need to make sure we're one step ahead of her and inform on her movements. Together, we'll set a trap, and she'll no longer be a threat. This is standard espionage."

"Why don't you do it, then? You're the Vympel agent. Isn't this what your kind specializes in?"

Samara shook her head. "We're on bad terms with her. We'd just be viewed with suspicion and probably killed."

"What'd you do?"

"We tried to steal the God Hand from her. It didn't work out well. There were two others in our group, also knights-errant. Janus Eicke and Juan Diaz de Villavilla. They turned on us and let Mezeta know of our plans. Now they're in her inner circle, and we're on the run."

"I'm surprised you betrayed her and lived."

"Barely," Samara said. "But now the screw's turned. We're all here, and we want to deliver some comeuppance. So, Taki Natalis, Imperial Paragon, are you in?"

Taki was silent in thought. He didn't relish being under Hecaton's command yet again and furthermore recoiled at the thought of being gutted for being a spy. *But this time, it'll be me screwing her. And that's far, far better than any tumble.* He reached a hand out to shake. "I'm in."

* * * *

Chiseled and scraped from the rhyolite atop a volcano long extinguished, the Ring stood before Taki as he finally surmounted the lip of the caldera. It was firmly midday, and the clouds had retreated from their perch over the ancient city. Now they only surrounded the small island in the middle of the crater's lake, from which the broken remains of a spire poked to the sky. Surprisingly, the curtain wall surrounding the Ring was of only middling height and crumbling in many places, as if the city's inhabitants had considered perimeter defense an afterthought. Taki squinted, trying to make out any obvious sentry towers or patrols, but found none nearby. For all the talk of a ravaging army occupying the place, it looked almost abandoned.

Taki had traveled nearly a fortnight since leaving Tsam. Ringo and Samara had left the city separately and on different nights, wary of Hecaton's army spies. How they had planned to locate Chronicler much less convince him to trust them was unclear, but Taki had decided he enough to worry about. His task was to travel to the Ring and join the inner circle. Samara and Ringo had given him an intensive crash course in the islanders' language, and now he could hold a somewhat respectable conversation in the foreign tongue.

He dismounted from his panting animal and led it onward by the reins. The winding path he'd taken up the mountainside had been long and arduous. Ancient cairns made of piled thunder eggs and small boulders served to warn of sudden drop-offs and rock falls. When he drew closer to an open archway, the tip of his boot brushed up against one of the small rock piles and knocked it over.

"Halt!" someone ordered in the islander language.

Taki put his hands up as helmeted heads poked over the battlements and two more islanders emerged from the entrance with shortbows drawn and broadheads trained on him.

"How'd you come up here so brazenly?" one of them said as he eyed the donkey's saddlebags. "Give us all your stuff, and we might let you live."

"We should kill him anyway," another said. "Look how strange his face is, brother. He's obviously a Hungry Ghost! Do you want his curse to spread here? Sirin will kill us for that!"

Taki cracked a grin. *Sirin. Mezeta's original name.* He'd come to the right place. "You'll do no such thing. In fact, you're going to take me right to the boss. I am her long-lost disciple, and if you lay a hand on me, she'll skin you alive with her mind!"

"You're her disciple? Bullshit! Can you even channel, or are you just some weakling?"

"Watch me," Taki said, and balled a hand into a fist above his head. He intoned a quick *pyr* sutra and opened his fingers to unleash a geyser of flame skyward. In turn, he was rewarded with more shouts of surprise close by, and yet more rushing footfalls of summoned reinforcements. He set his hands on his hips and let loose a deep, somewhat theatric laugh. "What are you fools waiting for? Take me to Sirin this instant! My mistress longs for a real channeler to rub her feet and hoist her standard. Every second you delay compounds her wrath!"

A few minutes later, Taki strolled down a crowded avenue with no less than ten spearheads at his back and a crowd of hide-wrapped onlookers who either pointed and guffawed or tried their hardest to run their hands over his alien features. He did his best to keep an arrogant leer plastered on his face. The islanders respected strength above all, and posturing was a large part of one's strength.

At the end of the avenue, Taki passed under an ornately carved and painted gate and entered a courtyard paved in granite. At the end of an upward slope stood a throne room topped with a sweeping, gabled roof whose eaves were carved to resemble dragons. Marble fu-dog statues lined the way like divine guardsmen, their mouths and fangs daubed with crimson.

Hecaton Mezeta lounged on her side atop a golden throne upholstered in silk. She was draped with a motley collection of animal pelts and other blankets, and atop her head was an ornate, bangled crown that looked ill sized to her head. To Taki's consternation, he couldn't shake the thought that underneath the blanket pile, his former commander might be naked. She turned her head away from the book in her hands and raised an eyebrow.

"Lord Sirin!" Taki's captors announced. One of them jammed the muzzle of a flintlock against Taki's head. "We captured this mongrel skulking around, and he claims to be your long-lost disciple. Would you like to kill him now?"

Hecaton rolled her eyes. "You couldn't have killed him outside? Why do I keep you around if I have to do all the murder?"

Taki stepped forward and bowed with a flourish. "Indeed, Mistress Hecaton, these degenerates expect you to do everything for them and then praise them for such a lackadaisical attitude. I, on the other hand, am a man of action and promise to serve you well!"

"Taki Natalis," Hecaton said with a sigh. "Whatever are you doing here? I don't remember letting you on my boat."

"Mistress, allow me to join your army and conquer the world alongside you! I came here of my own accord and through my own means. I have become much stronger than when you left me. I served you once, and now I wish to serve you again."

"You want to join my army?" Heaton threw her head back and laughed. The badly fitted crown tipped off her head and clattered to the floor. "But why? You never wanted excitement and danger. Why, you did everything you could in the name of convenience and comfort."

Taki rose to his feet and punched a fist into his palm. "Of all the commanders I have ever served, I most admire you, Mistress Hecaton! You told once what was good in life. I was young and a fool back then, so I couldn't comprehend your answer. But now I truly understand. There is no pleasure in life that comes close to crushing my enemies. To seeing them scattered and driven before me. To hear the lamentations of their families. You were my first teacher and the only one who spoke the truth."

155

Before Hecaton could reply, another spoke, and in perfect Ursalan. "Milady Hecaton, believe not this Imperial cur. He's clearly hiding his true purpose, which is to undermine our efforts."

Almost immediately, Taki was surrounded by a circle of spears and cocked crossbows. He glowered through his surprise at seeing another non-islander. Tall and finely featured, with a wiry moustache and well-trimmed goatee, the man regarded Taki with unveiled disdain.

"Who are you, sir, who knows me well enough to cast aspersions on my character?" Taki demanded.

"Juan Diaz de Villavilla, an honorable chevalier of Ordo Naranja and servant of milady the duquessa. And you...you are an Imperial by your manner. Imperials cannot be trusted. Imperials are not...human."

"You are correct on one part, Sir Juan. I once marched among the ranks of the padishah's army. I fought with them all the way to Versailles, where I climbed the spire and thus was reborn in these lands."

"You were in Versailles?" Juan bared his teeth. "Such lies! At least choose your falsehoods more carefully before stating a factual impossibility! Duquessa Hecaton, this man is not only a liar, he is also an imbecile!"

Taki laughed. "It is you who are in for a shock, Sir Juan. Your beloved Sanctissimus Rex is dead. The Imperium occupies your capital while your nobles murder each other for the remnants. Why, I was with Padishah Chronicler the First when he slew the man."

Juan drew his rapier and took a step forward.

Hecaton held up a hand. "Put up your sword before I brain you, Juan. I was getting bored, but *this* is interesting news, at long last. Taki, are you saying that the old fart's conquered the entire world?"

"Yes, Mistress," Taki said. "If you believe Murrikania to be mere legend."

"How annoying," Hecaton said, and shuffled upright. Her bare legs dangled off the edge of the throne. "I'd hoped to wallow here for a while longer, if not for that damnable man. Now, I'll have to punish him. I take it since you're here kowtowing to me, that you want a piece of the action?"

"Nothing would make me happier, Mistress," Taki said with another sweeping bow.

"Do you really believe this...this vagrant? This upstart?" Juan's face was nearly purple with rage.

"I tell nothing but the truth!" Taki said. He jammed the barrel of his Herstal against his head and cocked the hammer. "If you think I'm lying, Mistress Hecaton, then I'll kill myself without hesitation!"

"Don't dirty the floor," Hecaton said with a dismissive wave. "I'm more interested in seeing your gift. You *did* bring a gift, right?"

Shit. Taki clenched his buttocks to prevent his knees from shaking. *I didn't bring anything noteworthy besides some jerky. And what the hell would actually impress Mezeta, anyway?*

"Ah, you are a pauper in addition to a liar," Juan said with a mirthless chuckle.

Only because she stole my grad, Taki thought, bitterly. Then, sudden inspiration hit him. If he had nothing, he'd make up for it with gall.

"Mistress," Taki said, "my gift is five hundred Luger milligrad from the coffers of Tirefire the Lesser. *Paid in advance!*"

For a second, Hecaton's expression was inscrutable. The hairs on the back of Taki's neck rose. Any moment, he expected to be struck with lightning. To his surprise, Hecaton laughed.

"Taki Natalis, you little shit!" She slapped her knee and grinned. "You *are* right about one thing. You've grown since we last saw each other. I wonder if other parts of you have grown as well," she said with a leer.

"Thank you for accepting my gift." Taki's bluster stood on its last legs.

Hecaton seemed not to notice. "I have something for you to do, Natalis. My boys and girls here need to learn Imperial for when we invade the mainland. You are now Brother Number Eight, in charge of the propaganda division. Kill the other seven brothers and you'll be Number One and get first pick of all the loot. But keep a level head and don't cause more trouble than you're worth. I see you as maybe Number Four before you screw up."

"I am unworthy of this honor," Taki said, kowtowing. "But I accept!"

"Good," Hecaton said. She clapped her hands twice. "This demands a feast. Brothers and sisters, fire up the grills!"

9

Taki sat cross-legged on a brocade cushion that had once belonged to royalty and stuffed his face with greasy kebabs. He occupied a spot at one of the circular, low-set tables that were standard for the islands. The feast hall was constructed in the same style as the throne room had been, with large, load-bearing timbers supporting a heavy, gabled roof. Overhead, carved images of dragons and other, stranger members of the heavenly host cavorted and chased each other's tails.

Finished with another hunk of meat, Taki tossed his iron skewer into the growing pile in the middle of the table and took another swig of pocha. No matter how many times he'd had it now, the stuff never sat right with him. But since the vile purple liquid seemed to be everyone's replacement for water in these parts, there was nothing to do but hold his nose and recall good times had with beer.

"Have some more, little brother." A squat, ruddy-faced islander in hides passed Taki another kebab dripping oil and blood.

Though he was nearing fullness, Taki accepted it gracefully. "My thanks..."

"Jiang," the man said. "Brother Number One."

"It's an honor to meet you," Taki said. *Even though he doesn't look all that special.*

"You speak well for a barbarian," Jiang said with a laugh. "Better than some of the other narrow-faced ghosts."

Taki's hackles rose. Besides Juan, he hadn't seen any other non-islanders. "Uh, are there any more of my kind? Besides Sir Juan?"

"You mean Brother Number Seven? There have been a few more," Jiang said, furrowing his brow in thought. "There was a Brother Number Eight before you. Ringo was his name. There was Sister Three, who was wife to Brother Eight, but in my opinion she'd married down. Both were banished, though, after plotting against us. Finally, there's Brother Number Six, Janus. He is a barbarian who enjoys tinkering with things. Lord Sirin keeps him at the harbor to work on her sea-chariot, so he does not visit us often. When he does, he is…awkward."

Probably means the Ooss, Taki reasoned. *So she stole it after all.* He shook his head. For some reason, the desecration of the Dominion's most sacred holy site seemed not to affect him. Of course, while Polaris guarded the walls, they'd never been allowed inside, either.

But more pressing than past religious discrimination was the question of how he'd get back in contact with Ringo and Samara. In truth, Taki hadn't planned anything beyond simply becoming one of Hecaton's cronies. Samara had merely told him to stay vigilant; she hadn't offered any concrete plans. There was no telling how long he'd have to keep up the act, either. Tensions between him and Juan certainly didn't help, especially if the man was his senior in Hecaton's gang.

Before Taki could ruminate further, the far end of the feast hall erupted in a cacophony of stomping feet, chiming gongs, and throaty hurrahs. He looked up from his half-eaten kebab to see Hecaton gaily stomping down the hall to the mounting cheers of the regulars. She wore a fur gambeson trimmed in ermine and sported an oversized beaver hat on which bells dangled from every pointed end. When she reached Taki's table, she hopped onto it, turned, and waved a hand for silence.

"Many of you know that we welcome a new brother to the fold today! His name is Taki Natalis, and though he's never been with a woman, you should listen to his orders because he doesn't have the pox!"

Taki's face burned as the hall was wracked with laughter.

"He'll teach you lot the language of our enemies, so you can tell them to stick their heads in their own bungs and spread their arseholes for us! The chosen few! The twice born!"

Thunderous applause and cheering set the trenchers dancing on the tabletop.

"Soon, we will take down the wall of storms and open a path to the fat, indolent, mainland. We have a duty to punish the entire world for its decadence. *Uukhai!*"

"*Uukhai!*" the crowd roared.

Hecaton reached to her waist and drew a gleaming pistol from its holster. She waved it in the air by its peculiar broom-handled grip and started a throaty rendition of what Taki figured to be a duet.

Ш илээ цасыг хайлан,
Ш илгээтэл урсаж л байдаг.

Fire erupted from Hecaton's muzzle, and the shell casing landed in Taki's lap. The feasting army cheered and drank gulps of *arkhi*, while some shot their own guns into the gabled roof. Jiang clapped Taki on the back and proffered a large mug of the pungent liquor. Seeing no other alternative, Taki put the mug to his lips and downed it all in one go.

Шинэхэн ногоо нь ургаж л байдаг,

Хөхөө шувуу донгодож л байдаг.

More shots, and more *arkhi*. Jiang seemed to be gifted with an endless supply of the stuff.

Үнэхээрийн сонин сайхан баяхан

буурал Алтай хангай хоёр минь ээ.

Though he couldn't understand the dialect, Taki grinned stupidly and tried to chant along. The liquor ran hot in his veins, and he'd forgotten that he was still a spy deep behind enemy lines. He burped and was rewarded with vile, burning backwash. He'd need to vomit before he drank more—that was simple common sense.

He stumbled away from the table and walked toward a gap in the timbers. While it wasn't a true entrance, it was a convenient way to slip away without a crowd of well-wishers shadowing his every movement. He walked a short distance toward a pile of stacked barrels and got to his knees to shimmy over to a stone edge. Then, he vomited all the kebab and wine onto the steps below.

"Disgusting."

Taki blearily turned his head and caught sight of a pair of feet. He turned further to see a scullion standing next to him with a basket laden with mugs and trenchers. Her face was mostly obscured by a scarf and headwrap. Still, he recognized the voice.

"S-samara? That you?"

"Keep quiet, you godrotting lush," Samara said, and crouched to set her basket down. "Yes, it's me. Looks like you held to your end of the deal, if just barely."

"I nearly died," Taki griped. "They're all feral, drunken assholes. And they call *me* the barbarian?"

"You poor thing," Samara said with a roll of her eyes. She lowered her voice. "More importantly, we found *Ba'gshnar*. He's willing to help us."

"What..." Taki tried to get to his feet and swayed dangerously close to the precipice. "What's the plan?"

"The plan is that you don't kill yourself in the stupidest way possible," Samara hissed, and wrenched him toward more solid ground. "You're not here to drink and cavort. Juan will gut you the moment you let your guard down. I can't be here all the time to watch you. For the time being, I'll leave you messages. Each of the brothers has his own private crapping stall. Check under the washbucket for your orders. Do not write to us unless you've got something to back it up."

"Wait," Taki said in annoyance, "if you can just sneak in here at will, then why're you making me do all this spying nonsense?"

"Because if I babysat you all the time, when would I ever find time to stalk my husband?"

"You *stalk* him? For what possible reason?"

"To make sure he isn't getting into trouble," Samara said. "Or courting another woman."

"Men need alone time, you know."

"Ringo needs to be watched, *especially* when he's alone. Otherwise, he might pleasure himself."

Taki rolled his eyes. "So what if he does?"

"Then he's not pleasuring me."

"You're...you're some kind of fiend."

Laughter and footfalls sounded nearby. Samara cursed.

"Grab my arse," she said.

"Huh? Why—whatever." Taki shook his head and did as he was told.

Samara let out a squeal just as two islanders rounded a corner and came into view. She stumbled away from Taki and pushed past the newcomers, much to their laughter.

"Brother Number Eight!" one called over. "Stop diddling the servants and come back already! Teach us how to say 'I want to fuck' in your language! Ha!"

Taki forced a jovial smile. At least one question of his had been answered, but the stakes had just shot up tenfold.

* * * *

The next morning, Taki awoke on his stomach with one of his arms trapped at an awkward angle under his belly and atop a smelly pallet of furs. His face was slick with frigid drool, and everything smelled of *arkhi* and stale farts. With some flailing, he rolled over onto his back to free his trapped arm and sat up. This proved to be a mistake, however, as he instantly felt as if an iron spike had been driven into his head between his eyes. The world spun, and he wanted to vomit.

I'm hungover and don't know where the hell I am, he realized. He rubbed his face in an effort to calm the pain and slowly took a look around. As far as he could tell, he was in another part of the palace complex, one with nowhere near the elegance of the throne room. The space he occupied was about as small as one of the sleeping closets he'd bunked in during his time as a Polaris, save for the fact that there was no Draco snoring right next to him and using his ankles as a pillow.

Aside from the fur pallet and a dusty, low-set writing desk, the space was bare. A sturdy wooden door sealed him off from the rest of the world. Were these his quarters, as Brother Number Eight? Private quarters were probably a luxury afforded to the inner circle. This would make it easier for him to communicate with Samara, though, since he could draft messages without concern over prying eyes. All he had to do was obtain something to write with and something to write on. Mounting discomfort assailed his stomach, and he remembered Samara's directions. *Might as well take care of two things at once.*

Taki exited, noting with some annoyance that there seemed to be no lock for his quarters. When drafting missives, he'd have to write with his back to the door. His room opened to a sandy outdoor courtyard ringed with other quarters. Over his door was a crudely carved wooden placard, marked with what he deduced was the symbol for his new rank. He quickly memorized the symbol and then walked into the yard in search of the jakes. In the center, lolling nearby a cluster of denuded trees, a pair of islanders diced against each other.

"The jakes, where are they?" Taki asked.

One of the men bowed overly obsequiously and pointed. Taki nodded his thanks.

"Brother Number Eight," the other began with a giggle. "What is the barbarian word for man's smelly member?"

"Cock," Taki said, and walked off. After some meandering and the realization that the islander's earlier direction had been essentially garbage, he finally found the jakes in a separate courtyard nearby. Above each stall, the same symbols appeared. By now, the urge to go was overpowering.

"A moment, Imperial," Juan said from behind him. He wiped his hands with a rag and shuffled over.

Taki waved and kept walking. "Beg pardon, but I must answer the call."

Inconveniently, the stalls had no doors. *Everyone and God can watch me. Great.* He pulled down his leggings and squatted over a jagged-edged hole. The washbucket rested nearby, filled with dusty but clean-smelling water. He started to reach for it, only to realize that Juan waited no more than an arm's length away, and right in front of Taki's stall.

Taki frowned and hurriedly lowered a hand to cover himself. "Do you mind, Sir Juan?"

"Not at all," Juan said. "I will wait for you."

Is he serious? Taki shifted on his feet. "Why are you doing this?"

"Doing what? I wish to discuss important matters. You wish to attend to your functions. I will accommodate."

"Don't you think it's a little strange, not to mention impolite, to hover next to someone on the privy?"

"Why, not at all. We are made in the Lord's image, no? We both must eat and drink, and thus we must both excrete. It bothers me not to watch an act of divine design, nor should it bring shame to you to eliminate."

Taki clenched his jaw. "I don't care how you feel. Get away from me!"

"I will not."

"You're a pervert! Leave at once, or I'll let the others know of this!"

Juan grabbed Taki by the throat. "I am not a deviant! I swear this on the garter of Princessa Phillippa! *You*, however, are clearly hiding something! You're in league with Sir Ringo and that spetsnaz wench, aren't you? Aren't you?"

"I don't know who you're talking about." Taki fixed a venomous stare at Juan's eyes. "Touch me again and I'll kill you!"

He shoved the muzzle of his Herstal against Juan's belly and drew the hammer back with an audible click.

The chevalier looked down and returned a hateful glare. Then, he backed away.

"I know you're a spy, *amigo*. Until next time, eh?"

Taki waited until Juan had vanished from view and then slowly let the hammer down before putting the gun back in its holster. Whatever urge he'd had to go was suppressed, at least for the time being. *Damn that fucking knight,* he thought, and hiked up his leggings. Almost as an afterthought, he took the washbucket and lifted it by the handle. Underneath was a small leather pouch of what smelled like snuff. He secreted it away into a pocket and hurried back to his quarters.

With heart still pounding, he closed the door once inside and braced his back against the wood. Then, he opened the snuff pouch and shook it out. Chunks of moistened, pungent tobacco powder fell into the palm of his hand, followed by a small, crumpled piece of paper that could easily have passed for excess packaging. He let the snuff fall to the floor and smoothed out the paper.

"We're blowing the God Hand over the Ring. Make HM stay put. Burn this."

Taki let out a ragged breath. The plan made sense. The God Hand could eliminate entire armies in one blow and instill real fear in men like Chronicler. Hecaton was likely no different. But if Taki's job was to keep her occupied until the Hand struck…

He crumpled the paper in his fist and sank into a squat. *Does she expect me to sit and wait for a godrotting nuclear missile to go up my arse? Fuck her! Fuck Ringo! And most of all, fuck that old bastard Chronicler!*

Taki leaned back and thumped the back of his head against the door. There was always the option of simply confessing everything to Hecaton. But she was still an unknown quantity, just as likely to hang him by his toenails as she was to pardon his treachery. Plus, Juan would seize upon any excuse to kill him. Simple escape was a possibility. *But then where would I be? Hunted endlessly in a strange land with no connections and no way of getting home? Worse than death. Think, Taki Natalis! Think harder!*

He ground his scalp against the rough-hewn planks and closed his eyes. He tried not to envision the faces of his companions, for fear of weeping. He tried not to remember Enilna's touch, for fear of sinking into despair. And most of all, he desperately tried not to relive what Lotte had smelled like, tasted like, for fear of going mad.

After a long time spent hugging his knees to his chest, Taki put the paper back into the pouch, along with whatever fallen snuff he could scrape off the floor. He'd decided against burning the message, or taking any course of action, until his head had cleared. If the God Hand struck, there wasn't anything to do about it, anyway. He took a deep breath, patted the dust from his clothing, and left his quarters.

Jiang stood outside in full lamellar plate with a massive dao sword resting across his shoulders.

Taki tensed. "Brother Number One, what's going on?"

"There's a problem," Jiang said. "I hate to work you while you're hungover, Brother Number Eight, but I need you and Brother Number Seven to ride out with a company of horse and investigate the barbarian ship."

Taki felt all his sphincters loosen at once. "Barbarian ship? You mean the *Ooss*?"

"Yes, I think I've heard your kind call it that. Miscreants have been skulking around the ship. I need you to go and flush them out. Your senior brothers and I need to go and deal with some Birchen holdouts, so it's up to you both. I know your job is to teach, but you wouldn't be here if you couldn't fight well."

"You honor me with your trust, Brother Number One," Taki said, and bowed deeply. "I'll make sure the ship is safe."

"Make sure you do. It's going to be our flagship," Jiang said with a laugh. With that, Jiang turned and left. Taki straightened, his back newly sore. He wasn't used to keeping bowed so long, though that was the usual etiquette when dealing with a superior. Samara had taught him that during his crash course on the islanders' ways.

It was no mystery who was supposedly skulking around the *Ooss*. Jiang's assignment had been an unexpected blessing—now Taki was in a position to screw up Chronicler's plans. If they wanted to be rid of Hecaton so badly, then they'd have to renegotiate terms. Terms that included Taki not being mere bait. *And I'm definitely making sure I have a way home. Because fuck staying in this place.*

The only problem was Juan, of course. Taki's fingers brushed against the hidden snuff pouch. Though Taki had never been a tobacco aficionado, Juan had the smell strongly about him. Not burning the missive had been a wise decision, in retrospect. Now, he knew exactly what to do with it.

* * * *

Hecaton's people were horsemen above all. They lived, ate, slept, fought, and died atop their mounts, with the latter considered the highest honor possible under Tengri's blue sky. Thus, Taki rode not a donkey but an actual steppe charger, born and bred for war. At the head of a thundering vanguard of two hundred lancers, Taki wondered if he could grow addicted to the thrill.

The only problem, of course, was Juan's presence. Every so often, the chevalier would throw a poisonous glance back at Taki, as if willing him to fall from his horse and break his neck. Because Juan was a rank above Taki in Hecaton's brotherhood, he was compelled to take point, which Taki did not mind so much. It was better to stay behind an enemy at all times and not fear a sudden flash of steel in one's back.

On horseback, it had only taken a few bells to reach the narrow harbor where Hecaton had moored the *Ooss*. With high walls formed from cliffsides and a strong palisade, the small port stronghold had perfect natural defenses. Watched over by twice born, it was virtually impenetrable. Or it would have been, if not for the smoke rising from beyond the palisade and the bodies strewn near the entrance.

"In the name of God!" Juan shouted. "Imperial! Sound the horn!"

Taki lifted the oxhorn bugle to his lips and blew to order a charge at full tilt. The men behind him roared their approval, lowered their lances, and spurred on their mounts. Taki pushed his fur-lined helm down to make sure it didn't fly away and then tapped his horse's flanks. It rocketed forth in the direction of the shattered gates. A wedge charge like the one Taki had ordered was strong enough to break any infantry formation, even a fully braced pike square. He held tight to his reins, relishing the power he wielded.

No massed charge awaited them inside. Instead, all there was to be found was simple desolation. The wedge split in two, and the disappointed lancers slowed their horses to a circling canter. Juan and Taki trotted to the center of the courtyard and surveyed their surroundings.

"Damnation," Juan growled. "This place should have a hundred men at all times. Come with me, *amigo,* we need to see about the *Ooss.*"

They dismounted their horses and ran toward the water. Making sure that Juan was ahead of him, Taki jogged down the rickety wooden stairs leading to the dock. Now, though, he could see there was no need to hurry. The harbor was completely without a trace of any ship, much less a functional nuclear submarine.

Juan shouted and ran over to a nearby body, lying prone near the foot of the stairs, in the middle of a pool of coagulating blood. Taki followed.

"Dios mio!" Juan said, and turned the corpulent form over onto its back. "Sir Janus, they've killed you! *Pendejos!"*

The obese man's eyes fluttered open; he coughed, sending black clots from his nose and mouth. Juan got to his knees and shook the man by his shoulders.

"Have a care," Taki warned. "He's wounded! You'll make him worse."

"Silence, inferior being!" Juan said. He turned his attention back to the wounded man. "Sir Janus! Sir Janus! Speak to me! Who stole the *Ooss?*"

"Sir Juan, is that you?" Janus whispered. "Everything's so dark, forgive me…"

"No need, my friend," Juan said. "What happened here?"

"Samara came back to me," Janus said, with a bloody smile. "I knew she would, Sir Juan!"

"Did that cur steal the ship?"

"I don't know. She was with that famous old Imperial, Chronicler, though. Maybe he stole the ship. But that's not important. I held her again, Sir Juan. She told me everything would be okay from now on."

Juan's eyes widened. "Chronicler? This is worse than I thought. How about the God Hand? Janus, speak to me!"

"It was on board, but..." Janus grasped at the end of a chain necklace he wore and pulled. From beneath his tunic emerged a small, blood-smeared object that Taki instantly recognized. Essentially a spyglass with buttons attached, it was the only way to direct the God Hand to its destination. "Can't launch without this..."

Dear God, a Behelit. Now I really have to eliminate this knight. But how?

Janus gave a dreamy, wide-eyed smile. "Sir Juan...I must confess that I love her...I know it's an affront to the virtues...but I'm thinking of...renouncing my vows and...marrying that girl..." His breaths, shallow and rapid, abruptly stopped.

Juan knelt in stunned silence and let the body drop. He took the Behelit and stared at it. Then he stood and walked toward Taki and the stairs.

"Sir Juan, we should bring his body up," Taki said. "I'll have the men make a litter."

"Shut up," Juan said, and strung the Behelit around his own neck. "We're done here. I am now Brother Number Six, so keep that in mind."

"Shouldn't we at least bury him?" Taki asked, glancing at Janus.

"The crows can have him," Juan said. "He was useless to the end."

"That's not the right way to treat a fellow, especially between chevaliers."

"Didn't you hear him?" Juan let out a chuckle. "He wanted to renounce his vows. And for what? For an abomination that calls itself a woman? Imperial swine aren't human. They are beneath dogs! Sir Janus died a blasphemer and a pervert. He can rot under the sun."

Taki crossed his arms. "If you won't display dignity befitting of your station, then I will. I'll drag him up if I have to."

"No. I'm not letting you out of my sight," Juan said, and shoved Taki toward the stairs.

Taki stumbled but then stood firm. "We're not leaving till we give the body proper honors."

Juan's foot crashed into Taki's midsection, making him double over in pain. Then, Juan took Taki by the ear and bashed a fist into his jaw.

Taki reeled and collapsed against the stairs. Floaters starred his vision, and he fought to urge to lose control of his bowels. Juan was on top of him now. Before Taki could draw his Herstal, Juan had already ripped the gun from its holster and mashed the muzzle against Taki's head.

"I remember," Juan said with a malicious grin, "that you were going to kill me next time I touched you. Well? I'm waiting."

"This isn't the time or place," Taki sputtered. "God damn you, a companion of yours just died!"

"He was no companion of mine," Juan said. "Actually, he was competition."

"You've no honor," Taki said.

"And you've no stones," Juan said. He slipped a hand into Taki's leggings and squeezed hard.

Taki gnashed his teeth and tried his hardest not to scream. *The pouch! The pouch!* The mental effort of searching through his pockets for the snuff pouch distracted him somewhat from the pain. His shaking fingers grasped the leather.

"Confess!" Juan said. "Admit that you are an Imperial spy, or I will render you a woman and use you as such!"

Tears streamed from Taki's eyes as he felt his insides twist and tear. He brought his hands up to Juan's gambeson and tapped against it. The pouch slipped into one of the front pockets, right under the embroidered rose of Naranja.

"I confess!" Taki blubbered. "I am in league with Sir Ringo and Lady Samara! I came here to infiltrate Hecaton Mezeta's army! Is that enough?"

Juan loosened his grip and stepped back. "I knew it. Ha! Still, I am disappointed. I haven't had a shapely boy like you in quite a while."

Taki writhed and rolled over onto his side. The world spun, and he retched. "So what're you going to do now? Execute me?"

"I would like to," Juan said. "But first you will be judged by the duquessa. She should know that I served her well."

By now, the commotion had attracted the attention of many of the lancers, who peered over the precipice with interest.

"Brother Number Eight has confessed to foul treason," Juan said. "Strip him of his arms and bind him. There will be blood tonight!"

* * * *

Taki tried not to slump over and not to shiver. Both were difficult tasks, considering that he was stripped completely bare save for a heavy wooden cangue clapped around his neck and secured to the chilly stone floor with thick chains. The chains were short enough to prevent him from being able to stand, twist, or do anything but kneel or squat. Hecaton lounged on her throne with an expression of pure disinterest.

"Natalis," Hecaton said, and sucked her teeth. "What the hell happened to your balls? They're not supposed to be purple."

"Duquessa Hecaton," Juan said, with a deep bow, "this Imperial scum entered your demesne under false pretenses. He pledged loyalty to you and your cause, but in truth, he was in league with those disgraced traitors, Sir Ringo and the abomination Samara. He is also responsible for the death of Sir Janus Eicke and planned all this time to assassinate you. He has confessed everything under interrogation. I have many lancers who witnessed this. I beg you to let me punish him for this crime and to recognize my service to you."

Hecaton squinted. "Is this true, Natalis?"

Taki looked up at her. "I confess that I had words with Sir Ringo and Lady Samara. But I am not in league with them. I do know, however, that they have sent a traitor into the ranks of the brotherhood."

Juan reached over and slapped Taki across the face. "Don't mince words, you spy! You are in league with them, and the traitor is you!"

"No!" Taki tried to stand, only to be stopped by the cangue. "Mistress Hecaton, the real traitor is none other than Sir Juan!"

"Preposterous!" Juan drew back a fist.

"Stop!" Hecaton shouted. Thunder cracked in the background, and the air grew still and pregnant. "Taki Natalis, if you're wasting my time, you'll regret it. I'll have you done in by lingchi. Do you have proof of Juan's treason?"

Taki smiled. "Sir Juan wears around his neck a Behelit, which he has failed to inform you of. Surely you remember what those are used for. In the meantime, Sir Ringo and Lady Samara, with Lord Chronicler, have stolen your *Ooss* and its God Hand. Sir Juan is obviously in league with them and presents a grave threat to your rightful rule."

"That's just happenstance," Hecaton said. "Not good enough."

"I will perform the death sentence myself, Duquessa," Juan said with another bow. "Give the order!"

Taki spat. "In Sir Juan's breast pocket there is a snuff pouch. I have often seen him use from it, and I recently saw him take out a piece of correspondence and read it. I believe those are enemy orders from Sir Ringo. Please, search him for this!"

Juan was livid. "The prisoner's gone mad. Men, take him to the tower. This is a direct order from your Brother Number Six!"

"Hold," Hecaton said. "Search Brother Juan."

"Duquessa?" Juan wheeled around. "Why? This is madness!"

Before Juan could react further, two of the senior brothers grasped him by the arms, while Jiang slipped a hand into the breast pocket of Juan's gambeson, right under the Naranja rose.

"Lord Sirin," Jiang said. "It is a snuff pouch, as Brother Taki has said."

"Open it."

Jiang shook the contents out to the floor. He bent over and picked up a wadded-up piece of paper and carefully unfolded it. His brow furrowed, and he passed it to Hecaton.

"So, Juan," Hecaton said with a smirk. "You were supposed to keep me in place until Shastirch and his cronies could blow me up."

Juan whitened. "That's not my pouch! I swear to you on the garter of Princessa Phillippa! The spy Natalis put it there! He must have!"

"But you're the only one of us who uses snuff," Jiang said, as he rubbed the powder between his fingers. "I've never seen Brother Taki use it, so why would he have such a nice pouch?"

"It's not mine! It's this Imperial's fault!" Juan's knees were shaking. "I swore my loyalty to you! Believe me!"

Hecaton nodded to Jiang. "Take the irons off Natalis and give him back his clothes and weapons. Then take Sir Juan to the lookout and pitch him off."

Taki breathed a sigh of relief as the cangue finally came off and two of the brothers helped him to his feet and draped him with a cloak. Juan started to scream, until one of the brothers slapped a gag over his mouth.

"Natalis," Hecaton said, "your name is cleared and your honor restored. Do you bear resentment?"

Taki bowed deeply. "Nay, Mistress. Instead, I thank you from the bottom of my heart! And before Sir Juan meets his punishment, I request a boon. I wish to have a private word with him beforehand."

"Fine, whatever," Hecaton said. "Have a kiss or whatever you barbarians do. I've got matters to attend to."

A while later, after Taki had cleaned himself, applied a poultice to his sore parts, and dressed again, he emerged from his now-nicer quarters and marched to the lookout point where Juan awaited. The lookout was constructed at the top of one of the Ring's surviving high towers set into the perimeter wall and served both as a means of surveying the land as well as a means of punishment for misdeeds. Getting to the top required a long, twisting ascent up narrow stairs, and by the time Taki emerged at the top, he'd worked up a sweat.

Juan knelt sullenly before a wide gap in the ramparts, his arms and ankles bound in chains. A handful of islanders with spears stood at the ready. Taki nodded to the men and signaled for them to leave. They bowed and wordlessly filed out.

"I got the pouch back," Taki said, and tied it around Juan's neck. "Refilled it, even. Snuff's expensive."

"I'll gut you in hell, you son of a bitch," Juan growled. "Do you really think you can take on the likes of the duquessa? She'll crush you like a bug. This, I swear on the garter of Princessa Ph—"

"The princessa's dead," Taki said. "Sir Aslatiel killed her and set her corpse on fire."

Juan's eyes widened. "You bastard! You'll all burn for this!"

"I took the liberty of writing a reply to Sir Ringo and Lady Samara. It's in that snuff pouch of yours. I'd ask you to tell them, but I'm sure they'll figure it out." Taki stepped back, drew his Herstal, and aimed at Juan's head. "One more thing. What did I tell you would happen if you touched me again?"

"F—"

Juan's curse was cut short when Taki pulled the trigger. The body slumped forward and pitched off the edge of the lookout. A few seconds later, Taki heard a dull, distant thump. He reholstered his pistol and took in the panorama. The midafternoon sun had dissipated most of the clouds obscuring the lands around the caldera.

Unlike in Taki's native land, most of the Blue Sky Land had been left untouched by man. Amid the rolling hills, herds of wild horses roamed freely, nibbling at the grass and lapping from glacial streams. A formation of birds passed nearby, flapping sinewy wings and calling to each other in strangely melodic song. The sky above—Tengri's sky—was unmarred and shamelessly blue.

10

"We congratulate you, Taki Natalis of the barbarian horde!" Jiang announced in a warbling tenor. He poured from a porcelain bottle of *arkhi* into a clay bowl in Taki's hands. "For exposing the treachery of Brother Number Seven and avenging Brother Number Six, Lord Sirin names you Heavenly Warrior Attendant, in charge of the antitreachery division! Rise, Brother Number Six!"

Taki rose from where he knelt and hoisted the full bowl to Hecaton on her throne. "Thank you, Mistress! I will work tirelessly against your enemies and extinguish betrayers in your name!"

He downed the contents in one gulp, as did the hundred twice-born islanders gathered around him. The *arkhi* burned pleasantly down his throat. When he finished, he threw the bowl down and shattered it. A second later, the islanders did the same, covering the ground with shards.

"Natalis, you have a habit of leaving bodies in your wake," Hecaton said. "But that's why I like you."

"What are your orders, my Mistress?"

"Somehow, my bumbling ex-husband found his way here and stole my ship. I want you to go and take it back from him. If you can punish those two miscreants, Ringo and Samara, then do so. But above all, get the ship back. If you absolutely have to, sink the damned thing. I'll take care of raising it back up."

Taki bowed. "I will work my hardest to bring you victory."

"Good," Hecaton said. "You have until the end of the season. If you have not found the *Ooss* by then, I'll have your head. You may leave now."

Taki bowed again, took three steps back, and then turned around. The islanders clapped him on the back and shouted *arkhi*-scented congratulations, to which he tried to smile heartily back.

When he was free of the crowd and the palace, Taki jogged to where the jakes were and found the stall designated for Brother Number Six. The islanders' symbols for letters and numbers had come easily to him, and now he could read most of the signage around the grounds. He barely had time to feel proud before he promptly hurled.

After he was done, he reached into the nearby bucket and washed the foulness from his lips. At the very least, the stall didn't smell quite so rank as his earlier one, thanks to Janus never having used it. He lifted the bucket and poured the rest of it out to wash the place clean. A small message container made from horn rolled away and tapped against his boot.

Taki fought back another wave of nausea and hurriedly palmed the tube. He avoided the temptation to immediately look behind him. Samara was already long gone. *Natural-born stalker, that one. Does she watch me when I sleep?* He shuddered. Whatever was in the tube would spell either his salvation or his doom. He had not minced words in his correspondence to Samara and the others. If they cut him off, then Hecaton would have his head come the end of the season. He hurried back to the residences.

Now that he was Brother Number Six, he was allowed better quarters. Befitting the rank, the space was more generous than before. Instead of a smelly fur pallet, the room boasted an actual mattress topped with a silken comforter and down pillows. A lacquered chest at the foot of the bed could hold his belongings and, unlike the door, boasted a lock and key. Nearby stood a wardrobe of fragrant rosewood, within which was hung a fur overcoat that wasn't Taki's.

A dusky-eyed woman lounged atop the bed wearing a linen shift and smoking a rolled cigarillo. By islander standards, she was essentially naked. And if she was on his bed in his room, then there was no mistaking her intent.

"Brother Number One sent me," the woman said. "He is a good man who looks out for his inferiors."

Taki's eyes widened. "What's your name?"

"Whatever you want it to be. You can call me Sirin if you want. Many of the brothers do."

She got off the bed and strolled over. Taki stiffened as her hands slipped under his cloak and deftly undid the clasps. Then, she started to work on undoing his gambeson.

Taki sweated and fidgeted uncomfortably. The message tube in his palm might as well have been a live ember. *Why did this have to happen now? Shit!*

"Are you a virgin? Jiang says you are."

"Of course not," Taki said, more defensively than he wanted. *I need to look at the message.*

She laughed. "Too much chi makes men act strangely. I'll relieve you of some of it."

"No. I'm sorry," Taki said. He grabbed the overcoat out of the wardrobe and thrust it at the woman. "I actually need to be alone right now. Please send my thanks to Brother Number One."

"Huh? You have strange humor, barbarian."

"I'm not japing at you," Taki said, and opened the door. "Mistress Sirin's commanded me to find her *Ooss*. I don't have time for this."

"You don't have time to tumble?"

"No, I really don't." Taki pointed to the outside. "Leave."

With confusion written all over her face, the woman stepped out. Taki closed the door after her. Then, he went over to the lacquered chest and pushed it over to bar the entry shut. As a last, anxious touch, he then sat on it.

With fingers that felt like useless, floppy noodles, he unscrewed the cap from the message tube and unrolled the note inside. He squinted at the spidery text, written in Samara's hand.

"Fine, we'll do it your way. Boat's anchored a league offshore from northern Ainu-Mosir. Bring the Behelit. We'll deal with HM's boys."

Taki let out a ragged breath and sank into a slouch. If Samara could be trusted, then he was saved. Aside from an Ursalan spire, the *Ooss* was the only way to cross the storms that cut the islands off from the rest of the world. If Hecaton Mezeta had to follow the same rules, depriving her of the *Ooss* was the next best thing to killing her.

He gingerly grasped the message between his fingers and muttered an incantation. The onion paper trembled, smoked, and then dissolved into white ash. He would have to bide his time. Going right up to Hecaton with the location of the *Ooss* was tantamount to a full confession of treason. For a moment, Taki considered attempting to find Jiang's gift woman again. He quickly decided against it, however. The islanders respected conviction.

* * * *

Two fortnights later, Taki knelt before the throne again.

"Mistress, I have found your *Ooss*, and with it lies the God Hand," he said.

Hecaton crossed her arms. "Took you long enough. You've spent the last month doing nothing but wandering. I was starting to look for good chopping blocks. There are precious few which fit your large, round head. So, where is my boat?"

"It is still within your demesne, though barely. A full three days' journey to the northernmost point of the Ainu-Mosir, and with the aid of a spyglass you should see it anchored at sea, just barely peeking over the surface with its holy promontory. In my opinion—"

"No need to ask," Hecaton said, cutting him off. "The rest of your brothers and I shall ride out with you. The court shall make preparations for my absence. We will depart immediately!"

"Mistress," Taki said, "I...I am grateful for your personal attention to this matter, but are you sure you need to accompany us?"

"Never, *ever* ask me again if I'm sure of my decisions. Of course I'm riding out. Every ruler who's foisted off important tasks on mere lackeys has ended up wearing her own insides as a hat. If you want to make sure something's done right, you do it yourself. Am I clear?"

Taki bowed. "Absolutely, Mistress. I will be ready to depart momentarily."

"One last thing."

"Yes, Mistress?"

Hecaton flashed him a feral grin and a thumbs-up. "Good job!"

Taki suppressed a shudder, backed three steps away, and then turned to leave.

He raced back to his quarters, where he quickly threw his belongings into a set of saddlebags. A quick inspection of his ammunition stores revealed twelve shots left. His islander currency was down to two steel discs and a smattering of silver change. When he'd feigned riding up north to scout for the *Ooss*, he'd stopped in many taverns and sampled the menu. By now, he couldn't imagine drinking anything but pocha and was starting to crave new and novel vegetables. *High time I leave this place,* Taki thought with a chuckle.

Lastly, he made sure the Behelit was hung securely from his neck and then sat at the writing desk. He pulled out a thin strip of onion paper and wrote.

"You have three days. We're all coming. HM too."

He rolled the paper and slipped it into the horn message tube. Samara had told him not to try to contact her, but he reasoned that this was an occasion to break the rules.

He exited his quarters, sure that he'd never see them again, and went over to the jakes, where he pretended to relieve himself and then slipped the tube under the washbucket. He reasoned that if anyone but Samara found it, word would get to Hecaton too late to make a difference.

At the Ring's entrance, Taki found the brothers mounted and ready to ride, along with a company of a hundred mounted archers and lancers. Hecaton's destrier chomped at the bit at the head of the formation.

"Taki!" Jiang trotted over and gave Taki a friendly clap on the shoulder.

"Yes, Brother Number One?"

"Oh, enough with the formality. You can call me by my name when we're among friends."

Taki shifted on his saddle. "Thank you, Jia—Older Brother."

Jiang laughed. "I think you must have some of my people's blood in your veins. Familiarity with our betters does not come easily to us like it does to barbarians."

"I appreciate the sentiment," Taki said. *Though you still call me a barbarian.*

"You know, when I first laid eyes on you, I had my doubts. But I like you better than the other two barbarians. They were smelly, nasty men incapable of self-reflection. Full of bluster and always, always scheming. But you, Taki, are different. I think that you could even lead the army one day, if I were ever to fall in battle."

"You honor me too much, Older Brother."

"Nay," Jiang said. "I speak truth. Lord Sirin shares my view, and above all, she is forthright. I have served a number of lords and generals in the past. Many are—what is the word in your language?—duplicitous. They say one thing and mean another. They use good men and then discard them. But Lord Sirin will never engage in such disgraceful conduct. In fact, some accuse her of being too honest. That, however, is what I love about her, and why I will follow her to the end of my days on earth."

"Older Brother," Taki said, looking away. "What does she want with the lands west of here, anyway? What will she do once she invades? Does she intend to kill off my people and replace them with her own?"

Jiang shook his head. "They say that long before we men fell, our people once tried to conquer the world. We destroyed what we had to destroy but saved all we could. When a man attempts to extinguish a tribe of other men, Tengri will always strike him down. Lord Sirin understands this well, and thus her quarrel is not with the barbarians but with Shastirch. I believe you call him Chronicler in your tongue. He has become something unholy. Something profane that must be eliminated for the good of all."

"I suppose that's fair," Taki said. "And all the more reason to find him."

* * * *

The Ring and lands south of it had been chilly, but at least they were dry. Ainu-Mosir, on the other hand, was not only frigid but also wet. The last day of their trek north, the company of Hecaton and her brothers had ridden through rain and fog, which had bogged down the horses and slowed progress. Finally, however, they had made it to the northernmost point, a cliff overlooking a gravelly, decidedly inhospitable beach.

Taki knelt at the grassy edge and scanned the dark, still sea through an ancient spyglass. Fortunately, the rain had abated, allowing him a clear view through the somewhat distorted glass. Jiang and the others waited expectantly nearby, miffed that they weren't able to start cookfires or warm themselves.

Should be here, unless I've been betrayed, Taki thought. He clenched his jaw to still his anxiety. If he'd made Hecaton come all the way out here for nothing, then it would be his head. He panned across the seascape again. Past the horizon was the omnipresent maelstrom that seemed to surround the islands in every direction. A seemingly solid mass of roiling thunderclouds and seaspouts, the Storm Wall was something one could stare at for hours, mesmerized by the constant flashes of lightning emanating from within. Taki, however, had no time to ponder its mysteries. He looked again, desperately, for the *Ooss*. A subtle disturbance flashed across his view. He stopped and jerked back to center it in his vision. *Thank God!*

He looked up from the spyglass and pointed. "Mistress Sirin! It's here!"

Hecaton snatched the glass from Taki and peered through it. Then she gave it back to him and shouted over to the men. "Make ready some rafts and oars! We'll push the damned thing here if need be!"

Over the next few bells, the islanders set on a stand of spruce and fir nearby where the horses were tethered. As the timbers fell, their branches were expertly stripped and the trunks stuck together with pegs and lashed together with ropes. The rafts were then toted down a gently sloping path leading down from the cliff to the beach. Normally, the timbers and bindings would have been sealed with tar, but smoke was a dead giveaway. The rafts only had a few days' worth of life, but that was all that was required.

"Brothers, get on the rafts and row out to the *Ooss*," Hecaton ordered. "I'll stay here and make a nice storm to shield your approach. Blow a hole in the thing if you need to, and kill everyone inside."

She tromped up to the edge of the cliff, sat cross-legged in the grass, and closed her eyes. The world quickly darkened, and raindrops started to fall. At first only a light dusting, the precipitation quickly turned to fist-sized gobs of water that poured from the swirling clouds above. The sea started to froth white, and before Taki set foot on the beach, lightning flashed overhead and struck the sea nearby. The islanders roared in approval and enthusiastically shoved the rafts into the water and jumped aboard.

A swell washed over the beach and hit Taki square in the midsection. He stumbled and fell back, unable to find his footing in the agitated sand. Just before his head disappeared under the backflow, Jiang's meaty hand grasped the back of his collar and jerked him upright.

"Be careful, Taki," Jiang said with a chuckle. "You haven't grown up diving into these waters for pearls. Do I need to make you a leash?"

"Thanks, but it won't be necessary, Older Brother," Taki said, and climbed aboard the nearby raft. Jiang followed, seemingly effortlessly for his bulk. Then, he took one of the massive, crudely fashioned oars and started to row.

Just how strong is he? Taki marveled as the raft not just moved but lurched away from the beach at a speed normally reserved for sleek naval cutters. The most disconcerting thing was that the other ramshackle boats were making similar speed. *Only that Lucatiel woman could've done something like this. Is this entire island filled with people as strong as she is? We don't stand a godrotting chance against them!*

The sea was a wrathful, churning mess that pitched and buffeted the rafts with fury that would've broken the keel of an Imperial war galleon. With every swell, Taki reflexively tensed his gut in anticipation of sure destruction. Yet the timbers, lashed together as inelegantly as they were, somehow seemed to tolerate the constant abuse, and before long, the ancient, rune-covered surface of the *Ooss* was within reach.

"Surround the ship and tether it!" Jiang roared. "Do not allow it to sink and retreat!"

With surprising seamanship, the small flotilla split into two columns that rowed along both sides of the floating reliquary. Between the rafts, the islanders spooled out lengths of rope that they let sink into the water to wrap around the bottom of the hull. Then they exchanged the ends of the ropes and lashed the rafts securely to the top deck.

"It's time," Jiang said to Taki, and stepped off his raft and onto the ancient metal. "We couldn't have done this without you, Little Brother. Now come—we will earn our glory together!"

"Aye," Taki said. His teeth chattered, but not from cold. He set foot on the ancient metal deck and drew his sword. Fortunately, the *Ooss* was much more stable of a platform than the rafts had been, and his nausea faded quickly. *What's the plan, Samara? Surely you must've noticed us!*

Cautiously, Jiang and the brothers padded their way toward the massive, fin-like tower near the bow. Jiang signaled, and one of the brothers climbed up a nearby ladder. He squatted and started to work. Before long came the sound of squealing metal. The brother stood and turned to look down at the others.

"Brother Number One! The hatch is open! I'm going in!"

Jiang raised a hand. "Wait for—"

The tip of an islander saber erupted from the brother's chest, and the man sank to his knees. Chronicler lifted the body by the cloak and pitched the man into the waters off the side. Then, he flicked the blood away from his sword and onto the aghast fighters below.

"This ship belongs to the Imperium," Chronicler said. "And this land belongs to *me*."

Behind Hecaton's men, the smooth deck of the *Ooss* rumbled as previously unseen hatches opened in orderly rows along its surface. From the open hatches, islanders in boiled leather and peaked helms leapt out with their weapons ready.

"They've recruited Birchen scum!" Jiang hissed. "Brothers! Kill the enemies and take this ship!"

Both groups of islanders roared and then charged at each other. A moment later, they met in a thunderous clash of sparking steel, shattering wood, and billowing gunsmoke.

Taki raised his blade just in time to deflect a spear thrust and countered with a burst of his *khala* sutra. The compressed blast of air hit his Birchen opponent in the chest and flung the man into the choppy water off the side of the *Ooss*. Taki hopped back just in time to avoid a sweeping saber blow and started his riposte, when a fellow brother blasted the attacker with a handheld musket.

"What the hell are you doing?" Samara hissed in Taki's ear, and whisked him quickly behind the sail tower, where Ringo waited, wide-eyed. "Those are *our* men! Your allies!"

"I had to defend myself," Taki said. "Took you both long enough to show!"

"We're no match for them hand-to-hand. Let the Birchen men finish Mezeta's off. Do you have the Behelit?"

Taki pulled it out. "I admit, I thought you wouldn't honor our deal."

"What do you take us for?" Ringo snarled. "Honor is the foremost of the chivalric virtues! We're going to kill Mezeta and get us all back home like we promised."

"Oh, my darling, I'm glad you said 'us.' That makes me happy," Samara said, and kissed Ringo on the cheek.

"D-don't presume! We're getting a divorce the moment we hit land."

"That's not what you said last night after we—"

"Dammit, not in front of him!"

"Okay, okay!" Samara smirked. "Natalis, aim the Behelit. The countdown's started already."

Taki nodded and got on one knee to steady himself. He sighted the edge of the distant cliff and pressed one of the buttons on the side of the device. *I once did this to Chronicler. Now I'm doing it to Hecaton Mezeta. Funny how things end up.* The Behelit clicked and rattled, and Taki lowered it. The deed was done. Hecaton was as good as dead.

On the other side of the sail, the sounds of battle had mostly died down. Before Samara and Ringo could stop him, Taki edged back toward the fray.

The deck was stained with crimson and littered with broken helms, shattered muskets, and snapped spears. Bodies, both Birchen and Kvara, bobbed nearby amidst the waves. Of Hecaton's brothers, only Jiang still stood. Blood ran freely from gashes in his scalp, and his lamellar armor was rent and torn. The massive dao blade lay snapped in pieces on the deck, leaving Jiang with only his fists and feet. Chronicler tossed aside his own saber, dabbed at a trickle of blood from a split lip, and sank into a defensive stance.

"Shastirch, my old friend. There is still time to surrender," Jiang said with a laugh that provoked a froth of pink spittle. "Lord Sirin has often expressed a wistful longing for your presence at her side."

"Jiang, I urge caution," Chronicler said. "Should Sirin ever hear you utter those words, we'd both be cast to the lowest reaches of hell."

"Your technique has grown rusty. Those barbarians rely overmuch on their guns. I wonder if that's rubbed off on you."

Chronicler smiled. "My friend, if the barbarians have done one thing right, it is adapt to overcome their weaknesses. That is why they are taking over and we are dying out. We would all do well to take their example to heart."

"What a scene this would make on silk!" Jiang said. "Us two philosophizing atop a barbarian relic in a storm."

"I promise you that I will paint it."

"That warms me to hear it, Shastirch. I was worried that you'd forgotten how."

Jiang shifted his weight and leapt at Chronicler, who bounded forward to meet the attack. Faster than Taki could process, the two men blinked by each other and then ended up on opposite sides. Chronicler and Jiang rose from their stances and bowed. Then, Jiang sank to his knees, clutched his chest, and fell to his side, dead.

Just behind where Jiang lay, a final hatch opened to spew a geyser of flame and smoke. A white blur shot skyward, belched a jet of flame behind it, and then screamed toward the coast.

"Shit! Get inside now!" Samara bellowed, and started to climb the ladder up.

Taki followed quickly behind Ringo and pulled himself up over the edge. Before he set foot into the open hatch, he glanced one last time at the cliff. Even if Hecaton had noticed the launch or the missile streaking toward her, there was nothing she could do to avoid her fate. Taki howled and pumped his fist in the air in jubilation. *I hope you see me, Hecaton Mezeta! I hope you see me and realize that I, a powerless worm, killed you!*

Light flashed from the cliff, and for a moment, Taki felt as if the world had turned to molasses. A beat later, he shielded his eyes, expecting the heat and shockwave to come any moment. Instead, he saw the God Hand streak right back toward him.

His eyes widened, and he instinctively ducked, though by the time he'd bent his knees, the missile was dozens of meters above his head. He whirled in disbelief as it rocketed away from the ship and toward the roiling darkness of the Storm Wall.

"But…" Taki croaked.

The God Hand slipped into the thunderheads. A second later, a blinding flash of light and pressure bowled him over. An avalanche of unbearable heat and noise washed over him next, working its way in through his nose and mouth and every other orifice until he wished, more than anything else, to die. And then, just as abruptly, the torment faded.

Taki cracked an eye open and lifted his head. Far in the distance, where the Storm Wall had been, was now a column of pure white, larger than anything he'd ever imagined could exist. A cloud rose languidly to the heavens, glowing precipitation falling underneath. To Taki's amazement, it resembled something he'd seen many times in the wild: a mushroom.

He tore his eyes away from the sight and scrabbled toward the hatch. Nothing mattered besides getting to that hatch. His knees, jelly-like, refused to work in synchrony with his arms. Madly, he pulled himself toward the opening. From the mushroom cloud, an impossible high wall of solid white bore down on the *Ooss*. Taki reached for the hatch.

"I have no tolerance for those who fail me," Chronicler said, and jerked Taki away from the hatch by the back of his gambeson.

"Your Majesty! Mercy! Please!" Taki blubbered, to no avail. With a flick of Chronicler's wrist, Taki flew away from the hatch and splashed into the choppy waves. A moment later, the *Ooss* started to submerge.

Taki reached out as the water lapped at his face and blended with his snot and tears. He felt no urge to swim and had not the strength. The last thing he saw was the solid front of a tidal wave right in front of his face. Then all was darkness.

11

Taki coughed, rolled over on his side, and promptly retched up enough seawater to fill a milk pail. Salt stung at all of his sensitive places: his eyes, his sinuses, the back of his throat, and even where he pissed from. But at the very least, he was no longer cold. In fact, sodden as he was, he was even a touch uncomfortably warm.

He blinked and wiped at his eyes. Around him, the ground seemed to writhe and stank to high heaven. Taki flailed around in an effort to sit up, and he coughed and retched some more. Pain lanced through a finger and he pulled back, only to find that a crab had caught the digit in its pincer. He grimaced, shook the creature away, and then gasped.

He lay on the grassy knoll near where Hecaton had been meditating. Around him, however, the grass was littered with sea life. Dying fish gasped for air and flapped fruitlessly while crustaceans skittered around like decapitated fowl. Shredded seaweed hung from the branches of nearby trees, glinting translucent and green in the light of the sun. Finally, Taki looked out toward the ocean. Where the Storm Wall had once blocked further view of the horizon, he only saw uninterrupted sky.

Next to Taki, Hecaton Mezeta sat cross-legged, her clothing soaked through but her tobacco dry, as evidenced by the smoke coming from the bowl of her pipe. Crackling in front of her was a small driftwood fire, over which she unevenly roasted a viciously fanged fish skewered on a stick. She looked over at him and motioned with her cookery.

"I'm not sharing, if you're wondering. I caught this guy fair and square."

Taki looked at her and shook his head. He had neither the energy nor the will to hide the truth from her anymore. "What happened? Why did the God Hand turn around?"

Hecaton snorted derisively. "Because I made it turn around."

Bryan Choi & Erica Carson

Taki let out a despairing laugh. "I thought I'd finally screwed you back, but I guess that was always a foolish hope. The likes of me...the captain, Draco, Mikkelsen, Gillette...we can't do shit to your kind, can we? We'll never be more than mere ants."

He drew his knees to his chest and rested his forehead against them. "Why did I even come here? Nothing *any* of us did mattered in the end! It was all shit! Why did we even try? Why did *I* even try?"

He felt Hecaton's hand rest on his back.

"Just get it over with," Taki said, hugging his knees. "And do it right. That's all I ask."

"Stewing in self-pity doesn't befit a warrior of the Blue Sky Land," Hecaton said. "You have to set a good example for your younger brothers, because the moment they see you cry like a little bitch, they'll gut you."

Taki looked up in confusion. "What? Why are you lecturing me? Just kill me already."

"Kill you? Stop spewing nonsense, you damned barbarian. I don't want to kill you; I want to offer you a promotion. You offed every other brother ahead of you, so you'd be the new Brother Number One. I told you how the system worked when you came here."

"Don't you understand? I'm a traitor and a spy," Taki snarled. "I was in league with Sir Ringo and Lady Samara. I sent the God Hand right at you. I wanted to blow you up! I was working against you *from the beginning!*"

"Yeah, but you're kinda cute, so I still like you. Against my better judgment, I might add. And unlike my silly, demon-possessed husband, I won't try to screw you at every opportunity. I offer fair terms, and I will always tell you the truth. Especially the truth you don't want to hear."

"You stole our pensions and left us to die," Taki snapped. "How does that show your fairness?"

Hecaton blinked. "And for that, I apologize."

Taki grimaced. "But?"

"No buts. I'm sorry."

"You're not going to try to justify yourself? Or tell me you were acting in our interests all along? Or...or..."

"No," Hecaton said.

Taki looked to the sky and gave a despairing laugh. "I didn't think I'd ever hear those words from you. Almost makes all the shit I endured to get here worth it. If only the captain were here. I guess I can accept your apology. After all, it's more than I ever expected."

184

"Moving on, do you accept my offer, or not?"

Taki's chest heaved and his eyes stung, though it wasn't the saltwater's doing. "I don't want your pity."

"Pity?" Hecaton turned and slapped Taki lightly across the cheek. "Who the hell do you think I am, young man? Pity is something a mother gives. And I'm definitely not your damned mother. I am your lord and master, and don't you forget it."

"And what would you have me do?"

Hecaton took a bite of her fish and spat it out a moment later. She tossed the skewer away with a disgusted look. "First of all, we're going to get the hell out of here, because the food stinks. Second, you're going to help me complete my conquest over the Islands. Third, we're going to sail across the sea and bring the fire down on Shastirch. I always knew he was an idiot, but I didn't think he'd actually go and sell his own damned soul to some demonic shithead. That kind of crap is what brings this entire world to a screaming end, and in the process makes everything smell like farts. I *hate* it when people fart on me."

"You don't need me for that," Taki said.

"Sure I do," Hecaton said. "You think the padishah and his cronies are going to let me march over there and wring my ex-husband's balls? No. This will be a bloody hell of an invasion. And I need a competent commander. Someone who can read. Someone who won't fritter his time away on whores. A man I can respect. Someone like you. So, are you in?" She extended a hand.

Taki sucked his snot in and regarded her incredulously. He'd traveled, fought, killed, and nearly died many times just to be where he was now. In his most sodden, painful, and desperate moments, he'd found solace in this moment: the chance to stick a dagger in her heart, even if he died in the attempt. A final "fuck you" to the woman who'd derailed his life. Hecaton wasn't stupid, he figured. She knew how he felt, too, and yet was willing to trust him with her plans? And even respect him for that?

He squeezed his eyes shut and wiped away the last of his tears with a sodden sleeve. Then, he took her hand in his.

"I'm in."

The thrilling conclusion to
The Polaris Chronicles arrives in 2017!

...as well as another Tale about a certain redheaded gun-nut...

Visit www.carsonchoi.com for updates, announcements, and bonus material!

There, you can follow us on Twitter, like us on Facebook, join our mailing list, and be the first to hear of deals and new releases.

Finally, if you enjoyed this book and want to see more in the series, leaving us a review on Amazon is the single best way to let us know.

www.ingramcontent.com/pod-product-compliance
Lightning Source LLC
Chambersburg PA
CBHW061230170626
46809CB00007B/2601